CHERRY BOMB

A Jacqueline "Jack" Daniels Mystery

CHERRY BOMB

J.A. KONRATH

HYPERION

NEW YORK

Library of Congress Cataloging-in-Publication Data

Konrath, Joe.
  Cherry bomb / J.A. Konrath.
    p. cm.
    1. Daniels, Jacqueline (Fictitious character)—Fiction.   2. Policewomen—
Illinois—Chicago—Fiction.   3. Fiancées—Crimes against—Fiction.
4. Chicago (Ill.)—Fiction.   5. Chick lit.   I. Title.
  PS3611.O587C48 2009
  813'.6—dc22
      2009010658

Hyperion books are available for special promotions and premiums.
For details contact the HarperCollins Special Markets Department
in the New York office at 212-207-7528, fax 212-207-7222,
or email spsales@harpercollins.com.

FIRST EDITION

10 9 8 7 6 5 4 3 2 1

SUSTAINABLE FORESTRY INITIATIVE Certified Fiber Sourcing www.sfiprogram.org

THIS LABEL APPLIES TO TEXT STOCK

We try to produce the most beautiful books possible, and we are also extremely concerned about
the impact of our manufacturing process on the forests of the world and the environment as a
whole. Accordingly, we've made sure that all of the paper we use has been certified as coming
from forests that are managed to insure the protection of the people and wildlife dependent upon
them.

This book is dedicated to my wife,
my one true love,
and my very best friend.
Happily, they're all the same person.
You're magic, Maria.

CHERRY BOMB

1 oz. vodka
1½ oz. white crème de cacao
¾ oz. grenadine
1 maraschino cherry

Shake vodka, crème de cacao,
and grenadine with ice.

Pour into a rocks glass.

Garnish with cherry.

CHERRY BOMB

CHAPTER 1

AT MY FIANCÉ'S FUNERAL I got a phone call from the woman who killed him.

"I checked the Weather Channel." Her tone was conversational, cheery. "It's raining in Chicago. That's appropriate, don't you think? Funerals on sunny days seem so wrong."

The pastor hit the switch, and the mechanical winch lowered Latham's casket into the ground on black canvas straps. Slow, like it was sinking into a swamp. The rain beaded up on the lacquered oak lid and I had an irrational urge to find a towel, wipe it dry. Latham didn't deserve to spend eternity wet.

"I'm coming after you," I whispered into the phone.

"That's what he said. Before I shot him. He said you'd come after me. Latham had faith in you until the very end, Jack. Like a puppy dog. Poor guy. Murdered, just for loving the wrong woman."

My partner, Sergeant Herb Benedict, had been staring at me since the phone rang. Herb's black suit was purchased back when he weighed less, the tightness making his large stomach seem even larger. His free hand—the one that wasn't holding the crutch—reached up and touched my shoulder.

Alex? he mouthed.

I nodded.

"Is this your grand plan, Alex? Calling me to make me feel guilty?"

"I don't need to make you feel guilty, Jack. You're already guilty. Latham was a good man. I would have preferred shooting you in the head, but our game isn't over yet. Later today I'm sending you a picture over the phone. Twelve hours from then, the man in the picture will die. Unless you can find him and save him. I hope, for his sake, you do a better job than you did with your fiancé."

I gripped the cell phone so hard my hand was shaking. Latham's casket dropped below ground level, and the tears on my face mingled with the rain. I managed to keep my voice even.

"And what if I don't want to play your game?"

"The man I'm going to kill has a wife and kids. Leading the kind of life that you might have led, if you weren't burying your future. If you don't make an effort to save him, the next picture I send you will be of a playground filled with children. How much more guilt can you handle before you crumble and blow away?"

I wiped my cheeks, then turned away from the grave. Latham's family stared hard at me. No pity in their eyes. Only disdain.

"Don't cry. And if I may be blunt, don't you think that skirt you're wearing is a little short? Not very appropriate, unless you're cruising the funeral for a rebound fuck."

I glanced down at my knee-length dress, then did a quick 360.

"Careful, Jack. You're spinning so fast you may knock your fat partner off his crutch."

I covered the phone and faced Herb. "She's here."

Herb hit his lapel mike, turning on his radio and calling for a perimeter sweep. There were more than fifty cops at the funeral. As they scattered I dug my .38 Colt out of my Gucci handbag and walked away from the grave site, scanning tombstones and monuments, heels sinking into the wet sod, worming my way through Latham's family while they shamed me with hateful glares.

"You brought a gun to a funeral, Jack?" Alex asked. "Were you expecting me to show up?"

"I was hoping."

The October wind kicked up, blowing dead leaves and cold air across my scalp, making my stitches sting. Twenty-plus years of on-the-job training made me keep low, a smaller target. Not that it mattered. Alex was a crack shot.

"Turn left," Alex said, "another few yards, next to the mausoleum. There's an angel watching over you."

I followed instructions, feeling like I had a bull's-eye on my forehead, and not minding much. I ran my eyes along the slanting granite roof of the stone structure, and noticed the statue of a cherub perched on top. Something was duct-taped to his hand. I moved in closer, gun arm extended, and saw it was a camera phone.

"Twelve hours, Jack. Then he dies. And keep your cell on. Never know when I might call with a hint. Don't fail him like you failed Latham."

Alex hung up. My legs decided they didn't want to support me anymore, and I fell to my knees, my gun hand dropping to my side, cursing the day I became a police officer.

CHAPTER 2

MILES AWAY, Alexandra Kork sits in a coffee store chain, sipping a tall black dark roast. Alex doesn't care for coffee, but the free WiFi access makes her Internet trail harder to trace. She moves a finger along her laptop touch-pad, and the camera zooms in on Lieutenant Jacqueline Daniels, kneeling in the mud. The image is in color, with a gorgeous 600 dpi resolution that is unfortunately blurred by the drizzle.

Behind the mesh veil, Alex smiles with half of her face. Like Jack, she wears funeral black, but her heels and her hemline are higher. The outfit is new, a Dolce & Gabbana two-button blazer with a matching skirt. No top underneath, just a push-up bra that reveals a lot of cleavage in the V-neck. The hat is vintage, purchased at a thrift store, wide brimmed and stylish in an Audrey Hepburn kind of way. The netting extends from the brim and curls down to beneath her chin, tickling her neck. For the discreet serial killer, it's the next best thing to a hockey mask.

Above the scents of coffee and cinnamon, Alex catches a whiff of Lagerfeld. It stings her sore nose. She powers off the computer just as the man approaches her small table. Mid-fifties, balding, short. His suit is tailored, expensive, but still can't hide the middle-age spread and the bullfrog chin. The gold wedding band is tight on his sausage finger.

"I noticed you sitting here, and I wanted to offer my condolences," he says, speaking to her breasts. Men are laughably predictable. If she were topless, she wouldn't even need the veil to hide her face—no man would bother looking above her collarbone.

"Thank you," Alex says. "I'd offer you a seat, but I was just leaving."

Alex stands. She's two inches taller than he, and his eyes follow her cleavage like laser scopes. He seems momentarily unable to speak, so Alex prompts him.

"This may sound rash, but I'm feeling vulnerable right now, and I could use some company. Would you walk me back to my hotel room?"

Now his eyes meet hers. They widen with possibilities.

"Of course. Let me get my things."

He hurries over to his table, grabbing his umbrella, reaching for the paper cup of coffee and open copy of the *Wall Street Journal* and then hesitating. Alex can almost see his thoughts pop up over his head in cartoon balloons. If he takes the paper and coffee, then he won't have a hand free to help console the poor widow. He chooses to leave them, then spins fast and bumps into another man who is also staring at Alex. They exchange glances, one gloating, the other envious, and then he slips past and offers Alex his arm.

Alex tucks her computer into the carrying case, pulls the strap over her shoulder, and links her fingers around his biceps, feeling the doughy fat beneath the fabric. There are six people in the coffee shop, three of whom watch them walk to the door.

"I'm staying at the Hyatt." Alex is louder than necessary. "It's right up the block."

The overcast day matches the hue of the stained sidewalk and dirty office buildings. Even the air smells gray, car exhaust melding with drizzle. Alex begins to stroke his arm. Her breath quickens in anticipation.

"I'm getting hot."

"Do you want me to hold your jacket?"

"Not that kind of hot."

Alex maneuvers him against the brick wall at the opening of an alley. She takes his hand, which is as pliant as a doll's, and runs it over her chest, down her trim belly, to between her legs.

"Sex and death," she whispers. "They're connected. Part of the same cycle."

His eyes bug out, and his jaw drops open, but he stays stock-still. She writhes against him, and he finally gets the hint, his chubby fingers beginning to explore her.

"Is it wrong?" Panting now. "That death turns me on?"

He moans something noncommittal, but the umbrella drops from his other hand and he grabs her left breast, seeking the nipple through the fabric.

"In the alley," she says. "Behind the Dumpster."

She leads him, walking backward, his hands stuck to her as if glued, and when the Dumpster shields them from the street view she runs a palm over the front of his pants and feels how much he wants her.

He reaches up, leaning his chubby face in, trying to lift up her veil and kiss her. She catches his wrist.

"You'd prefer it on," she says.

His eyebrow lifts in a question. His face is close now, and Alex senses that he can see through the mesh. She's wearing a lot of makeup, a special brand that fills in the indentations of scars, but it can't cover everything. His expression changes from lust to worry.

Alex grunts, working open his fly, pulling his cock out over the waistband of his tighty whities. It's long and hard and she digs her fingernails into the shaft. But his fingers have stopped moving, even as she tries to grind against them, and his eyes remain locked on her face.

She sighs, annoyed, and releases his wrist.

"Fine. You really want to see? Help yourself."

He lifts her veil. His worried expression explodes into revulsion.

"Oh . . . oh Jesus God . . ."

He tries to pull away, but Alex grips his shaft tight. Her free hand unclips the folder knife from her garter belt, using the thumb-stud to flick open the three-inch blade. She jabs it in sideways, under his balls, slicing through to the femur.

The man screams.

Alex twists the knife, severing the femoral artery, then spins on her heels and shoves him face-first into the wall. She pins his shoulders while blood sluices down the bricks. His hands are clamped on to the wound, but it won't help. She widens her stance as the pool of blood grows, avoiding stains on her Miu Miu pumps.

He struggles, and struggles hard, but Alex has both strength and leverage on her side. His moans are muffled by the wall and the traffic sounds. She's still turned on. Alex thinks about reaching down, forcing one of his hands between her legs, but she doesn't want to risk him getting loose.

"What do you think your family will say?" Alex gently chides. "Found dead in an alley with your prick hanging out?"

He strains against the wall. The harder he fights, the faster he loses blood. Alex leans in closer, whispers in his hairy ear.

"Maybe I'll pay your wife a visit. Tell her how much you wanted me before you died. I bet your driver's license has your address on it. Should I drop by the old homestead?"

He takes his hands off his crotch and pushes against the wall, grunting. The blood is really flowing now. His effort lasts less than a minute, then he slumps against the brick like a drunk embracing an old war buddy.

"I hope you were worth my time."

She tries the front pockets first. Keys, a tin container of breath mints. Alex opens the container, and instead of breath mints finds egg-shaped yellow pills. Tadalafil, for erectile dysfunction. Not that this guy seemed to have any problems. Then she digs into his back pocket, freeing his wallet. Three dollars. Three lousy dollars. And his credit cards all say SEE ID on the back signature line.

"Shit." Alex is no longer horny. Just irritated.

He's almost dead, probably in shock, but she takes some time to vent her frustrations out on him. When she's finished, his face looks a lot worse than hers ever did.

Then she squats next to a rain puddle and rinses off the folder before clipping it back to her garter belt. On her way out of the alley she picks up the dropped umbrella and opens it, shielding her face from the drizzle.

Alex needs money. The three bucks she just stole won't even buy hair dye. When the body is discovered and ID'ed, there's a chance it will lead back to the coffee shop. Cops will be looking for a blonde staying at the Hyatt who recently attended a funeral—all three false leads, once Miss Clairol gets involved.

Luckily, this is a big city, and money is everywhere if you know where to look. Alex checks her watch. She has some time before her date. More than enough time to make a few grand.

She heads uptown, a spring in her step, eyes searching for the perfect person to murder.

CHAPTER 3

URNING LATHAM'S FUNERAL into a crime scene didn't endear me any further to his relatives, but work was more productive than grief. I established the perimeter, organized teams to question the attendees and cemetery staff, bagged, tagged, and sent the camera phone to the Crime Lab, and led a search for Alex that proved fruitless.

My boss, Captain Steven Bains, waited for things to calm down before approaching me. He was short, stocky, with a crop of unnatural-looking black hair that may have been a weave, a toupee, a hair transplant, or some kind of dead animal.

"I'm sorry for your loss, Lieutenant."

"Thank you. And thanks for coming."

"When one of these perverts attacks one of our own, we make it personal. We will catch her."

"I know."

"The key word there is *we*. Not you. You're a victim. You can't be on the case. You're too good a cop to throw away your career on a personal vendetta."

I did my best to look neutral. This didn't surprise me, but it still rankled.

"Alex called you, right?"

"I gave my cell to Herb. He's working on tracing the number."

"Sergeant Benedict isn't part of this investigation either."

"He said he'd pass it along to Mankowski."

Bains searched my eyes. If he detected the lie, he didn't call me on it.

"I can't imagine how much you want this woman, Lieutenant. But if I find out you're trying to involve yourself in the investigation, your leave of absence will become permanent."

The wind kicked up a notch. I shivered, and the act made me feel weak. Bains gave me an awkward half hug, sort of slipping around me and patting my back. I got a good look at the top of his head but still couldn't tell what sort of hair he had up there. I fought the urge to touch it.

Bains eventually broke the embrace, and an impromptu line formed behind him, cop after cop shaking sad hands with me and offering words that meant nothing. I outranked most of them, and stayed stoic until I got to Herb.

"I should have done more," he said.

"Jesus, Herb. You did everything you could."

"So did you."

"It wasn't enough."

He grabbed me like a bear.

"You'll get through this, Jack. You're the strongest woman I ever met."

Like all strong women, I ignored compliments.

"If Bains asks about my cell phone, tell him you gave it to Mankowski."

"What?"

"I'll explain it later."

Herb released me, staring over my shoulder.

"Ah, shit. The assman cometh."

I followed Herb's gaze and saw Harry McGlade walking over to us. Harry was an ex-cop, and my ex-partner, currently eking out a living as a private detective. He looked as he always did: expensive tailored suit that needed to be pressed, three days' growth of beard, a Bogart hat, and a broad grin that made you think he was laughing at you. Which he usually was.

"Hi, Jackie. When are we going after the bitch?"

Harry had been there the night Latham died, and had his own reasons for hating Alex Kork, many of them just as valid as mine. But I'd worked with him in the past, and had no desire to repeat the experience.

"I'm on a leave of absence," I told him.

"Good. We can take turns driving the Winnebago."

"The what?"

"I just bought it. Stocked with all the latest spy shit. Phone tracers. Surveillance equipment. GPS trackers. It's like a crime lab on wheels. If her ass is hiding in a Stuckey's shitter in Mobile, Alabama, I'll be able to find it."

He grinned, winked, then nodded at Herb.

"How's the knee?" Harry asked.

"Hurts."

I hid my surprise. It was the first time I'd ever seen Harry and Herb be civil to each other.

"I see the pain hasn't kept you from eating." Harry rubbed his chin. "You're going to give Rudolph and the other eight reindeer hernias."

Herb smiled, but it held no humor. "The police report will say you lost your teeth resisting arrest. Bad for you, but good for your boyfriend."

"Guys—" I stepped between them.

Harry stuck his head over my shoulder.

"I'm a heterosexual. Ask your mom. But you . . . you're a hipposexual. How does it even work? Does Mrs. Claus hang above you in some kind of harness?"

Herb brought up his crutch like a sword. Harry snatched it in his prosthetic hand. There was a whirring, mechanical sound, and the aluminum frame bent in Harry's metal fingers.

Herb smiled for real this time. "It's time for a physics lesson."

He shoved, knocking Harry onto his back. Several cops still in attendance came over, but Herb warned them away. He gripped the top of the crutch and leaned on it, forcing the end into Harry's diaphragm.

"This would be a good time to apologize."

"I'm sorry," Harry croaked, struggling to breathe. "Maybe you're not fat. Maybe you're just pregnant with a wildebeest."

Bernice, Herb's better half, gently took her husband's arm and led him away, probably saving Harry's life. Harry grinned up at me.

"I'm glad his trainer stopped him before he ate us all."

I shook my head. "You're an idiot."

"And you're my sister. But, disgusting as it sounds, I still can't help looking up your skirt."

I'd recently discovered that Harry might, *might*, be my half brother—a troubling fact that DNA testing would either confirm or deny in the next few days. If it turned out we were related, I'd have to double my weekly therapy sessions. Once I bothered to find a therapist.

"Go away, Harry. I don't want to deal with you right now."

"I'll call you later. We can eat in the Winnebago. It's got a kitchenette. You can cook stuff."

I started to walk away, back to the casket.

"When you come over, bring food!" he called after me. "I haven't bought any food yet! Pick up some steaks! Or a ham!"

"Shut up!" someone yelled. "It's a funeral! Show a little respect for the dead!"

"Who the hell are you, Big Nose?"

"I'm Latham's cousin Ray!"

"Well, I was with Latham the night he died, and his last words were: 'My big-nosed cousin Ray is a dick!'"

Swearing ensued, and probably a scuffle. I didn't look back to find out.

Mom stood at the edge of Latham's grave, peering down. We'd spent six hours shopping for her dress, Mom dismissing one after another, convinced that Latham wouldn't have liked them. They'd been close.

I reached out, held her hand, feeling swollen knuckles beneath thin, cool skin. I tried to recall the exact moment when Mom had become an old lady, and wondered when I'd reach that point myself. I stared at my hand, looking for signs of arthritis, and instead focused on my engagement ring.

The pain threatened to erupt. I shook with the effort to keep it buried.

"You have to mourn sometime, Jacqueline."

Mom's voice left no doubt she was following her own advice.

"I need to find her, Mom."

My mom turned away from the grave, her red-rimmed eyes finding mine. The softness of her tone didn't undermine its strength.

"I could tell you that revenge won't bring him back. Or I could tell you that letting go is the only way you'll be able to get on with your life. Or I could even plead with you to not chase Alex, because I can't bear to lose you. But instead of all that I'm just going to say that when you need me, I'll be there."

I managed to choke out, "Thanks."

We were silent for a moment, focusing on Latham's final resting place.

Mom broke the silence.

"Revenge won't bring him back."

"I know."

"You need to grieve and accept. It's the only way you'll get through this."

"I know."

"And if anything . . . happens . . . to you . . ."

I hugged my mother, her tears warm on my neck.

"I know, Mom. I know."

After a few deep sobs, Mom stiffened. She held me at arm's length, her face hard and set. The face she wore as a cop, decades ago.

"Don't try to arrest her this time, Jacqueline. When you have the chance, send her to hell where she belongs."

I nodded, but I didn't really want to think about that right now. What I had to say next didn't come easy.

"Mom . . . I need you to go away for a while."

Instead of showing anger, Mom smiled.

"I've already booked a cruise. Two weeks in Alaska. I'm leaving tomorrow."

Color me surprised.

"Really? I thought I'd have to threaten you."

"It doesn't make sense for both of us to be worried about each other. Alex won't be able to get me while I'm on a boat. And seeing glaciers and polar bears will help me forget that my daughter is hunting a maniac."

"It will?"

Mom shook her head sadly.

"No. You'd better come back to me, young lady. Don't make me strap on my gun and put her in the ground myself."

Again I faced an internal battle to hold back the tears.

"I'll be fine," I managed.

"I assume Harry's going with you."

"Probably not."

"You need help, Jacqueline. Someone to watch your back."

"Harry is a . . ." My mind searched for a softer word than *shithead*. ". . . he's difficult to work with."

"He's an obnoxious pig, and I say that knowing he might be my son. But he cares about you in his way, and you can use him."

"Going on the road with Harry McGlade . . . I think I'd rather dance at a strip club for sex offenders."

"You need someone. Herb won't be any good to you with his bad leg. How about that other fellow who helped us? Phineas Troutt?"

"This isn't his fight, Mom."

"Alex seemed just as eager to kill him as she did us. Call him."

"If you want me to."

"Pinky swear."

"Jesus, Mom. I'm forty-seven years old."

She held up a gnarled pinky. I hooked mine around it.

"Fine. I pinky swear."

Mom stared at the grave for another minute, said good-bye to Latham under her breath, then turned to leave.

"I'm going to Shirley's. Your partner said he'd give me a ride. You sure you don't want to come?"

Latham's cousin was having a reception at his house following the funeral. Mom was invited. I wasn't. I considered going anyway, weighing the pros and cons of being spat on by his family and friends. Much as I deserved it, I'd be a disruptive presence.

"I need to be alone for a little bit. If I don't see you, have fun on your cruise."

"I intend to. I'm hoping I'll meet a nice man. Those tiny little cabins are much cozier when you're sharing a bed."

Mom winked, and touched my cheek. Then she headed back into the throng of mourners, which had now dwindled to only a few. I silently wished for someone, anyone, to come up to me and blame me for Latham's death. Call me names. Even throw a punch. I was prepared not to defend myself.

Except for a few sour looks cast in my direction, I was ignored. I faced Latham again.

"I'm sorry," I mumbled for the thousandth time.

I tried to get my lips to say good-bye, as my mother had done. They refused. I wasn't ready to let go just yet. So I simply stood there and stared.

After a while, the grave digger came by with a backhoe and began filling in the dirt. Methodical. Disinterested. The elaborate ceremony of death, meant to offer comfort to loved ones, reduced to menial labor. I watched, staying put as the drizzle became heavy rain, cold, relentless, and unforgiving.

CHAPTER 4

THE MAN'S WRINKLES are caked with filth, and the layers of soiled clothing wrapped around his thin body smell of BO, urine, and worse. Alex takes no joy in slitting his throat. She mixes business with pleasure when possible, but for this old crazy bum it's a mercy killing. Alex derives no pleasure from mercy.

She holds his shoulder, keeps him turned away so the spray of the carotid doesn't splash her Dolce & Gabbana. He moans a little, but resigns himself to his fate quickly, collapsing into a clump of bloody, dirty rags. The alley, like most in the area, is narrow and deserted.

Alex lights a cigarette and waits for him to stop breathing. She doesn't inhale, because she doesn't smoke. If someone happens to walk by, a nicotine break is a good excuse for standing around in an alley.

Two minutes pass. No one walks by. For a population of six hundred thousand, there aren't many people on the street. Maybe it's the crummy weather.

"D . . . deh . . . deh . . ."

The bum is trying to talk, but he's having some problems; most of his breath is bubbling out through the hole in his neck. She nudges a patch of unbloodied clothing with her toe.

"Last words are important. Try to finish."

"D . . . deh . . . *devil*," he manages, somewhere between a whisper and a gurgle.

Alex smiles, but only the right side of her face moves.

"The devil isn't real, buddy. I am."

The bum expires, rheumy eyes going dull, and the blood finally stops pumping. Breaking his neck would have been quicker, but that would have meant getting behind him, finding a good grip. Changing her hair color is annoying enough. Alex doesn't want to fuss with lice shampoo as well.

Alex peels back his sweatshirt, and the smell gets so bad it activates her gag reflex. She removed the bandage from her nose a few days ago, not because the break was fully healed, but because it drew more attention than her scars, even under a veil. Now she wishes she'd waited; a nose brace and plugs would have prevented this awful odor from assaulting her.

The money roll is in his pants pocket, almost the diameter of a soda can. During her stint in the marines, she knew of an MP who would roll drug dealers and pimps when he needed fast cash, the logic being they always had a wad. The downside was they also carried weapons, and had unsavory friends.

When Alex needed money, her solution was less complicated. Homeless people carry their entire fortunes on them. Though some were drunks and druggies, spending their last nickels to score, the schizos and psychotics tended to hoard cash. It took her less than an hour to find one on the street, muttering to himself. When she shoved him into the alley, he was more interested in protecting his plastic bags full of precious cans than his own throat.

She flips through the bills, which are surprisingly clean and crisp, and concludes she's just made around six hundred bucks. Alex tucks the roll into her laptop bag, checks the sidewalk for pedestrians, then steps out of the alley and heads for her car. It's parked on the street next to a small bookstore. A recent model Honda Accord, so popular it's anonymous. In her younger years, she preferred to steal sports cars. But those are conspicuous.

Or perhaps, Alex thinks, *I'm simply mellowing with age.*

She approaches it from behind and inspects the trunk, satisfied that the car's previous owner hasn't begun to leak any bodily fluids. Since killing Jack's fiancé three weeks ago, Alex has switched vehicles three times. Perhaps a bit overly cautious, but she doesn't want to leave Jack such obvious bread crumbs. She prefers to keep the lieutenant guessing.

Exactly twenty days have passed since Alex was a guest of the Heathrow Facility, a maximum security prison for the criminally insane. She'd been put there by Jack, who had torn off half of her face in the process. The skin grafts, done by unskilled surgeons on the public dime, left Alex pink and mottled from her eye to her chin. She looked like a crazy quilt made out of Spam.

While in Heathrow, Alex had a lot of time to think. About revenge. And about the future. She planned two elaborate schemes. The first was to exact some payback. The second was larger in scope, but would be even more satisfying than killing Jack and company.

After a dramatic escape, Alex paid the lieutenant a visit, intending to kill her and everyone she cared about, including Jack's mother; her partner, Herb; her fiancé; and two old friends, Harry McGlade and Phineas Troutt. But there were . . . complications, and everything went to hell.

Alex had been thinking about that night a lot. About how it could have gone differently. Jack and her friends got very lucky, no doubt. But Jack had also stood toe-to-toe with Alex, and broken her nose.

Alex had been in scores of fights, with both men and women. But no one had ever broken her nose before.

So, scheme number one got flushed down the toilet. But scheme number two is still viable. Scheme number two will make everything right. And there's room for Jack to take a big role in it.

A very big role.

Alex takes out her keys and presses the button to open the car door. After she climbs in and buckles up, she considers her next move. It's a little past two p.m. There's time to buy some dye, do her hair, before her four o'clock date. Alex uses the onboard GPS system and searches for *drugstore,* finding one less than a mile away.

She chooses red for her new hair color. The dead bum would have approved.

Then Alex heads toward the Old Stone Inn near the airport, picked because the name is absolutely perfect, and muses about all of the people who are going to die in the next few days.

There will be quite a few.

CHAPTER 5

I WANTED TO GET GOOD AND DRUNK, but I'd been pretty much good and drunk for the last few weeks. Mourning. Hating myself. Wallowing in a pool of alcohol, antidepressants, and self-pity, biding time until I was able get my shit together.

The time had finally come.

I walked past acres of tombstones through freezing rain, exited the Graceland Cemetery on Clark and Irving, and hailed a taxi.

"UIC on Roosevelt."

The cabbie glanced up at me in the rearview. I was soaked and shivering, my clothes sticking to me like they'd been painted on, my nipples jutting out like gun barrels.

"Wet out there," he said.

I didn't answer. He turned up the heat without being asked. I didn't deserve warming up, but I had no will to argue.

Forty blocks later and thirty bucks lighter, I was spit out by the cab at the University of Illinois Chicago. The rain had changed its style of attack, cold fat drops replaced by wind-driven drizzle, which stung like needle pricks. The campus, normally gorgeous in the autumn, looked barren and dead. The trees were skeletons, their leafy skins shed in clumps all over the ground, brown and wet as mud.

The Illinois Forensic Science Center was on the south side of the street. Before it merged with the state police more than a decade ago, it was just known as the Crime Lab. One of the most advanced in the country, containing over fifty thousand square feet of crime-busting technology.

I showed my badge at the front desk, declined the offer of paper towels, and took the stairs to the second floor and Officer Scott Hajek, whom I'd phoned earlier.

Hajek had a roundish face and large blue eyes magnified to cartoonish extreme by his thick glasses. The top of his head came up to my nose. He had a crush on me, and had asked me out several times over the years. I always deferred, saying I already had a boyfriend. Hopefully he'd have the tact not to ask me again.

Per our call, I met Hajek in one of the many labs, this one crammed with computer equipment, expensive-looking electronic devices, and an impressive collection of empty pizza boxes stacked neatly in the corner.

Hajek, sitting in a swivel chair and peering at a computer, glanced over his shoulder at me when I entered.

"Still raining?"

I held my thumb and index finger an inch apart, indicating a wee bit.

"There are some take-out napkins on the table there, next to that container of Parmesan cheese."

"I'm fine." My teeth were only chattering a little.

"You hungry? I still got some pizza left over from lunch. Double pepperoni."

"No thanks."

"You don't like pizza?"

"I just came from a funeral. I'm not very hungry."

Hajek stared at me, and for a moment I saw his eyes flicker to my boobs, which felt ready to fire two shots across his bow.

"Maybe later tonight? You have to eat, and if you want to talk, I'm a good listener."

"Thanks for offering, Scott." I tried to sound genuine, even though I was tired and he was annoying me, squinting to see through my dress. "Tell me what you got on the cell phone I sent over."

Hajek blinked, swallowed, and turned back to his desk.

"It's a PP Tangsung 117EX. Quad-band, GSM 1900 network, MMS and EMS. Or, in non-geek terms, a pay-as-you-go model with enhanced video and messaging capabilities, and a good antenna. I lifted two prints, both belonging to Alexandra Kork, but you probably already knew that."

I shivered. "Traceable?"

Hajek swiveled to face me, except his eyes didn't meet mine.

"She bought the phone at the mall in Gurnee, Illinois, six days ago. I called them, spoke to the employee who sold it to her. Said it was a tall woman, well built, with bandages on her face. Used a credit card in the name of Shanna Arnold. I ran a check; Mrs. Arnold was recently reported missing by her husband."

"Were you able to trace the call? Where Alex called from? Her number?"

Hajek didn't answer. His eyes were having a telepathic conversation with my breasts. I folded my arms over my chest.

"Officer Hajek?"

He blinked.

"Captain Bains called me. Said you're on a leave of absence. You're not part of this investigation."

My demeanor grew as cold as my skin.

"So you're not going to tell me?"

"I could get into trouble, Lieutenant."

"She killed my fiancé, Scott."

"I'm sorry about that."

I could have gone all superior officer on him, but instead I lowered my arms, knowing he'd look at my boobs again. Girl power.

"Please, Scott. Between you and me."

He licked his lips, then slowly nodded.

"There isn't a record of her activating the phone. That means she unlocked it, and used a different SIM card as a new number." He cleared his throat. "Then she spoofed the caller ID."

"In non-geek, please."

"Basically, she hacked the phone to make it usable with any network, then put in a stolen Subscriber Identity Module so the calls are being billed to someone else's account." He held up the cell. "This phone is using Shanna Arnold's SIM."

"Can we find out the number Alex called from?"

"No. Because of the spoof. Alex used this phone as a remote camera, switching it on by calling it. When I checked out the caller ID recorded on the SIM card, it showed that fake number Hollywood uses in movies, 555-5555."

I'd seen the 555 number myself, on calls from Alex. She probably thought it was funny. "How is that possible?"

"There are Internet services you can sign up for that let you place a call and leave false caller ID numbers and names. You use a VoIP—a Voice-over Internet Protocol service—and punch in the ten-digit number you're calling, plus the ten-digit number and name you'd like the recipient to see."

I frowned. I'd been hoping there was a way to trace it through the provider.

"Can we get all the names of customers who had phones recently stolen, see if we can connect Alex with one of those?"

"Do you know how many people lose their phones every day? And not everyone who does reports it. In Mrs. Arnold's case . . ."

He let the words trail off. I knew what he meant. Shanna Arnold was probably dead. It wouldn't be beneath Alex to kill just to get a cell phone.

"So there's no way to find out where she called from?"

Hajek grinned shyly, like a schoolboy.

"Tell me, Scott."

"You sure you don't want to have a bite to eat later? I live real close."

The little extortionist. If I hadn't been on a mandatory leave of absence and warned away from this case, I would have gotten seriously pissed.

"Not tonight, Scott. But I'll have some free time next week."

"Tuesday?"

I shrugged. "Sure."

He grinned. Something was caught in his two front teeth. Probably double pepperoni.

"MMS sent through GSM is stored on the SIM card, which also records the unique TAP/CIBER, which can be put into the HLR database—"

I held up my palm. "The bottom line."

"If Alex sends video or text messages, I can use the SIM card to get the phone number and basic location of the phone she called from. She activated this camera from a phone in Deer Park."

"Do you have the phone number?"

"There's a problem."

"What problem?"

"I tried calling the number already. When I did, this one rang." He held up the phone from the cemetery.

"Meaning?"

"Alex must have known the SIM cards could be traced, so she set up a call-forwarding daisy chain. She calls phone number one, and it automatically forwards the call to number two, and so on, to as many phones as she wants, until the last one in the chain receives the call."

"But if I find the phone, I can bring it to you, and you can trace it to the next one?"

"Sure. But it won't be easy to find. A cell phone can only be traced to within three hundred meters of its location. It could be in a hotel room, in a parked car, or plugged into an outlet in some public place, like a library or a bus station. She bought twelve phones in Gurnee, plus she could keep adding more to the chain."

"I'll chance it. Gimme the number."

"You need help, Lieutenant. A big team, working on this, is the best way to go."

I chewed my lower lip, which still was sore from the same encounter with Alex that resulted in twenty-six stitches on my scalp.

"What if we had a phone that wasn't part of the daisy chain? That was a direct link to Alex?"

"What do you mean?"

Alex had sent me a cell phone in a floral arrangement, during my hospital recuperation. I hadn't told anyone, even Herb, because I didn't want it taken away. I wasn't on Latham's murder investigation, but I wasn't about to give up my only link to Alex.

Unfortunately, I needed Hajek's expertise, and that meant disclosure. I didn't know if I trusted Hajek. He'd done good by me in the past, but he was a by-the-book kind of guy, all about protocol and chain of evidence and forms in triplicate.

I weighed my choices, realized I had none, and took a leap of faith.

"Alex gave me one of those twelve phones. She's called me, text messaged me, a few times. Could we get her location from the SIM card?"

Hajek's face fell. "She gave you a phone?"

He sounded a bit more upset than I would have liked.

"I just said that. Can we get her phone number from it?"

Hajek rolled his chair a few inches backward, like I'd suddenly become a leper.

"Withholding evidence in a murder investigation is a felony, Lieutenant. Obstruction of justice."

"Blame stress."

"How long have you had the phone?"

The look on his face told me he'd gone from ally to adversary. I pulled the friendship card.

"Scott, this is really important to me."

"I've followed this case. Read all the files for research. She's seriously evil, and totally dangerous. If you've had the phone for more than a day or two, keeping it to yourself might have cost the lives of several people."

I switched to the sympathy card.

"If that's the case, I'll head straight for the hundred and third floor of the Sears Tower with a glass cutter and a laminated photo ID so they can identify my body afterward. Come on, Scott. Alex killed the man I loved."

He shook his head. "You have to turn it in."

I tried the vamp card, walking up to him with a forced smile and trying my damnedest to get my voice low like Kathleen Turner in *Body Heat*.

"I'd be really grateful if you could help me out, Scott."

Instead of melting into putty, Hajek grabbed for the landline on his desk.

"I'm not losing my job over you, Lieutenant. It's my duty as a police officer to inform your captain that—"

I played my last card. The tough bitch card.

"Officer Hajek." There was so much steel in my words that he flinched as if hit. "Put down that phone right now or this is going to get ugly."

Hajek obeyed.

"Give me the number."

"I . . . uh—"

"Now!"

Hajek grabbed a sheet of paper off his desk and offered it meekly. I spun on my heels and headed for the door, hearing him pick up the phone again as I left.

CHAPTER 6

AN ASTHMATIC BLOWS HARDER than the complimentary hair dryer in room 114 at the Old Stone Inn, but Alex makes do, brushing out her new strawberry red color while standing in front of the bathroom sink. She tilts her head forward, shaking out her long bangs, straightening while drying. When she finishes, her hair is still in front of her face. Alex looks into the mirror, then parts the bangs with her fingers, pushing the right side behind her ear and letting the left side hang flat. Covering her scars.

Alex stares. Sees someone she recognizes. Someone she hasn't seen in a while. A beautiful old friend who has gone away and is never coming back. Fit. Trim. Still attractive, even a year shy of forty.

"I miss you."

She kisses the tip of her index finger, then touches the glass, running it down the reflection of her jawline. Her hair falls back, revealing the pink ugliness underneath.

Without telegraphing the move, without even changing expression, Alex makes a fist and drives it into the mirror. Her image shatters.

She feels like there are coiled springs nestling in her muscles, bursting to be set loose. Naked, she lifts her arms above her head and rolls into a handstand, walking over to the area the bed used to occupy before she pushed it into the corner. She tilts farther forward, her feet touching the wall, and begins to do reverse chin-ups, her head touching the carpet with every dip.

When she reaches seventeen, the sweat comes, rolling down her ears and soaking into her hair.

Her arms begin to wobble at forty-six. She starts to pant, oxygenating her muscles, the lactic acid building and burning.

Alex pushes on to sixty, even though her arms are shaking so badly her balance is wavering.

By seventy-three, her left arm gives out, causing her to collapse onto her side. She rolls with the fall, tucking in her head, using momentum to get to her feet. Alex turns and launches into an explosive tae kwon do kata, kicking, twisting, and punching.

Her mind is both focused and clear as she forces her body through the moves, grunting exhalations called *ki-hops* with each blow. Her muscles remember every thrust and spin. The particular form she uses is traditionally done with four assistants, who hold boards at various heights to be broken by hands, feet, and head.

Rather than boards, she flails at the air, directing each strike at the unscarred face of Jack Daniels.

The kata ends in the splits, the toes on the forward leg pointed skyward, hands clenched into fists and spread out like wings. Her body glistens with sweat, and her breath comes in gasps.

With her heart rate still up, Alex flips over and begins a set of fingertip push-ups. She knocks off a hundred, rolls gracefully to her feet, and pads into the bathroom to towel off.

The cracked mirror tells her she's still ugly. As if she needed the reminder.

The clock on the nightstand reads ten after three. Her date isn't due until four, but from experience she knows he usually comes early. In more ways than one.

Alex doesn't dress. Instead, she digs into her gym bag and removes a fresh roll of duct tape, a package of rubber bands, a box cutter, a Cheetah stun gun, and a handheld butane torch. The stun gun is pink, the shape and size of a cigarette pack. The torch looks like a phaser from *Star Trek*. It's also pink, which delighted Alex when she found it at the home supply store. A girl has got to know how to accessorize.

Then she sits on the bed, lotus style, and waits.

Ten minutes later, David "Lance" Strang knocks on her motel door. She confirms it with the peephole.

"I've been waiting for you, Lance."

She opens the door, lets him ogle her. Lance hasn't changed much in the fifteen years since she's last seen him. Same broad shoulders. Same strong chin. His thick brown hair has receded just a bit, and now it's salted with gray, but other than that he's exactly as she remembered him from their Geiger days.

Lance takes Alex in, staring at her legs, her tits, before moving up to her face. When he sees the scar, his grin falters.

"Yeah, sorry about that, Lance. And about this."

Alex brings up the Cheetah and hits David Strang in the gut, applying a million volts to his nervous system. He jerks forward, and all two hundred and twenty fit pounds of him crumple to the carpeting.

CHAPTER 7

CABBED IT from the Crime Lab, heading for the nearest Washington Mutual bank branch. Again, the driver commented on how soaked I was. Next time it rained, I'd indulge in a thicker bra. Or an umbrella.

During the ride I made some calls. One I didn't want to make. The other I *really* didn't want to make. I began with the easier one.

"Wilbur? It's Jack."

"How are you holding up, sweetheart?"

"I've been better. Thanks for respecting my wishes and not attending the funeral. Mom would have shot you if she saw you."

"Um, about that . . ."

I took a deep breath—never a wise move in a Chicago cab. This one smelled like gym socks and cheap incense.

"Tell me you weren't there, Wilbur."

Pause.

"Wilbur . . ."

"Your fiancé died. Of course I was going to come."

"I didn't see you there."

"You didn't see me at any of your graduations or your wedding either, Jacqueline. I'm good at being discreet. Look, I know I only met Latham once, when you brought him over, but for what it's worth I really liked him. I'm so sorry for your loss, sweetheart. If there's anything I can do . . ."

My voice got harder. "There is, Wilbur. In fact, there is."

"Name it."

"I need you to go away for a while. The person who killed Latham, she has a habit of targeting people close to me."

Wilbur paused.

"Thank you, Jacqueline."

"For sending you away?"

"For saying that I might actually be close to you. I know I've been an absentee father. I know how much I've missed out on. These past few months, as we've gotten to know each other, have been the best of my life. I mean that."

"Good. Then you'll get out of town for a few weeks, until this gets resolved."

"Absolutely."

"I mean it this time, Wilbur. No saying one thing and doing the other."

"It's already taken care of. In fact, I just booked a vacation. I'm taking an Alaskan cruise. It's shipping out tomorrow."

"Really?" Mom was also going on an Alaskan cruise tomorrow. I thought about mentioning it, but the chances that they would both be on the same ship were a zillion to one. Instead I said, "Good. Have fun."

"I intend to. Maybe I'll find a nice man on board."

Mom said the same thing.

"Remember to wear protection. Or make sure he wears protection." I wasn't sure how my father's relationships actually worked, and wasn't sure that I ever needed to know.

"I promise. And speaking of protection, please make sure you protect yourself when you're chasing Alex."

"I will."

"You're going to kill her, aren't you?"

I'd been wondering the same thing, but hearing a kindly old man say it made it sound horribly wrong.

"I'm . . . going to stop her."

"I've saved every press clipping you've ever been in, Jacqueline. You arrested her before. She escaped. You can't risk that again."

"It's . . . it's complicated."

"This isn't murder, sweetheart."

Jesus. The M word. I had a hard enough time living with myself as it was. I became a cop to catch murderers, because murder, in every single case, was wrong. Even in cases of revenge.

Every night since Latham's death, I've lain awake in bed conjuring up scenarios where I blew Alex's head off. Alex was always armed, trying to kill me as well. I evened the score, while also retaining my morality and humanity. But if I had the chance to murder her, in cold blood, would I take it?

"She's a rabid dog, Jacqueline. It's not murder. It's mercy."

I doubted the courts would see it that way. I doubted *I* would see it that way.

"Have a good time in Alaska, Dad. Call me when you get back."

"You know, my heart gets a little bigger every time you call me Dad. I love you, sweetheart."

Since Wilbur reappeared in my life, he'd accepted our relationship much more easily than I had. He'd been saying "I love you" for a few weeks now, but I wasn't ready to return the sentiment yet. Being abandoned for thirty-plus years, even understanding the reason why, wasn't easy to forgive.

"We'll talk soon," I said, and disconnected. Now for the hard call. His number wasn't in my cell address book, so I had to use directory assistance. I hoped I'd get a machine, then I could leave a message, clear my conscience, without having to talk.

Just my luck, he picked up on the first ring.

"This is Alan."

"Hi, Alan. It's me."

There was a pause. I wondered if he was thinking what I was thinking. About our years being married. About our recent affair. About him leaving me for a second time.

"I'm sorry about Latham."

"Did Mom tell you?"

"I haven't, uh, talked to your mother since we saw each other last.

I signed up for this thing on the Internet. Google News. Every time you're mentioned in the paper, they send me a link to the article."

I was touched.

"You're checking on me?"

"More like waiting for the obituary."

Ouch.

"Well, sorry to disappoint you, but I'm still among the living."

"Jesus, Jack. You know I don't mean it like that."

"Then what did you mean?"

"You need a reminder? The reason our marriage ended was because I couldn't stand worrying about you all the time. Do you know what it's like to lose someone you love?"

"Yeah." My teeth clenched. "I just came from his funeral."

"Oh, hell. Shit. I'm sorry. I'm an insensitive bastard."

"Yes. Yes you are."

"Good. We agree on something. So why the call?"

I searched my mind for the right words, the words that would make him listen to me. The silence stretched.

"I'm sorry, Jack. You can't come here."

Being cold and wet didn't stop me from blushing. "Excuse me?"

"I feel bad for you. And I still love you. But you know my feelings. We can't be together unless you quit the force."

If I still carried around any remnants of affection for this man I was once married to, they were now gone. The conceit, the nerve . . .

"Have you quit?" Alan's voice went from accusatory to hopeful. "Tell me you've quit."

I recovered, found my spine. "No, Alan, I haven't quit, and I don't want to be with you. I don't want to see you. I don't even want to talk to you."

"Then why are you calling? You think it's easy for me to talk to you?"

"I'm . . ." I took a deep breath, let it out slow. "I'm calling to warn you. The psycho who killed Latham might be targeting people in my life."

"You're kidding."

"It would be best if you went away for a few weeks."

"You're fucking kidding me."

"Alan, I don't like it any more than—"

"Are you serious?" He'd gone up an octave. "Are you fucking serious? Your job just killed your boyfriend. That could have been me. If we were still married, I'd be the dead one. How many times have we talked about your fucking career, about how dangerous it is?"

I shut my eyes, trying to stay professional even though it would have hurt less if he were in the cab with me, stabbing me with a fork.

"Alan, I'm sorry, but you really need to leave town."

"You're unbelievable. Unbefuckinglievable. You know what? All these years, I've been waiting to say I told you so. Well, here it is, Jack. *I told you so.* Who's next? Herb? Your mother? Your best friends from grammar school? All because you chase killers for a living?"

Professionalism flew out the window.

"This killer is chasing me, Alan! It doesn't matter if I quit my job, move to Tibet, join a goddamn monastery! She's after me, and she may go after you too! So, please. *Please.* Take a long vacation and let me fix this."

"I can take care of myself, Jack. In fact, I've been doing that quite well since you drove me away. It's too bad, for Latham's sake, you didn't drive him away too."

The fork twisted so hard that tears came.

"Please get out of town, Alan."

"Don't call me again. Ever."

"Alan—"

He hung up. The tears became sobs, and pretty soon I was bawling so bad my nose was running down my chin.

"Miss? I try not to eavesdrop on my fares' conversations, even when they're yelling like you were, but I noticed you said something about being chased by a killer."

"Don't worry," I told the taxi driver between sniffles. "I'm sure you're safe."

"I hope so. We've had a dark sedan following us since you got in the cab. Turns every time we do."

CHAPTER 8

STUN GUNS WORK on two levels. The first is through pain compliance. Being hit with a million volts hurts like hell, comparable to being jabbed with a hot poker. But unlike a hot poker, the electric current also overrides a person's muscles, causing them to twitch uncontrollably while simultaneously being unable to fight back.

Alex holds the stun gun against Lance's stomach long enough to drop him to his knees. Before he can recover, she hits him in the temple with the meat of her palm, hard enough to jerk his head to the side. He collapses.

She drags Lance into the hotel room, locks the door behind her, and muscles him over to the bed. He's heavy, cumbersome, but she lifts with her legs and jerks him onto the mattress. He begins to moan, so she juices him with the Cheetah stun gun again, causing his limbs to twitch and contract. She holds it there for a few seconds, and when she kills the power he's limp and a line of drool is running down his chin.

It takes a few seconds to start the roll of duct tape, but when she does she uses a long strip to bind his left wrist to the leg of the bed. The other limbs follow suit, until he's spread-eagled and immobilized.

Using the box cutter, she starts at the cuff of his jeans and slices the fabric upward to his belt line, careful not to nick his skin. Then she does the other leg. Then his shirt, until all he has on are his shoes, socks, and Duff Beer boxer shorts. Alex tosses the knife aside and tears off the shorts with her hands, feeling the excitement build, feeling herself get wet.

It isn't necessary for Lance to be naked. Alex could have gotten what she wanted just by unzipping his fly. But she likes seeing men naked. Especially good-looking men. It's been a long time.

Since being out of prison, no one has stepped up to the plate. One came close, until he got a good look at her face and sarcastically demanded she wear two bags over her head, "in case one fell off." She left him in a Chicago bar with two teeth in his mouth and a broken pelvis.

But things are definitely looking up. Alex runs her fingernails through Lance's chest hair, then pinches his nipples. He stirs, glassy eyes focusing, and calls her a name he knew her by.

"Hi, Lance. It's been a long time."

Lance tries to move, sees he's taped to the bed.

"What's going on?"

"Shh." Alex puts a fingertip to his lips. "No talking, or I'll gag you. I need a few things from you, Lance. First, I need you to fuck me. Hard. Then I need to know where your EOD lieut lives, where he keeps his van, and what kind of toys you boys have in there."

"What the hell are you—"

Alex grabs his ear, jerks his head to the side.

"I said no talking."

He looks terrified, which is a terrific turn-on. Alex wants to kiss him, but doesn't want to risk being bitten, or worse, rebuffed. Instead she runs her teeth across his neck and nibbles her way down his body, across his chest, to his belly button. He tastes good, like a man, tangy and hot. Alex grabs him, feels that he's responding even though he's frightened. This pleases her; she won't have to use the tadalafil she liberated from the coffee shop guy.

She moves her head down, holding his cock in both hands, running her tongue up along the side of the shaft. A thought hits her: *Will I be able to function normally?* Half of her face muscles are gone. But when she takes him in her mouth he offers no objections to her technique. And as she lowers her head farther, opening her throat, Lance's hips begin to pump.

Alex matches his thrusts for several strokes, then releases him, both of them breathing heavy. She's hot, hot and wet, and she wants to climb on and impale herself. But they have done this dance, many times, in the past. And though Lance may have gotten better since those days, Alex doesn't want to have to rely on his staying power. She reaches for the nightstand, tears open the bag of rubber bands, and winds a fat one around the base of his dick.

Lance makes a noise of protest, and Alex gives the rubber band a snap, shutting him up.

She straddles him, guides him into her, and moves down slowly, deliciously, until she's filled. Hands on his chest, she begins to raise and lower her hips. Easy at first. No need to rush. At the bottom of each stroke she presses into him, grinding her hips, which makes her gasp with pleasure each time.

Alex wants to draw it out, to tease herself. But it's been too long and the rhythm becomes involuntary, unstoppable. She pushes into him, harder, faster, and all too quickly the first spike of orgasm seizes her, building into a large peak that forces a cry, and then spreading to envelop her entire body like a shock wave, prompting a throaty scream that makes her feel whole again.

Alex doesn't stop at one. Or two. Or four. She goes at him from many positions, and he's so into it that by the second hour he's begging her to undo the rubber band, to let him come. Alex promises she will, and as she rides his face and his probing tongue works her into a frenzy she orgasms a fifth time and almost considers keeping her promise.

Instead, Alex climbs off the bed, heart hammering and legs shaky, and gives him a gentle pat on the cheek.

"Jesus, I really needed that."

"What about me, babe?" Lance looks so desperate, so pathetic. He *wants* her, even though she's a hideous freak.

"Consider it payback for all the times when you got yours and I didn't get mine. Now it's time to move on to the second part of the evening. If you tell me what I need to know, I promise I won't kill your wife and family. Hell, you may even live through this, if Jack is fast enough."

Lance stares at her, his face a snapshot of confusion. Alex goes to the nightstand. She flicks on the butane torch, adjusts it to a blue flame, and gives him a quick, two-second taste on his thigh.

Lance howls.

"That's nothing. I can keep it there for a lot longer. Or move to more sensitive parts."

She gives his erection a playful flick with her finger.

"What . . . what the hell do you want?"

"I've followed your career. You've done well with the police department. Been in the papers several times. Always were a bit of an adrenaline junkie, Lance. Is that why you picked the EOD?"

He stays silent. Alex brings the torch up to his face. The flame makes a hissing sound, like a snake. Lance quickly nods.

"Most squads have a van or a truck with their equipment in it. They don't like to leave dangerous materials at work. Too risky. So they take it home. Does your boss have one?"

Another nod.

"Truck or a van?"

"A van."

"What sort of goodies are you boys packing?"

Lance opens his mouth but nothing comes out. His eyes are locked on the torch.

"Dammit, Lance. Focus. What kind of caps?"

"Bridgewire."

"Sun cord?"

"Maybe three hundred feet on a spool."

"Got a pigstick?"

"Yeah."

"Rounds?"

"Two cases. Assorted."

"How about initiators?"

"Yeah."

"It sounds like you've got a very well-stocked van, Lance. Now tell me about the big stuff."

"My . . . throat's dry."

"That's because you're afraid I'm going to burn you again. And I will, Lance, unless you focus. What else you got?"

"PENO."

"Nice. That's Finnish, isn't it?"

"Yeah."

"How many bricks?"

"Six."

"Anything else? Tell the truth now, Lance, or we're gonna have a weenie roast."

"We . . . we got a few M18A1s."

Alex raises her good eyebrow.

"Really? Wow. That's impressive. So far, so good. Now, the moment of truth."

Alex leans forward, peering into his eyes.

"Where's the van?"

Lance doesn't say anything.

"You sure you want to play hard to get, Lance?"

His Adam's apple bobbles up and down like a tetherball.

"If . . . *if* . . . I tell you, what are . . . what are you going to do to him?"

"I just want to borrow his van."

"I don't want him or his daughter to get hurt."

Alex sits on the bed, running her hand over Lance's chest.

"What is he to you? Best friend? Father figure? Fuck buddy? Caring about people never leads to anything but pain, Lance. Trust me. I know from experience. That's why I'm going to tell you the truth. Lieutenant Lucky Andringa is as good as dead. And if his wife and daughter are home when I stop by, they'll die too."

Alex lightly pinches one of his nipples. Lance begins to cry.

"No tears, Lance. I just gave you a gift. I freed you from having to worry about him. It's not your fault he's dead. I'm the one that's going to kill him. And there's nothing you can do to prevent it. Now tell me where he lives."

Lance turns away, burying his face in the pillow.

"You sure you don't want to tell me? You're going to tell me eventually."

Nothing.

"Okay. Your choice."

Alex picks up the duct tape, tears off a strip, and sticks it over his mouth while he thrashes back and forth. She runs her fingers through his hair, still sweaty from their sex.

"Thank you, Lance. I was hoping I'd get to try this out. Will you look how cute this pink handle is? It matches my nails."

She smiles her half smile, then descends with the blowtorch.

CHAPTER 9

"STOP THE CAB."

"You sure you don't want me to call the police?"

"I am the police."

The cabbie didn't wait to see my badge. He pulled over. I threw some money at him, yanked my gun from my purse, and climbed out. The rain had come back, a downpour with more oomph than my vibrating shower head. The sedan parked behind the cab, and I stalked over, ready to shoot someone.

The driver opened his window.

"It's raining."

Were all men this tuned in to the obvious?

"What the hell do you want, Dailey?"

"I'm Special Agent Coursey. That's Special Agent Dailey."

Coursey used a head motion, indicating his passenger. They were both dressed identically in gray suits, blue ties, and silver Timexes. Age was tough to determine, since neither of them ever made any sort of facial expression that could cause wrinkles.

One of them, I forget which, once told me that they weren't related, even though they looked more alike than most twins. I had a fanciful notion that our government grew Feebies in a lab somewhere, using some kind of genetic Jell-O mold.

"What the hell do you guys want?"

Coursey hit a button, and the back door lock snapped open.

"I don't want to go anywhere with you. I'm on a leave of absence."

"Is that why you went to the Forensic Science Center?"

When cornered, attack.

"Don't you have anything better to do than follow me around? Like maybe catch some criminals? I hear you guys have a most wanted list with a few names on it. How's that Bin Laden hunt going?"

They exchanged a glance, possibly communicating using their FBI brain implants, and then Dailey said, "We think we may know where Alexandra Kork is."

I got in. The car was nice. Leather interior. Heated seats. Much better than my car. Especially since I didn't have a car anymore. My Chevy Nova, a classic 1985 model, was recently towed to the scrap yard. Unlike those TV commercials where they pay you cash for your used vehicle, I had to pay them to take it away.

I leaned forward.

"Where's Alex?"

Neither Coursey nor Dailey so much as glanced at my boobs. I wasn't sure if I should be grateful, or insulted.

"We want some information first," said Dailey.

"You help us, we help you," said Coursey.

"Quid pro quo," said Dailey.

"You guys learned that term from watching *Silence of the Lambs*."

Dailey put his arm over the back of his seat and faced me.

"We know you're looking for her, Lieutenant. We want to help you."

"Fine. Where is she?"

"Are you willing to trade information?"

"What kind of information are you looking for?"

Coursey handed Dailey an 8×10 mug shot, and he passed it back to me.

"We're looking for this man."

I studied the photo. White. Blond hair. Blue eyes. Mid-thirties.

"What about him?" I asked.

"You arrested him several years ago."

"I arrest a lot of people."

They stared at me. I stared back. Feds are masters at staring. But so am I. I didn't get to the rank of lieutenant by being easily intimidated. I can go days without blinking.

The staring contest continued, and I remembered the bank was going to close soon.

"What did he do?" I finally asked.

"Bank robbery. He tied three road flares together, walked into the drive-through lane, and placed the flares in the vacuum tube container."

"Live flares?"

"No. Unlit flares. Along with a note saying it was dynamite, and he would set it off unless they gave him two thousand dollars."

Coursey handed me a photo taken by the bank surveillance camera. The man stood outside the bank window, holding a small black box with an antenna sticking out of the top. He was smiling and waving.

"That's a remote control car radio," I said.

"The tellers didn't know that."

"They gave him the money?"

"Yes. Then he returned the container and asked for his road flares back."

I shook my head, amazed. "He told them they were road flares?"

"He did. Then he apologized for deceiving them, and sent them a package of cookies."

I suppressed a smirk. "Sounds like Public Enemy Number One."

"Bank robbery is a federal crime, Lieutenant."

"Did you canvass nearby convenience stores? You might also be able to nail him for trafficking in stolen Oreos."

I watched Coursey actually write that down. Maybe my government Jell-O mold idea wasn't as fanciful as I thought.

"So what do you extra-special agents want from me?"

"This guy's off the grid. No address. No job. Doesn't pay taxes or Social Security. According to his record, he's only been arrested once," said Dailey.

"By you," said Coursey.

"Like I said, I arrest a lot of people," said I.

"So you don't know where he lives?"

"I don't know where he lives."

More staring. If they scrutinized me any harder, I might fall asleep.

"Look, if I knew where he lived, we could all drive to his place right now. I'd even spring for the milk to dunk those cookies."

Coursey and Dailey shared another telepathy glance.

"So where's Alex?"

"We have reason to believe she's in Knoxville," said Coursey.

"Knoxville," I repeated.

"Tennessee," said Dailey.

"How did you learn this? Witness? Informer?"

"Vicky."

I almost slapped myself in the forehead. Vicky is the Violent Criminal Apprehension Team Computer.

"Vicky is the Violent Criminal Apprehension Team Computer," said Coursey.

"We've had this conversation before, guys."

"She compiles information, creates suspect profiles, and predicts future movements."

Vicky cost the taxpayers sixty-five million dollars, and she couldn't predict the time an hour from now.

I feng shuied my many negative thoughts and calmly asked, "Why does Vicky think Alex is in Knoxville, Tennessee?"

"She compiled information and—"

"I got that part. What led Vicky to believe this?"

They were silent. I heard a faint, mechanical sound, which may have been the gears in their robotic brain implants failing.

Coursey finally said, "There's Dollywood."

I blinked. "Dollywood?"

"It's only thirty-five miles southeast of Knoxville," said Dailey.

"You think Alex Kork went to Dollywood?"

More silence.

"Why would she go to Dollywood?" I thought it was a reasonable question.

"Everyone likes Western-themed rides and attractions," said Coursey.

"And Southern hospitality at affordable family prices," said Dailey.

I rubbed my eyes. "You rehearsed this. You planned this whole gag, and you're going to laugh about this later on. Right?"

They exchanged another glance.

"Vicky cost sixty-five million dollars," Coursey said.

My phone rang. The one Alex gave me.

"Excuse me, guys. I have to take this. Good luck with that cookie robber guy."

I pulled on the door handle. Naturally, it didn't open. Federal, state, city, or town—cop cars were all the same.

A second ring.

"You want to let me out?"

"Alexandra Kork has committed felonies in six states," said Dailey. "So the Bureau is very interested in bringing her to justice."

The phone rang a third time. I still didn't pick it up.

"I promise I'll check Dolly's cleavage when I'm in Knoxville."

"If you find her, call us," said Coursey.

"We mean Alex, not Dolly," said Dailey.

"If she contacts me, you'll be the first to know."

The door unlocked. I walked briskly away from the car, the rain a faucet on my head.

"It's Jack," I said into the phone.

No answer. I missed the call. I couldn't call back, because the call would just forward to this number, giving me a busy signal. Shit. Then the phone beeped, telling me I had a text message. I accessed it.

THIS IS LANCE. HE'S A COP.

There was a picture. A man, from the waist up, duct-taped to a bed. Short brown hair. Brown eyes. Late thirties or early forties. He had no shirt, and his bare chest was covered with black and red marks.

Burns.

On the bed, dangling over his forehead, was some sort of metal arm, holding what looked like a microphone a foot above his face.

Though he had tape over his mouth, I could tell he was screaming when the picture was taken: A feminine hand with a pink manicure held a miniature blowtorch against his nipple.

A beep. Then a second text message came through.

HE DIES IN TWELVE HOURS.

I checked my watch: 5:33. He'd be dead by morning.

The phone was getting seriously wet, so I shoved it into my purse. The Feds were gone. But by some huge stroke of fortune, a cab came up the street. I stuck up my hand and waved. He only slowed down enough to splash curb water on me.

The WaMu was only four blocks away. Since I couldn't get any colder, or wetter, I walked.

I didn't want this phone taken from me. It was my only link to Alex, the only way I could find her. But now I didn't have a choice. A man's life was at stake, and the clock was ticking. Detective Tom Mankowski was running the Kork investigation. He was a good cop. Plus he had a team behind him. Resources. Equipment. Funding. They could do more with the phone than I could. They'd have a better shot at saving that poor schmuck tied to the bed.

It was the right decision, morally and legally. Mankowski owed me a favor, so he'd keep me in the loop. I had to turn in the phone—the sooner, the better.

But I didn't.

God help me, I didn't.

CHAPTER 10

ALEX HAS THE CAR RADIO cranked to the max, singing along with the Red Hot Chili Peppers' ode to Magic Johnson. It ends too soon, and some rap shit comes on. She hits a few presets, but the car's previous owner apparently had a hard-on for hip-hop. A quick search of the glove compartment finds it crammed with every single goddamn CD MC Ice Koffee every recorded, plus three albums of other rappers doing MC Ice Koffee songs. She tries listening to one. After thirty excruciating seconds she chucks it out the window and fantasizes MC Ice Koffee is the one dead in the trunk.

She's dressed in Levi's, a Cubs hoodie she bought at the same thrift store she got the funeral hat, and some steel-toed Doc Martens. Her hair is in a ponytail under the hood, and an oversized pair of movie star sunglasses covers most of her face. From the sidewalk, from other cars, she's ageless, sexless, anonymous, invisible. A lioness creeping through the high grass, unseen and unheard.

The GPS advises Alex to turn right in three hundred feet. She does. Bay View is one of the nicer neighborhoods in the city. Row after row of Late Victorian–style houses, tall green trees, well-maintained lawns.

"Arriving at destination."

Alex pats the GPS screen and says, "Thanks." She parks the Honda across the street from a white two-story bungalow. An American flag hangs above the front door, next to the obligatory porch swing. Alex half expects Aunt Bea to stick her head out the window and call Opie home for supper.

She pulls her purse onto her shoulder and subconsciously checks herself in the mirror, a habit she wishes she could break because it always sours her mood. This time is no exception.

"You need duct tape and rubber bands to get men to fuck you," she says to her reflection.

Annoyed, Alex exits the car and walks up to the front door of the bungalow, giving the solid wooden door a firm knock.

A teenage girl, sixteen or seventeen, answers. She's wearing a belly shirt that exposes a piercing, tight jeans that ride just above her crotch, and more makeup than Boy George in his heyday. Her hair is as blond as the bottles can get.

"You must be Leena. I'm Sergeant Friday. I'm working on a case with your father."

Alex flashes Lance's police badge and ID, her finger partially obscuring his picture. She needn't have bothered; Leena's eyes are glued to Alex's face.

"What happened to you? Were you, like, burned or something?"

"Don't you think it's rude to ask that?"

Leena cocks out a hip.

"I think it's rude to walk around looking like Freddy Krueger."

Alex smiles, only half of her mouth moving.

"Is your dad home?"

A yawn. Alex is boring her.

"He doesn't get home until six."

"Mom?"

"Mom's dead."

"That's hard."

Alex knows this from experience. She helped to kill her own mother, and the bitch didn't die easy.

"It's a quarter to six," Alex says. "I'll wait for your father inside."

She tries to enter, but Leena blocks her path.

"You can wait on the porch."

Alex almost laughs.

"You're not a very nice little girl."

Cue the eye roll. "Whatever."

Alex leans in closer.

"I bet you get your way all the time, don't you, Leena? Shake your perfect little boobies, stick out your size zero ass, and the men fall all over themselves trying to please you. I hope you're getting it now. Because it doesn't last."

Leena doesn't seem to know if that was an insult or not.

"I go to rainbow parties," she says. "I've hooked up with plenty of boys."

Alex glances left, looking up the street.

"Rainbow parties. I think I saw that on Oprah. You and your girlfriends take turns giving some guy head. What a waste."

"You're the waste."

Alex looks right, down the street. All clear.

"It's too bad you'll never learn, Leena. Being a woman isn't about giving." Alex winks her good eye. "It's about *taking*."

Leena shrugs. "Are we done?"

"Almost. I was listening to MC Ice Koffee in the car. Do you like him?"

"Yeah. Ice is da bomb."

Alex hits Leena hard enough to break the girl's nose. Then she enters the house and shuts the door behind her.

"You ugly bitch!" Leena screams, hand pinching nostrils to stop the bleeding.

Alex takes Lance's 9mm from her purse and puts a round through Leena's flawless face, killing her before she hits the floor. Then Alex goes into the kitchen, prepares herself a ham sandwich and a glass of milk, and waits on the sofa for Dad to come home.

As Leena predicted, Lieutenant Lucky Andringa pulls into the garage at three minutes to six. When he steps into the house, Alex greets him with a bullet in the head, and another in the chest after he falls. Not very lucky at all. She takes his wallet, gun, and car keys, and marches into the garage.

The van is a new Toyota hybrid, meant to conserve gas and preserve the environment. Ironic, considering what it's hauling. In the back there's a custom storage trunk with ten locked compartments. Alex spends a few moments fussing with the keys, opening drawers and doors.

There's everything Lance said there would be. Everything and more. Alex runs her fingertips over the PENO.

It gives her chills.

CHAPTER 11

"I WAS WONDERING when you'd call, Jackie. Did you buy a ham?"

"Haven't had the chance. We need to meet. Where are you?"

"The Crimebago is mobile, sis. I can meet you anywhere."

I winced. "*Crimebago?*"

"*Crime* plus *Winnebago. Crim-e-bago.* I was gonna have the name painted on the side, along with a chick in a garter belt riding a Harley, but since I'm using it for detecting, it's better to keep things inconspicuous."

As if a motor home was inconspicuous.

"Can you clone a cell phone?"

"Hell yeah, I can clone a cell phone."

"Okay, meet me at the Washington Mutual bank on Diversey and Clark."

"You got it, sis. I'll—"

I hung up on him, crossed the street, and entered the WaMu, grateful they were open until six. The woman in line ahead of me had a pillowcase full of coins, and the teller fussed over her, both of them making predictions about the dollar value.

I finger-combed my wet hair back, probing the stitches on my scalp. They itched. I probably had an infection. Hopefully I wouldn't die until I saw this through.

The change-counting machine spit out a receipt, and the teller gave the woman some cash, including a few coins, which went directly into the empty pillowcase. There was a metaphor for life somewhere in there, but I was too preoccupied to look for it.

"Can I help you?"

"I need to close an account."

I gave the teller Latham's bank card. After we became engaged, we added our names to each other's bank account. I never touched his money, but Latham insisted on this as a precaution. Wills meant the IRS took a chunk, and probate took time. He said this was easier.

Practical Latham. I hadn't given much thought about what I'd do with his money. I didn't feel like I deserved any. I figured I'd split it among his relatives, maybe give some to charity. I didn't have much of my own in the bank, but it was important I paid for his funeral out of my funds. The least I could do.

"Both the checking and the savings, Ms. Daniels?"

"Yes, please."

The teller pressed some buttons.

"Are you sure you want to take all of it out?"

"Yes." I paused, considered my reason. "I'm going hunting."

Since Alex's call this morning, I figured that would be the best use of Latham's money.

"I need to speak to my supervisor to authorize a cashier's check for this amount. Can you hold on for a moment, Ms. Daniels?"

"Sure. Out of curiosity, how much is the amount?"

"Four hundred and eighty thousand, six hundred and thirty-six dollars."

I was sure I didn't hear that right.

"Excuse me?"

She swiveled around the monitor so I could see. Latham had close to a half a million dollars in his accounts.

While Latham never seemed to hurt financially—he lived in a nice condo, had nice things—he never mentioned having this much money. I tried to recall any conversation we had that would explain this. And then I remembered one, from a few weeks ago.

"My CDs just matured. I think instead of letting them roll over, I'm going to try my hand at the stock market. What do you think?"

"You're the accountant. I don't know anything about investments. I'm just a lowly cop."

"We could just take it all to Vegas, bet it on a single roulette spin."

"You hate Las Vegas."

"But wouldn't that be exciting? A whole life's work, doubled or lost in the blink of an eye."

"I'd never do that. I can't afford to lose the whole three hundred bucks."

Then he'd told me he had three hundred in his wallet, and coyly asked if I'd like to double my net worth. We'd gone into the bedroom.

The last time we'd ever made love.

I couldn't hold the tears back. I flat-out lost it in the middle of a WaMu, sobbing so hard it burned my tear ducts, crumpling to the floor and burying my face in my hands and hating myself so much that I barely even noticed as some strangers half carried me to a chair.

I cried until my mouth went dry.

A foghorn brought me back. I looked around, wondering if it was the bank alarm, hoping some ski-masked robbers had broken in so I could beg one to shoot me.

The horn blared again. Coming from the street.

The Crimebago.

And suddenly, I had a reason to live. I pushed the pain back, deep inside, and vowed not to let it out again. I'd deal with it later.

Someone offered me a box of tissues. I took a handful, filled them up with liquid self-pity, and tossed them in a can under a desk. Then I cleared my throat, stood up, and held my chin high.

My voice was steady when I said, "I'll just take a five-thousand-dollar withdrawal. Cash."

Another honk. I fished out my cell and called Harry.

"If you honk one more time, I'm going to impale you on the steering column."

"Sounds fun."

"I'll be out in a minute."

"See if they have any extra pens. I don't have any pens."

I hung up and waited at the counter while a teller counted out a never-ending stack of hundreds. First using the automatic bill counter, then by hand.

"Anything else, Ms. Daniels?"

The pen on the counter had one of those chains on it, so I sheepishly asked, "Does your bank have any pens?"

She handed me one with the bank phone number printed on it. I crammed the money into my purse, thanked her, and walked out to greet Harry McGlade.

The Crimebago was obscenely huge, the size and shape of a bus, white with blue and red stripes. There were six windows on the side facing me. I rapped on the center one attached to the trailer door.

The door swung out and a grinning, leering McGlade offered me a hand up. I chose to grip the door frame instead.

"Welcome aboard, Jackie. Did you grab me a fistful of pens?"

I handed him the pen.

"Only one? Weren't they free?"

Unsurprisingly, the interior smelled like the same aftershave Harry apparently bathed in, so strong it made my nostril hairs curl. Also, for reasons only known to McGlade, the air-conditioning was on, making every pore on my body pucker into gooseflesh.

"So, you like it?"

"It's freezing."

"Yeah, I'm having some climate control problems. I've got the oven on to offset that. You want a tour?"

"I need you to clone a cell phone first."

"That can wait."

"It can't wait."

"It has to. Cloning a phone ain't easy. I've got a reader that can copy the SIM and put it on a new card, but it takes a few hours. What do you need it for?"

"Alex is going to kill a cop. She gave me a phone, and she sends me clues. I can't give it up, because it's my only link to her. But I can't keep the phone from the police."

Harry scratched himself someplace I didn't want or need or like to see.

"Cloning won't work. If a phone gets cloned, only one can work at a time. The cops couldn't listen in, and they wouldn't get Alex's messages. Or you wouldn't—it depends who is closest to a cell tower."

Shit.

McGlade took my elbow and walked me past a large sofa to the rear of the cabin. The floor was carpeted. The walls were trimmed in dark wood that matched the cabinets.

"This is the galley. It's called a galley, not a kitchen. And this is the bathroom, but it's called the head. I like that name. Head."

"Can you trace a cell phone call?"

He shrugged. "Yes and no. I could get the number she's calling from, but could only pinpoint it to within a few hundred yards."

"What if she spoofed it?" I asked.

"Then no. This is the bedroom. There's no bed, because it's in the wall and comes out when I press the button to activate the sideout. It's totally James Bond cool. Wanna see?"

"Not really."

McGlade pressed the button anyway. The wall extended outward and a Murphy bed levered down. King size, with red velour sheets.

"You're a chick. Does seeing this make you want to get naked?"

"No."

"I'm getting a mirror installed on the ceiling next week. Would that seal the deal?"

"There's no way to trace it through the phone company?"

He pressed the button again. The bed began to rise.

"You know how cell phones work, right? By radio transmission. So they need antennas. Chicago has a few, and each handles thousands of calls every second. We'd have to contact every cell phone provider in the country, get their records, and go through each billing minute one at a time to find out which one matched Alex's call to get the ID number. There had to be tens, maybe hundreds of thousands of calls at that time."

The small amount of hope I'd brought with me was quickly fading away. Then I remembered what Hajek said.

"Could you trace it by analyzing the SIM card? If she's sending text messages?"

Harry looked thoughtful, then scratched himself again. It was like he had a metal hand and a pair of magnets in his scrotum.

Actually, he did have a metal hand. But he didn't use that for scratching, and probably with good reason. I'd seen Harry accidentally crush a doorknob with that hand.

"That might actually work, sis, because texts are saved on the card. The spoof fools caller ID, but it might not fool the SIM."

Harry walked past, into the lounge area opposite the sofa. He flipped a switch on the wall and a cabinet opened, a table coming down. It had a built-in keyboard and a flat-screen monitor, which flipped up. He dug a small white box out of a drawer and attached a cord to one end, plugging the other into a USB slot on the keyboard.

"Open the back of the phone and gimme the SIM."

I pried out the little data card and handed it over, then spent a minute tracking down the vent that was blowing cold air in my face. I closed it, but that only made the other vents blow even harder.

"You like my screen saver?"

I glanced at the monitor, expecting to see some naked girl eating a banana. Instead it was a pic of Harry with his arm around my mother. Both were smiling. I felt myself wince.

"It's . . . nice," I managed.

"Me and Mom have a lot of catching up to do. Mother and son stuff."

"You know, the DNA results haven't come—"

"Gotcha, you little bastard! There's the TAP/CIBER, and now I run the decryption program. This will take a few seconds. You get Mom anything for her birthday? I'm thinking a cat."

Speaking of non sequiturs.

"We've already got a cat."

"I know. Mr. Friskers, right? Is he still meaner than spit?"

"He's currently in a kitty motel. It's seventy-five bucks a day, plus we have to pay for injuries to the staff."

"That could get pricey."

"Hopefully that groomer won't need eye surgery."

"Does Mom like dogs? Or maybe a monkey? I'd like to have a monkey. You can teach them to fetch you things, like beer. A beer monkey. That would be cool. We could smoke cigars and watch *King Kong* together. I love the remake. It's got the extended footage, which means it's seventeen hours long. We can watch it later, on Blu-ray, if you want."

"Were you ever tested for ADHD?" I asked.

"Yeah. But the Ritalin makes me hyper. Okay, the decryption is finished, and . . . there's the phone number. I'm amazing."

Harry pointed at it, and I wanted to punch the screen. It was the same Deer Park number Hajek had given me. My phone wasn't a direct link to Alex, as I'd hoped. It was part of that call-forwarding daisy chain he had mentioned. I explained this to Harry.

"All's not lost, sis. I can find the phone in Deer Park, get the SIM, and then locate the next phone in the chain. It will lead to Alex eventually."

"There could be ten phones in the chain, Harry. You said you can only pinpoint the call within a few hundred yards, and she could have these hidden all over the country."

"It's a start. I've got an RF detector. I can find the phones."

I closed my eyes, thinking. Normally, when I was chasing a perp, there were witnesses to interview, evidence to examine, clues to follow up on. Alex was effectively invisible, and could be anywhere. How the hell do you find a person who only shows you what she wants you to see?

"I can't believe I'm saying this, but you're our only hope here, Harry. There's no other way to find her."

"I can do it. It'll just take some time."

"Time is something we don't have."

"So I see."

Harry brought the picture up on the monitor, of Lance taped to the bed and screaming. I checked my watch.

"Unless we can find him, he's dead in just over eleven hours."

Harry didn't say anything, which was out of character. I wondered if the picture brought him back to the time he was Alex's captive. She was the reason he had a prosthetic hand, and though he never talked about it, I knew a blowtorch played a part.

"We'll find him," Harry eventually said.

"How, if we can't trace her calls?"

"She left us a clue."

"What clue?"

"He's a cop named Lance. Probably hundreds of those in the U.S. But how many have one of these?"

Harry pointed to the metal tripod, which held the thing that looked like a microphone over Lance's head. I leaned in closer, squinting, and couldn't believe I missed it earlier.

"It's a pigstick," I said.

"Yeah. Looks like old Lance is on the Bomb Squad. The pigstick is armed with a shotgun shell, attached to a blasting cap. That wire is shock tube, probably leading to a timer. When the time is up, the round fires into poor Lance's face."

If Alex was being honest. For all I knew, Lance might already be dead. Or he might not be named Lance at all. I stared at his face again, his agony forever frozen in time. I wondered if Alex was still burning him.

"Alex sent me an earlier text, a few weeks ago. Said she was in Milwaukee. I don't know if she's telling the truth or not."

"She's a lying crazy psycho bitch. Believing her is a mistake."

"She bought this phone in Gurnee, which is on the way to Milwaukee. Maybe we should start heading up there."

"If she's lying, we could be heading in the wrong direction."

I chewed my lower lip.

"You need to bring in the troops on this, Jackie. They can send out a bulletin to other cop shops. Maybe even get his face on TV."

Harry must have noticed my reaction, because he shook his head.

"We don't have to give them the phone. Or even a clone of the phone. We can forward the pictures and texts to one of their phones. Send it to fatso. He'll take care of it."

"Fine." I held out my hand. "Give me the card back."

"Let me save this first. Resolution is for shit. Maybe I can tweak it, get a serial number on the pigstick. Can't be that many of those out there."

Harry opened up a photo program, but my mind was elsewhere. I'd met a few Explosive Ordnance Disposal cops. Serious, professional guys. A pigstick was a portable arm that held a shell or a high-pressure water jet, used to remotely detonate suspicious devices. Detonation wire, shock tube, and blasting caps were tools of the EOD. But they weren't the only tools.

Most bomb squads had bigger, more dangerous devices.

If Alex had a pigstick, what else could she have?

CHAPTER 12

THE JORDAN HISTORICAL SOCIETY, located only a mile from the beach, has closed for the day. It's dark and quiet.

Alex drives past the empty parking lot, over the grass, and pulls to a stop behind some fir trees. She kills the engine, grabs her army surplus duffel bag, and leaves the Honda, walking back toward the main building. The night has cooled off to the mid-forties. She tucks her hair under the hood and pulls the cords tight around her face. It's doubtful anyone is watching, but it never hurts to be careful.

The M4 Sherman tank sits in front of the building on a dais of concrete, just like in the Web site pictures. Alex walks up to it, touches the cold green steel. It's smaller than she expects, several yards shorter and half the weight of the MI Abrams. The 60mm gun on the turret is pointed east, poised to protect the shoreline from approaching enemy armadas. Metaphorically, of course, because the barrel is filled with concrete.

Alex rests the duffel bag on the front tread fender and sticks a mini Maglite in her teeth. Pointing downward, she tears the paper off a brick of PENO. The plastic explosive is gray, without odor, heavy for its size. Alex pulls off a fist-sized hunk and rolls it between her palms. It's stickier, and slightly stiffer, than modeling clay. She forms it into a pyramid shape, then places the base against the frontal hull of the tank, which the Internet says is sixty-one millimeters thick.

Returning to the duffel bag, she removes a bridgewire detonator and loops the bag's strap over her shoulder. The blasting cap is pushed into the tip of the pyramid, and Alex attaches a shock tube to that and plays line out of the spool until she's fifty yards away, behind the side of the building. She crimps the detonation cord into an electric sparker and smiles her half smile.

"Fire in the hole."

The explosion shakes the ground and momentarily deafens her. She remembers to open her mouth like she was taught, which equalizes the pressure on both sides of her eardrums. It still hurts, almost like getting struck in the head. The ringing continues as she approaches the tank, winding the now empty shock tube around her arm as she goes. There's no fire, and the smoke has almost dissipated. Alex points her flashlight at the hull and sees a jagged twenty-inch hole where armor used to be. It smells like hot coals and melted iron.

"Perfect," she says, but can't hear herself say it. She stuffs the used tubing back into her duffel bag and heads for the car.

Phase one of the plan is finished. Time to start phase two.

CHAPTER 13

"YOU SHOULD TURN THE PHONE IN, Jack."

Herb Benedict. We'd been partners for over a decade, and often played conscience for each other. But right now I needed an enabler.

"I have to see this through, Herb. Start with Milwaukee PD. See if anyone on their Bomb Squad is named Lance."

"How do you expect to find her? Track her cell phone?"

"It can't be tracked. Not directly. Long story."

"Then how? She could be anywhere. You're just going to sit around and wait for her to send you clues?"

"That's all I can do right now. That and prepare for when I'll have a shot at her. Does your cell accept pictures and text?"

"You've seen my cell. I think it's the very first one. It uses rotary."

I sat on Harry's sofa, shivering, and switched the phone to my other ear. The leather under my butt was cold.

"I want to send you what Alex is sending me. I know you're off the case too, but I'm hoping you can be my ears while I'm gone."

I could picture Herb thinking, probably rubbing his mustache with his thumb and forefinger. "Bernice has one of those new Motorola phones, the kind that does everything except make you a sandwich. Send it to her."

He gave me the number.

"Thanks, Herb. I owe you so many I'll never pay them all back."

"There's this mail order steak place. Grade-A prime-cut Angus beef. Ships them to you frozen. Their number is 1-800-MEATS4U. The *4* is a number and the *U* is the letter *U*."

"Consider it done."

"I like rib-eyes. And T-bones. And New York strips. And filets. Basically I like everything. They also sell Turduckinlux. That's a turkey breast, stuffed with a duck breast, stuffed with a chicken breast, stuffed with bacon-wrapped hamburger patties."

"I'll call them as soon as we get off the phone." I swallowed, hating to say what came next. "Look, Herb, I know you're being cautious, but Alex might take a shot at you. Or your wife."

"I could have Bernice stay with her mother, come and help you out."

"No way."

"My leg's not that bad, Jack. I can move fast if I have to."

Herb was loyal, smart, and tough. But he could never be called fast. And with his injury, all he'd be doing was putting himself in danger.

"Stay with your wife and heal. That's an order."

"What if I had some psycho killer after me? Would you stay out of it?"

"My psycho killer, my rules. I need you to stay close to the investigation, Herb. Keep me in the loop. Besides, I have some help."

"That idiot McGlade? He's a card-carrying asshole. I'm serious. He once showed me the card."

I eyed Harry, who was squinting at porn on the computer screen.

"He's not that bad," I said.

"Please don't tell me you're with him in that stupid RV."

"It has really good air-conditioning."

"Want me to turn it up?" Harry asked, never taking his eyes off the screen. A gorilla had joined the party. No—just a guy in a gorilla suit. What ever happened to normal, old-fashioned porn?

"Jesus, Jack. How am I supposed to sleep knowing that bonehead has your back?"

"I'm getting more help."

"Who? The criminal guy? Phineas something?"

"Troutt."

"What makes you think he'll help you?"

I got an image in my mind, of the last time I saw Phin. He had hugged me, holding it longer than our friendship warranted.

"He'll help."

Herb sighed, loud and dramatic.

"I want you to call me. Every evening at seven. If you don't call, I'm coming after you."

"Thanks, Herb. We'll talk soon."

"We'll talk tomorrow. At seven. Sooner if I hear anything. And tell that asshole McGlade to sit on his mechanical thumb and spin."

Herb hung up, and I tucked the phone back into my purse.

"How's the partner?" Harry asked. "Still fat?"

"He says hi. Can you send the picture and texts to him?"

I handed Bernice's cell number to Harry.

"Sure. I got a program that can do it from the computer."

"We also need to go to Wrigleyville. Joe's Pool Hall, to see if Phin is there."

"Check and roger."

"And turn off the porn."

Harry batted his eyelashes. "Anything else I can do for you, Your Highness?"

"Yes," I said, thinking of Alex. "Take me to the nearest gun shop. I need to exercise my second amendment rights to bear arms."

CHAPTER 14

ALEX SITS IN A BOOKSTORE CAFÉ, dressed in her funeral best. The WiFi is free, and her laptop is open. Her back is to the wall so no one can see her screen.

She uses a search engine to find her next victim. First the name. Then the town. It takes less than three minutes to get a phone number, and another two minutes to find the address. *Scary how easy it is to find someone,* Alex muses. People should pay closer attention to protecting their privacy.

The drive will take a few hours. Alex decides to wait until morning before leaving. She can't go back to the Old Stone Inn, because her bed is currently occupied. She calls the cell phone using the computer program, and a window opens, showing her a live feed of Lance. The picture isn't very good—even with all the lights on, the room is pretty dim. The camera phone is taped up to the wall, offering a wide angle. She presses some buttons, zooms in on Lance's chest.

He's asleep. Or unconscious. The burns have stopped bleeding, begun to scab over. It makes the symbols easier to see. She saves a picture of her laptop screen as a JPEG, crops it in Photoshop, and uploads it to her cell, viewing it from various angles, and judging it clue-worthy.

It's all Greek to me, Alex thinks.

Jack will get a copy later tonight.

Alex hits the hibernate key, blanking out her screen, and lets her eyes prowl around.

The bookstore is one of those large chains, ten times bigger than the library in the town where she grew up. Alex's father hated libraries. Believed that people only needed one book, the Bible, and that all others led to Satan. But according to Father, pretty much everything led to Satan. He blamed the devil for his appetites. He should have learned to embrace them. Indulge them without remorse.

Like she does.

Alex yawns, stretches out her long legs, and leans back in the chair to scope out women.

One walks by, wiggling her hips, getting in line for coffee. The right build. Right age. She orders something called chai tea. Alex doesn't know what that is. It would be a good thing to use as a way of introduction. But when Alex stands she notices how short the woman is, and doesn't bother. She sits back down.

Another woman, tall enough, but too young. Some men, whom Alex barely glances at. Then, a brunette. Age and height fine. A big ass, but people can lose weight. Alex gets into line behind her.

The woman orders a large vanilla latte and a pecan Danish, neither of which will help narrow her gluteus maximus.

"Are the Danish good here?"

The woman glances over her shoulder.

Alex doesn't smile behind the veil. She knows how it contorts her face, makes her look even more freakish. It's a definite handicap. Smiles disarm people. Taking a smile away from a recreational killer is like taking a pinky from a major league pitcher.

"They're pretty good. Not as good as the coffee place on Prospect."

The woman faces the cashier again. She's either in a hurry, not wanting to chat, or Alex's veil has set off subconscious warning bells. Strangers aren't to be trusted. People who hide their face are hiding something else.

Alex moves in a little closer, watches as the woman digs into her purse for a wallet. Though her clothes are decent, expensive, her handbag looks more like a backpack than an accessory. Alex catches glimpses of a tissue pack, some children's Tylenol, and a large key ring attached to a Lucite-encased family photo.

No good. Alex returns to her table, and is surprised to find a little girl standing next to it. She's blond, perhaps eight years old, and staring at Alex's laptop screen.

"Is that man hurt?"

She points at the live feed of the hotel room. Lance has woken up, and he's thrashing around on the bed like Linda Blair in *The Exorcist*. The child must have pressed a key, brought the computer back from hibernation mode.

Alex closes the cover, then looks around to make sure no one else saw anything.

"It's a movie. He's pretending to be hurt."

"My favorite movie is *Toy Story*. Have you seen *Toy Story*? It's about a cowboy named Woody, who is really named Tom Hanks. There's also *Toy Story 2,* but we don't have it anymore because it got stuck in the DVD player and Mommy threw it out."

Alex stares at the girl. So small and fragile. Father would have liked her. Alex prefers adults to children. Nothing can induce a migraine like a little kid screaming hour after hour. Even gagged, the high pitch is piercing enough to call stray dogs.

"Melinda!"

A woman hurries over, her expression a mix of concern and disappointment. She's tall, thin, pretty, platinum blond. Alex notices how she moves, in an easy, assured way. Athlete. Possibly a dancer.

"What have I told you about wandering off? You were supposed to stay by the picture books."

"The lady has a computer like Daddy's."

Melinda points to Alex's laptop.

"It is like Daddy's, but that doesn't mean you can go and touch things that aren't yours." Her blue eyes measure Alex. There's no hesitation, no drop in confidence, even when she notices the veil. "I apologize. Melinda, she's a curious little bug. I hope she didn't disturb you or ruin anything."

"You might want to keep her on a tighter leash." Alex puts a bit of iron in her voice. "There are some pretty crazy people in the world."

"Tell me about it. Look, it's not my business, but is that blazer Dolce and Gabbana? It is freaking gorgeous."

"Yes, it is." Alex appraises the woman's outfit, jeans and a red top. "Those jeans are Italian, aren't they?"

The woman lights up. "Yes! You won't ever guess what they're called."

"They're called My Ass. I used to have a pair. The belt line in back dips down, like the top of a heart."

The woman spins on her toes and lifts her shirt, revealing the divot, along with an intricate lower back tattoo. No visible thong or panty lines. Her heels are three inches, gold lamé. Alex amends her initial assessment from dancer to stripper. She's the perfect height, and no wedding ring either.

"I used to love those jeans. I bet your husband does."

"I'm not married."

"My mistake. Melinda said *Daddy*, so I just assumed . . ."

"Daddy died," Melinda chirped in, just as cheerful as when she was talking about *Toy Story*.

"We were never married," the woman explained. "Her father died last year. Car accident."

Alex's interest rises several notches. She still isn't sure about the woman's sexual orientation, so she plays it coy.

"I'm new here, so I don't know where any of the shops are. Where can a girl buy Louis Vuitton in this town?"

"I love Louis Vuitton! See?"

She holds up her brown purse, which Alex had spotted immediately after noticing her.

"It's freaking gorgeous," Alex says. "I'm Gracie, by the way."

"Samantha. Sammy for short."

Sammy offers her hand, smirks. Her touch is soft, and she tickles her index finger on the inside of Alex's palm when she shakes.

"Look, Sammy, this may sound kind of forward, but I need some-one to help me shop. I've been hiding from the world for a while. Car accident. Really messed up my face. This is the only outfit I feel I can wear in public. I haven't been out of the house in months."

"God, Gracie, that's awful."

"Are you and Melinda free now? We could hit a few shops, then I'd buy you guys dinner."

"Shit, that would be fun. But my shift starts in an hour."

"Is Sammy your stage name?"

Sammy grins wide, revealing perfect caps.

"Stage name is Princess. You used to be in the life? You've got the body for it."

"I've worked a few poles in my day. Which club?"

"High Rollers. It's uptown."

"Long hours. Does Grandma watch Melinda while you dance?"

"Grandma is in heaven with Daddy," Melinda says.

Sammy puts both arms around her daughter, cradling her face. "Our neighbor watches the bug. I only work four nights a week."

"Money that good?"

"It'll do till I get my business degree. I'm taking some classes during the day, when she's in school."

No husband, no mother, and a stripper to boot. She's almost perfect.

"If tonight isn't good, maybe sometime later?"

"Definitely. Let's trade numbers."

Sammy digs a pen out of her purse, writes down Alex's cell phone number on the back of a McDonald's receipt. She rips the paper in half, and gives Alex her number.

"One more thing, Sammy. And this is embarrassing. When I was working, sometimes the customers would want a little extra attention, and I got busted. As a condition of my parole, I'm not allowed to associ-ate with any known criminals. If you've got a record . . ."

Sammy shakes her head.

"I'm clean as a whistle. High Rollers gets stung all the time, undercover cops coming in, trying to get the girls to do more than dance. Two of my friends got nailed, so I don't do that. Not that I think it's wrong or anything. Just can't risk getting arrested when I've got Melinda to look after."

"Cool. Good luck tonight. Make some money."

"I always do. Hopefully we can hook up soon, Gracie."

Alex smiles her half smile and pats Melinda on the head.

"You can count on it."

CHAPTER 15

PHIN WORE JEANS and a white T-shirt, an outfit I'd seen him in many times. When he was bald from the chemo, it made him look like Mr. Clean, right down to the broad chest and narrow hips. He was currently in remission and his hair was back, blond and cut short.

He was leaning over the pool table, lining up his shot using a bridge. I'd never seen him use a bridge before, but when I eased through the throng of bar patrons and got closer I saw the reason. His left arm was in a sling.

Phin glanced up at me, looked back down at the table, and worked the stick. The cue ball hit the six, which knocked the nine into a side pocket, winning the game. His opponent, a blue-collar guy with mean eyes and a fuzzy beard, swore and dropped ten bucks on the rail.

"Lucky shot, crip. Let's go again."

Phin laid down the cue and the money disappeared into his jeans.

"Some other time, pal. I've got some other competition."

"Like hell. We're going again. I got money to win back."

"I said later."

"I said now!"

Mean Eyes grabbed Phin by his bad arm, high on the biceps. Phin spun, so fast he was a blur, coming up behind the guy and snatching his hair. He yanked, flipping his attacker over an outstretched leg and onto his back. Phin placed a boot heel on his throat as Mean Eyes flailed his arms. The flailing stopped when Phin raised the cue, directly over the man's eye.

"I beat you at nine ball one-handed. You want me to kick your ass one-handed?"

Mean Eyes attempted to shake his head. Tough to do, when someone is stepping on your neck.

Phin raised his foot, and the guy scrambled away, pushing through the gawkers. Then Phin tilted up his head at me. My dress was still damp and clingy, and his stare lingered on my body in an unmistakably male way. I'd been gawked at by men all day, but this time it didn't bother me. Truth told, it made my skin flush, which warmed me up for the first time in hours. When Phin's eyes finally met mine, they were kind.

"Hi, Jack. Latham was a good guy. I'm sorry I couldn't go to the funeral."

I had expected Phin to make an appearance, after all we'd been through together. But my earlier chat with the Feebies explained his absence.

"Too many cops there," I said.

"Not my kind of crowd."

"Last time we spoke, you told me you weren't wanted for anything."

"You had enough on your mind, Jack. Didn't want to burden you."

I should have been pissed, but the smile was already on my lips.

"Road flares?"

Phin's face stayed blank.

"What are you referring to, Lieutenant?"

"You want to play coy? You weren't coy for the bank cameras. The Feds showed me a nice picture of you waving."

"Must have me confused with some other handsome guy." His voice betrayed nothing, but his eyes crinkled at the edges.

"You don't trust me, Phin? Think I'm wearing a wire?"

"I know you're not." His eyes moved down. "Not the way that dress is hugging you."

I blushed harder, hoped he didn't notice it, then wondered why I cared one way or another. Phin was a friend, and nothing more. He was also a criminal. Our relationship went as far as playing pool, and doing each other occasional favors. Sex was not among those favors, and it should have been the last thing on my mind at the moment.

I came closer, resting my hip against the table.

"How'd you hurt your arm?"

"Dislocated elbow. Happened that night with Alex."

"You never told me."

"You had enough on your mind. Didn't want to burden you."

He moved a step closer, until we were less than a foot apart. His expression was friendly, playful. In the bar lighting his blue eyes appeared deep purple.

"You here for a game?"

"No time. How bad is the elbow?"

Phin removed the sling, stretched out his arm. I watched his face. If he was in pain, I couldn't tell.

"I'm supposed to keep it immobile, but I have a full range of motion."

"Painkillers?"

"Nonprescription. Alex back?"

I nodded.

"Who's on our side?"

"Just me and McGlade."

"So now we're three. When are we starting?"

"Now. You free?"

Phin leaned in, until our bodies were almost touching. His friendly stare became something else.

"I'm always free for you, Jack."

His breath was warm, and smelled faintly of cinnamon. When he touched my hip, I moved away. I needed Phin's help, but unlike with Hajek, I wasn't willing to lead him on to get it. Not because I felt anything for Phin. But because, unlike with Hajek, I didn't think Phin would be dissuaded once he was encouraged.

"We need guns," I said.

Phin took the hint, gave me some space. "I know a guy."

I grinned. "I do too. He works at Sports Authority. Can you fire a rifle?"

"Haven't had much practice. But I'm a quick study."

"I meant with your injury."

"I'm good at coping. But I need to pick up some things first."

"No time. Latham's paying for this. We can get you clothes and toiletries at the store."

"Some things aren't for sale at the store."

I wondered what he meant, then wondered if I really wanted to know.

"We need to go now, Phin."

"Okay." Phin dug his hands into his pockets. "I'm yours."

We made our way through Joe's, weaving through laughing, happy people, and one who wasn't laughing or happy.

"Liar! You ain't crippled!"

Mean Eyes broke through the crowd and launched himself at Phin. I caught a glimpse of something in his hand, and my leg whipped around in a spin kick, my head snapping back to take aim. I planted my foot dead center in the guy's gut, as hard a blow as I've ever landed. He fell to his knees, dropped his knife, clutched his belly, and began puking up beer. I should have arrested him, but I didn't have my badge on me, didn't have any handcuffs, and didn't have the time.

I bent down and grabbed his knife, a four-inch folder with a serrated blade. Phin squatted next to me and picked up my heel, which had broken off.

"Nice. Red is my favorite color."

I didn't understand what he meant, because my dress and shoes were black.

Only when we walked outside did I remember that my panties were red. My dress must have ridden up while I was kicking.

I felt myself flush, embarrassed, even though I had no reason to be. Phin was a friend. Nothing more.

I kept saying that to myself, over and over, as we walked back to the Crimebago.

CHAPTER 16

A LEX CAN'T SLEEP.

True, it's only ten p.m. But it has been a pretty full day. She killed two people, got laid, tortured an old friend, killed two more people, flirted in a bookstore, and planned her next murder. She should be exhausted. But instead, she's wired.

The Motel 6 room she's in is nicer than the one where she left Lance. The bed is bigger, softer. The pillows fluffier. Sleep should come. But she stares at the ceiling, jaw set, unable to relax. Her mind refuses to shut off. The end is in sight. Not quite the home stretch, but each passing hour brings her closer to her goal. A goal that will fix everything in Alex's life.

Jack is no doubt on her way. That idiot McGlade is probably with her. And Phin, whom Alex finds dangerously attractive. She imagines having Phin tied to the bed, and predicts she wouldn't need to use a rubber band with him. If circumstances were different, she might not even need bindings. Phin wouldn't mind a woman with scars. Perhaps he'd even find them sexy. She senses in him the same predatory nature as Charles, her one true love.

People like Phin and Charles are rare and exotic as snow leopards, and just as hard to catch. Unfortunately, you can't put an ad in the personals that reads *Freakishly scarred serial killer looking for soul mate, must have great abs and enjoy guns, violence, and romantic candlelight dinners.*

But Phin is an enemy, and a serious threat, so he has to die. They all have to die. They killed her beloved Charles. They sent her to prison. They took her face.

Alex rolls onto her stomach. The room is dark. The sheets are cool and smell like laundry detergent. She closes her eyes and parts her legs.

Maybe Alex can plan it so she can give Phin a farewell fuck. See how many times he can get it up before she peels off his skin.

McGlade won't get a farewell fuck. While he's also an enemy, he doesn't pose the same danger as Phin and Jack. Alex decides to let him live—after she removes his other hand, his eyes, and his balls. And perhaps throws in some third-degree burns as well.

The idea of burning McGlade makes her tingle. She arches her back, then presses against the mattress.

An ambulance. Or hospital. She'll break into one sometime in the next few days. Steal some antibiotics, sutures, and a few IV bags. When she gets Harry McGlade alone, she wants to make sure he survives his extensive injuries to lead a horrible, disfigured, unhappy, and very long life.

Getting warm in here. Alex yanks off her cover blanket, reaches down.

Now Jack—Alex has spent hours obsessing over how Jack will die. First, emotional and psychological suffering. Alex wants to make Jack regret becoming a cop. To break her down until she has no will to live.

Then, when the physical suffering starts, Alex will prolong her death until she gets bored. Perhaps rent a cabin in the north woods, keep Jack chained there, visit her a few times a week for some female bonding over extended sessions of excruciating pain. *Maybe I'll pick up a paper,* Alex thinks, *check the real estate listings for someplace secluded.*

Revenge is best served cold, but fantasizing about what she'll do to Jack makes her hot. So hot that she considers going back to the Old Stone Inn and riding Lance again.

But Alex can't go back there. Time and again, Jack has proven herself a smart and worthy adversary. While Alex is pretty confident that

Jack won't find Lance in time, she doesn't want to risk the lieutenant bursting into the room while she's bouncing toward the Big O.

However, there are other ways for a horny girl to get her rocks off. Ways that are a lot more satisfying than self-gratification.

Alex rolls to the edge of the bed and flips on the light. The drive will take a few hours, but she's not tired. If her victim is home, and the setup looks good, Alex might even get laid tonight.

Sex and death. They go together like chocolate and peanut butter.

She dresses as fast as she can, jeans and a hoodie, grabs the things she needs, and hangs a Do Not Disturb sign on the doorknob before heading to the car.

It's time to go looking for a cop.

CHAPTER 17

"SO FAR," Herb's voice was tired, frustrated, "not a single bomb squad has responded saying they have a cop named Lance on their team."

"No hits on the picture?"

I was back in the Crimebago, and warm because of Phin. Not due to sexual tension, or anger, or embarrassment. Phin had been able to fix Harry's air conditioner.

"You know how hard it is to ID by pic, Jack. How differently people look in different situations. In Lance's case, he's got duct tape around half his head and he's screaming in agony. We might not even recognize him if he was eating a five-course Mongolian BBQ across from us."

Leave it to Herb to work food into the discussion.

"Any MIAs?" I switched my cell phone from my left hand to my right.

"One. A Detective Don Oakes, EOD out of North Carolina. Didn't report in today. His lieut said the pic sort of looks like him."

"Where in North Carolina?"

"Wilmington. On the coast."

"You've alerted their department?"

"Got an all points on Oakes. They're bringing in the Feds, suspected kidnapping."

"Thanks, Herb."

"Keep me in the loop. And don't forget my Turduckinlux."

Herb hung up. Harry plopped himself on the couch next to me. The aftershave smell made me wince.

"Alex told me she went through basic training in North Carolina." He scratched himself in a bad place. "Makes sense she'd go there."

Phin folded his arms. "I don't want to get within a mile of Alex without long-range backup. If we go to NC, we have to leave the rifles behind."

We'd just spent several thousand dollars of Latham's money at a local sporting goods store, buying two H-S Precision professional hunting rifles with twenty-six-inch barrels, chambered for .377. But no traveling cases for them, and no time to get any. My watch said 10:30 p.m. Lance would be dead in seven hours. Assuming we could get a late flight out, we wouldn't have much time to find him.

"You scared of a girl, Phin?" Harry asked.

"Yes," Phin said.

Harry nodded. "Me too. I vote we stay here, see if something else shakes loose. The WPD probably won't let us in on the investigation anyway."

"I agree with Harry. But this is your decision, Jack."

I squeezed my eyes shut, trying to force a brilliant thought. I settled for a semi-apparent one.

"How did Alex get the pigstick?"

Harry made a face. "Duh. She stole it from Lance, who's on a bomb squad somewhere."

"Did she just find a random EOD cop and follow him home?"

Phin leaned against the kitchen counter. Or the *galley* counter, in Harryspeak. "I get it. She knows him."

"Fatso hasn't found anyone named Lance on any bomb squad?"

I shook my head. "Not yet."

"Maybe he's not civilian." Harry scratched the stubble on his chin. "Maybe he's military police. Someone Alex knew when she was in the marines. Those guys would have pigsticks, det wire, all that shit."

Phin appraised Harry. "Did Alex talk about any old boyfriends?"

"I don't remember. She didn't mention her past much."

"How about her old unit?"

Harry grinned. "Heh heh. You said *unit*."

"Focus, Harry. You spent more time with Alex than we did. You have to know her better."

"If I knew her so well, think I'd have this?"

Harry held up his prosthetic hand. There was a whirring, mechanical sound, and his middle finger raised up. Crude way to make a point, but valid nonetheless. Alex had fooled us all. I met her under false pretenses, and actually considered her a friend up until the point she tried to kill me. She could lie and manipulate better than anyone I'd ever known.

I rubbed my eyes, which stung from all the crying I'd done today. "Okay, we stay put, follow the military angle. I'll call Herb, see if he can get access to Alex's records. Maybe we can find someone in her past named Lance."

Harry shook his head. "Lance is probably dead already. We should head to Deer Park, try to trace the first cell phone in the daisy chain. That's a sure path to Alex."

"Can't we do both?" Phin asked. "Split up?"

Harry rocked himself up off the couch and slapped an arm around Phin's shoulders.

"Good idea, Phin old buddy. Me and you. Two men on the open road. We can find the phone between marathon sessions of poker and drinking. Hell, with no women around we don't even have to bother showering or getting dressed."

"I'm going with Jack." Phin met my eyes. "If that's okay."

I shrugged. "It's a full night of going over reports, case histories, those shrink sessions while she was at Heathrow. Nothing exciting."

"Two can read faster than one. And if I'm there, we can keep each other up."

An unwarranted thought popped into my head, of Phin without his shirt. He had a terrific body. Defined pecs. Six-pack abs . . .

Focus, Jack, you're being an asshole. We were chasing a killer, Phin was a crook, and I was still mourning the man I loved. What the hell was up with my hormones lately? PMS?

I calculated when my period was due, and the answer startled me.

Last week. It should have been last week. And I was never late more than a day or two, not once since the age of twelve. I could set my watch by my cycle.

Stress. Could be stress. That's why I missed it.

Or it could be . . .

"You guys got a thing for each other?" Harry asked.

"We're just friends," I said quickly. Maybe too quickly.

"I hope so, because you're like twice his age. Besides, women over forty-five shouldn't have sex. Unless they're Cher."

"Ready to go?" I asked Phin, giving McGlade my back.

He put out his hand, helped me up off the couch. His palm was cool, soft, and he held on for longer than necessary. I gently disengaged, and we began to gather up all the stuff we bought at the sports store.

"You sure you want to go with her, Phin? I got a thirty-pack of Old Style in the fridge, and I just downloaded the entire Pink Floyd discography from a file sharing network."

Phin stared at me, hard. "I'm sure."

Harry shrugged. "Okay. Your loss. You want me to drop you off somewhere?"

"My truck. It's parked in a long-term lot on Addison."

"Gotcha. I'll be driving, anyone needs me."

Harry wandered up to the cab of the RV. A moment later Pink Floyd came on, shaking the walls and rattling the windows. I used the knife I'd liberated from Phin's pool buddy and opened up three plastic blister packages containing walkie-talkies. Then I inserted their batteries and made sure all were on the same frequency.

"I'm leaving you a radio," I yelled at Harry over "Dark Side of the Moon."

"What?"

"A radio!"

"Got a CD in already!"

Harry turned up the volume so high it vibrated my tonsils. I shoved the other two radios into a backpack with a portable GPS, two Bushnell rifle scopes, two forty-caliber Beretta semiautos, and several boxes of ammo. Phin was folding clothes. We'd both opted for T-shirts, sweatshirt hoodies, and sweatpants. Nikes and a sports bra for me. Boxer shorts for him. The sporting goods store also carried panties, but I figured I could get another day out of the French-cut red pair I had on. It had nothing to do with the fact that none of their panties were sexy. Or red. That Phin seemed to like red was completely irrelevant.

The RV jerked to a stop, jarring me off my feet. I reached out my hands to break my fall. Caught Phin. He gave me a look. I needed to nip this thing in the bud.

"Phin, we've got a lot of work to do and all this flirting bullshit has to—"

His mouth pressed against mine, cutting off my words. Phin's lips were firm, insistent, demanding, like I was the most important thing in the entire world and he had to have me. His tongue searched for mine, touched it gently, and I didn't pull away, instead meeting it with surprising urgency. One of his hands tangled itself in the back of my hair and the other cupped my ass and then my body betrayed me and I hooked my right leg around his and ground into him, a hungry moan escaping my throat.

I wanted his hands on me, his mouth on me, all over. I wanted to stop thinking and stop hating myself and stop being afraid and have him inside me, right away, right now. Was it wrong? Hell yes. When we were finished, I'd add it to the list of reasons I hated myself.

My fingers fumbled with the top button on his jeans, popped it free.

"Bed," I managed to gasp in the brief second I came up for air. "Harry's bed."

But I wasn't sure we'd make it to the bed. My dress was hiked up, and he already had my bra up, rough fingers teasing my nipple, making me want to do him right there standing up, and then there was a groaning sound and it was coming from me and it wasn't a happy sound at all.

Phin stopped kissing me. He drew back, a question on his face. My tears were on his cheeks.

I covered my eyes, not wanting to watch him watch me cry. My shoulders shook, and I clenched my teeth to keep the major sobs in, but a few of them got out anyway.

Phin put his arms around me again. There was no urgency this time. Only sympathy. I buried my face in his shoulder, wishing he was Latham, wishing it so bad it made my ears ring.

Or maybe that was the Floyd.

I caught my breath and forced the pain back. Disengaged myself from Phin. Couldn't look at him. Couldn't say anything. Pulled down my bra, then busied myself instead with gathering up the remainder of our purchases, feeling his pity like laser sights all over my body.

The music cut off mid-tune and Harry called to us.

"You kids know anyone in a dark sedan? They've been following us for five blocks."

I hurried up to the cab, checked the enormous side-view mirror.

The Feebies. Bastards must have tailed me. Which means they knew I was with Phin. Bad for me. Bad for him. Worst of all for Lance, if I had to spend all night answering questions about aiding and abetting a known felon.

"They're Feds, Harry. After Phin because he robbed a bank."

"Good for you, Phin!" Harry called behind him. "Win one for the little guy! You pay for gas next stop!"

I put my hand on Harry's shoulder.

"We need to lose them, Harry. If they find him with us, we're screwed."

Harry snorted. "Lose them? Jackie, we're driving an RV on a Friday night in one of the most traffic-congested cities in America."

"You have to try."

"It's not gonna happen. He can hide in the refrigerator. I made sure I got one big enough to fit into."

"Please, Harry." The word didn't want to leave my throat, but I said it anyway. "Bro."

Harry raised an eyebrow, grinned, and slammed down on the gas.

CHAPTER 18

THE HONDA'S SPEEDOMETER is up over ninety mph, and has been for close to half an hour, but Alex hasn't seen a single squad car on this stretch of highway. None hidden. None passing. Not even one coming in the other direction on the opposite side of the street.

It's discouraging. Don't cops have monthly quotas? Who's protecting our nation's roads from reckless drivers?

Finally, after blowing past an obvious speed trap semi-hidden by a cluster of bushes, Alex grows a red and blue tail. She waits for him to hit the siren before taking her foot off the accelerator and rolling to a stop. Traffic on the interstate is sparse at this time of night. They're past the city limits, in the country. No stores, houses, exits, or oases, for two miles in either direction. Just plains and trees, stretching out and fading into unpopulated darkness.

The cop parks behind her, but farther out on the shoulder, protecting himself from being accidentally run over. He aims his side-door spotlight directly in Alex's rearview. She angles it downward, deflecting the glare, and turns around in her seat to see him coming, hoping he's not too short or fat.

Alex likes speed, and because of that she has been stopped many times in the past. Flirting, flattering, showing some leg, has gotten her out of many a ticket. But with her face the way it is, no cop will be anxious to get her phone number.

This time, however, she's not looking for a free pass.

He climbs out of his car, and Alex is surprised. He is actually a she. Girl cop. Cool.

Alex digs into her purse, palms the stun gun. Waits.

"License and registration."

The cop is standing a foot behind the driver's-side door. One hand is on her belt, near her holster. Alex squints behind her, doesn't see a partner in the squad car. She opens the door.

"Stay in the car, ma'am."

It's an order, delivered with authority. The cop's hand has now un-snapped her holster and is on the butt of her pistol. It's hard to tell with the light silhouetting her, but Alex guesses her at about thirty years of age, tall, maybe a hundred and fifty pounds. A pro, by the way she's con-ducted the traffic stop so far.

But Alex is a pro too.

Alex fumbles with her purse, pretending to search for her wallet.

"Oh, Jesus, I'm sorry, I know I was speeding, I can't find my license, my boyfriend, he hit me—"

"Get back into the car, ma'am."

Alex takes a step toward her, hand still in her purse. The cop's name tag reads *Stark*.

"The hospital, I need the hospital, look what the bastard did to my face—"

Now Officer Stark draws her weapon, aims at Alex's chest.

"Drop the purse and hands above your head!"

"Why? I didn't do anything. My boyfriend—"

"Drop your purse and hands above your head! Now!"

Alex halts. She's excited, even a little scared. Alex drops the purse, slowly raises her hands.

"Turn in a complete circle!"

Alex complies, her shirt riding up, showing the cop there is nothing in her pockets or her belt.

"Get on your knees! Hands behind your head!"

Different cops arrest suspects in different ways. Some order them to palm the car or the wall. Some order them to lie facedown on the ground and spread out their arms and legs. Some prefer the knees and the hands behind the head routine.

Which Alex had been hoping for.

"On your knees! Hands behind your head!"

Alex nods quickly, getting down, the asphalt cold beneath her jeans. She puts her hands on her neck, under her long red hair. If Stark had ordered her to palm the hood of the car, Alex first would have fallen to her knees and faked sobbing, face in her hands. If Stark had wanted her to eat the tarmac, she would have complied, but put her hands behind her head. But any way it went down, Alex still would have been within easy reach of the stun gun she'd stuck in the hanging hood of her sweatshirt.

"Look the other way!"

Alex turns her head, knows that the cop will approach her from a different angle to keep her off balance. As expected, Officer Stark comes at Alex on her left side, snicks the cuff on Alex's right wrist with her left hand, grabbing Alex's thumb to hold her steady. But it's impossible to fully handcuff a suspect while holding a pistol. Stark has to holster her weapon before slapping on the other cuff. As she does this, Alex's free hand snakes into the hoodie and grabs the Cheetah. Alex tilts left, twisting around under her armpit, and jams the stun gun into the officer's hip, letting her feel a million volts.

Officer Stark folds in half and drops to the street. Alex reaches for the gun, but it's secured by a strap. She takes a second to find the release, then the pistol—a Sig Sauer .45—comes free. Alex sticks it in the back of her jeans.

A car whizzes by, doesn't slow down. The cop moans. Alex juices her again, then drags her between their cars, onto the dirt beyond the shoulder. She unclips a Maglite from Stark's belt and takes her pepper spray and radio. The handcuff keys are in her breast pocket, and Alex removes her bracelet and binds Stark's wrists. Then she waits.

The cop stirs, opens her eyes. Alex focuses the beam on her.

"Full name and car number."

"Ma'am . . . you're in a lot of trouble."

Cops like Maglites. Illumination is only one of the reasons why. Alex raises it, heavy with six D batteries, and brings it down on Officer Stark's leg. Not hard enough to break it—that would cause a delay—but hard enough to hurt like hell.

This produces a sound somewhere between a whimper and a howl. Alex repeats the question.

"Val . . . Val Stark. Car Five Victor Seven."

"Good. Now on your hands and knees. Back to your ride."

Alex follows while hunched over, keeping out of sight of the occasional passing car. She helps Officer Stark into the backseat.

"Be right back, cutie."

Alex winks and slams the door. Then she gathers up the items from the back of the Honda and transfers them into the passenger seat of the cop car, save for a fist-sized chunk of PENO, a pyrotechnic blasting cap, and four feet of pink thermalite fuse. She pushes in the Honda's cigarette lighter, then spends a few dirty minutes crawling under the chassis. Alex hums as she works, sticking the PENO to the gas tank, and the combined fuse and cap into the plastic. The road, and the undercarriage, are still damp from the earlier rain, but the explosive sticks like peanut butter.

Boom time.

Alex pops out the lighter, admiring the orange glow. She hesitates, savoring the moment, letting some anticipation build.

The fuse ignites, hissing and sparking and making Alex feel like she's ten years old again, behind Father's barn with Charles, lighting cherry bombs and blowing up tin cans.

Four feet of pink thermalite equals eighty seconds. Alex pockets the lighter and strolls to the police car, no hurry, and climbs into the driver's seat. Officer Stark has left her keys in the ignition, the car still running. The car computer—a laptop—is attached to the armrest, its white screen blinking. Alex shifts into reverse and backs up along the shoulder until she's a good hundred feet away from the Honda. Then she chews her lower lip and watches, eyes wide. Waits for it . . . waits for it . . .

Eighty seconds pass.

Nothing happens.

The radio squawks, making her jump.

"Five Victor Seven, status on the 10-73. Over."

Alex locates the handset, picks it up.

"This is Five Victor Seven." Alex's pitches her voice higher, to match Officer Stark's. "Standby, Central."

"Ten-four, Five Victor Seven."

Still no explosion. Alex wonders if the wet road snuffed out the fuse. Or if she grabbed an electric blasting cap by mistake. There could be a dozen reasons why it didn't go off, but going out and checking doesn't seem like the brightest of ideas.

"Check under the can, Alex. See if it's lit."

"You check, Charles. I don't have to know that bad."

But in this case, Alex has to know. Her prints are all over that car, and a quick peek at Officer Stark's computer shows it has been reported stolen. If the Honda doesn't explode, it will give Jack an unfair jump on Alex's location, and let the lieutenant know she has plastic explosives. Not to mention alert the local cops that an escaped serial killer is prowling the area.

Alex speaks into the radio, reading the call number off the screen.

"Central, this is Five Victor Seven. Negative on that 10-73. It was the owner, spent a few days out of town, forgot to call home, over. I'm giving her a warning. Over."

"Roger that, Five Victor Seven."

Alex turns around, faces the cop in the backseat.

"Officer Stark, I need you to check to see why my car hasn't blown up."

Officer Stark doesn't move, and her face reveals she isn't pleased with the idea.

"Chances are pretty good that it went out," Alex says, soothing. "I don't think it's going to blow up in your face."

"Then you go check."

"I have the gun, so I don't have to. Now, are you going to help a civilian out, or do I have to put two in your knees?"

"You're making it worse for yourself. You need to stop before this goes too far."

Alex considers this woman. She's tall enough, but the eyes are wrong.

"Are you married, Stark?"

"Yes. I have a husband and three kids. You don't want to do anything stupid."

"Exactly. Which is why you're the one who's going to check the fuse."

Alex exits the vehicle and walks around to Stark's door. One hand opens it. The other points the Sig.

"Check if the fuse died, or any other problem you can find."

"I don't know anything about explosives."

"It's easy. If you see a spark, run. And make sure you run this way, or I'll shoot you."

Stark pulls herself out of the backseat—not the easiest of tasks with cuffs on—and stands before Alex.

Alex extends her empty hand. Stark flinches, but Alex brings the gun up under her jaw to keep her still. She pushes a stray auburn bang out of Stark's face, tucks it behind her ear.

"Don't be afraid," Alex says. "Things happen beyond our control. We can't do anything to stop them. But we do have control over how we react. How we respond. Being afraid is a choice."

The speech seems to have the opposite effect on Stark, who begins to tremble. Alex rolls her eyes.

"Just get over there, 'fraidy cat."

Stark moves like a robot, joints stiff, head down, scanning the road. Alex waits behind the open door of the cruiser, one hand aiming the Sig, the other aiming the Maglite.

The closer Stark gets to the Honda, the slower she becomes. At this rate, the sun will be up before the car explodes.

"Let's pick up the pace, Officer Stark. I'm hoping to get laid tonight. You find the fuse?"

Stark mumbles something, the words lost in the night.

"Crouch lower," Alex says. "It's a skinny pink fuse."

Another mumble. Alex aims, fires a round over Stark's head, close enough for her to feel the wind. The cop drops to the ground.

"That's what I mean. Keep looking."

Another minute passes, along with three rubberneckers. One slows down enough to maybe see that things aren't right. The radio squawks again.

"Five Victor Seven, what's your twenty? Over."

Alex doesn't know radio call signals. And she can't trust Officer Stark to give her the correct response. She chooses to ignore it, hoping to get out of there shortly.

"See the fuse?" Alex calls to Stark, who is now on all fours next to the Honda, shaking so bad she looks like a wet dog.

"No."

"Check underneath, by the gas tank."

Stark doesn't budge. Alex shoots out the tire Stark is crouching next to, the *pop* almost as loud as the gunfire.

"I hate repeating myself, Val."

"Five Victor Seven, status."

Goddamn radio. Alex opens the front door, grabs the hand mike.

"Just finishing up here, Central. Computer problems."

She tosses the mike back inside, and notices Officer Stark is under the car. But there's a faint blue light under there with her.

The bitch has a cell phone. Probably one of those ultra-thin models for Alex to have missed it in the pat down.

"Five Victor Seven, do you have a 10-86? Over."

Dammit. Alex figures she said something wrong, which means another patrol car will cruise by any minute. She needs to get out of here, pronto.

"Throw away the phone, Val!"

Alex fires two rounds into the trunk of the car. The cop can't drop the phone fast enough, and it skitters across the pavement.

"Now grab the plastic explosive I put on the gas tank!"

Val cowers, hands covering her head, as if that will protect her from a forty-five-caliber bullet.

Alex takes a deep, calming breath, then exits the vehicle.

"I'm going to count to three. If I don't see the plastic in your hand, your children will grow up without a mother. One . . . two . . ."

Officer Stark holds up the PENO.

"Good. Now run back here. Move it, double time."

Stark half jogs/half stumbles to the squad car. Her face is wet.

"Gimme the plastic, and get in the backseat. Close the door behind you."

The cop follows orders. Alex studies the PENO. The fuse has fallen out. Alex frowns with half of her face. She places the PENO on the passenger seat.

"Now take your clothes off, Officer Stark."

"Why?"

"Because I said so. Faster would be better. If you follow directions, you'll live through this."

She uncuffs her and Officer Stark strips. Alex enjoys the show. From experience, she knows how difficult it is to undress a body. It's much easier, and quicker, when they undress themselves.

"Underwear too. This is just so you won't be able to follow me."

Alex gives Officer Stark credit for not losing it. There are tears, but no begging or sobbing. Tough broad. Not a bad body either.

"Very good, Officer Stark. Now I want you to get into the Honda. I'm going to leave you there."

Alex opens the door, checks for cars, then marches the cop to the Honda. Moving bodies is an even bigger pain in the ass than undressing them. Much easier to let them move themselves.

"Sit in the driver's seat, put your hands out."

Alex tucks the gun into her waistband. Naked, the cop has lost the will to fight back. It takes a few seconds to uncuff one of her wrists, then attach it to the steering wheel.

"Are you afraid, Val?"

Officer Stark stares hard at Alex.

"Yes. But I'm controlling it."

"Good. Good for you. Are your children proud of you? That their mother is a cop?"

Stark nods.

"They should be."

Alex hurries back to the squad car, picks up the PENO and two feet of thermalite fuse. Dispatch comes on the radio. Alex switches it off, concentrating on inserting the fuse into the blasting cap. Once she's satisfied it won't fall out, she returns to the Honda, stopping once to pick up Officer Stark's cell phone.

"Normally I savor things like this, Val, but I'm short on time."

Alex takes the cigarette lighter from her pocket, and leans across Stark to press it into the outlet.

"I'm using a forty-second fuse. I won't light it until your call goes through. Forty seconds probably isn't long enough to say good-bye to your kids, but it's an unfair world."

Alex hands Stark the phone. She looks deep into the cop's eyes, sees it all. Disbelief. Realization. Anger. Despair. Acceptance. Out of everyone Alex has killed today, this is the most memorable. Too bad she can't stick around to watch her face during the final moments.

The lighter pops out.

"Call home, Val."

Val's hands are shaking so badly she has to dial three times. Finally, she gets a connection.

"Honey? It's Mommy."

Alex caresses Val's hair. Then she lights the fuse and tosses the PENO under the Honda.

As she walks back to the patrol car, Alex wonders what she would do with only a few seconds left to live. What would she say?

Nothing. She'd say nothing, because she doesn't have anyone to call.

The explosion is loud, and rattles the police car, but there is no huge pyrotechnic fireball like on television. The car burns, but it's a small fire, won't last long.

Alex hits the siren and peels out. Mission accomplished. On to the next goal.

CHAPTER 19

THE CRIMEBAGO ACCELERATED with the speed and grace of a three-legged elephant, blowing through a red light and prompting a honking frenzy from all four corners of the intersection. Harry alternated between steering and punching buttons on the dashboard CD changer. I gave him a friendly tap on the back of the head to keep him focused.

"What the hell are you doing, McGlade? Watch the damn road!"

"I'm looking for car chase music."

"I'll do it. Pay attention to driving."

"Find Steppenwolf. It's disc five or six."

I pressed some random buttons, and Pink Floyd came on again.

"Too mellow!" McGlade yelled, jerking the wheel left and turning onto Halsted. I fell into the passenger seat, and Phin appeared and punched off the stereo.

"Is there a door to the roof?"

"Skylight opens. Latch is above the sofa. Why'd you kill the tunes?"

"Pull up next to a bus, then slow down and let them get close."

"You want to jump from the Crimebago to a bus?"

"Yeah."

"Motorhead would be perfect for that. I think it's disc eight."

Harry fussed with buttons. Phin locked eyes with me and said, "Make sure he does what I told him."

"I'm going with you."

It was slight, but he still smirked. It annoyed me. I shoved Phin to the side, grabbed a walkie-talkie, and turned it on.

Then the RV exploded, a deafening thunderclap that made my knees buckle.

"SACRIFICE! PAY THE PRICE!"

No, not an explosion. Harry had found the Motorhead CD.

I clawed my way up to the cockpit and smacked it off.

"I'm the driver, dammit! I pick the music!"

"Focus, McGlade. Get next to a bus and make sure the Feebies are right behind you, then come to a stop. They won't be able to see up onto the roof if they're hugging the bumper."

Harry reached for the stereo. I smacked his fake hand.

"Are you listening?"

"Jesus, sis, I got it the first time."

"We'll go on your say-so. Lead them around for another ten minutes, then pull over. Got it?"

"There better not be a body cavity search. I'll give you up if they threaten me with a body cavity search. My ass is exit only."

"Relax, Harry." Phin patted him on the shoulder. "They won't think I'm hiding up your ass."

Harry nodded, then accelerated to catch up to a bus several car lengths ahead. Phin and I went to the kitchenette, strapping on our backpacks. He smirked at me again. I frowned.

"I'm going with you to find Alex, Phin. That's the only reason."

"I know."

His grin didn't fade. I thought about mentioning the obstruction of justice charges I'd be facing if we were caught, along with accessory after the fact, all because he robbed a goddamn bank instead of getting an honest job. But instead I said, "What's so damn funny?"

He shook his head slightly. I realized he wasn't amused by the situation, or anything I was doing. He was staring at me the way Latham used to, the way Alan did before our marriage imploded. Not lust. Something even more dangerous.

Love.

A quick romp in bed was one thing. An actual relationship was something I couldn't even consider, especially at that moment. I wanted to smack him for being ten kinds of inappropriate.

"They're on my bumper!" McGlade yelled back.

"How close?" I turned away from Phin's stare but still could feel it.

"Close enough to give me a reach-around. Bus is on the left. You got about twenty seconds before the light turns green."

Phin shouldered the backpack and hopped onto the sofa, fussing with the latches on the ceiling panel. It swung upward on hinges. He stuck his arms through, got his palms onto the roof, and hoisted himself up. I hung my purse around my neck and cast a longing glance at the rifles. We'd have to leave them for the time being.

"Cross traffic is flashing the Don't Walk light," McGlade said.

A hand reached down. I stepped onto the sofa and grabbed Phin's wrist. His fingers locked onto my forearm and he yanked me through the opening, up onto my butt.

Vehicle exhaust soured my sinuses and cold city wind spit drizzle on my cheeks. I knelt on the roof, rainwater soaking through the seat of my sweatpants.

"The Don't Walk light is solid." McGlade's voice was muffled, competing with the sounds of the street. Engines, honking, a siren in the distance. I looked behind me, couldn't see the Feebies' sedan. We were too high and they were too close.

Phin pointed left, to the bus. A Chicago commuter, green on white, about a foot taller than the RV and too far away to jump onto.

But Phin wasn't reading my thoughts, and he sprinted up from a crouching position, took three big strides, then launched himself through the air.

His jump took him at least eight feet, and as his arc crested and waned I knew he didn't have enough height to make it. Phin must have realized it as well, because he tucked in his legs midair, and hit the roof of the bus on his knees, sliding across the top in a spray of dirty water.

I knew I couldn't follow. Too far.

"Yellow light!" McGlade warned.

Phin twisted around, beckoned me to jump. I got on my feet, but there was no way. Not without wings and a stack of mattresses. I shook my head.

"Green light!" Harry yelled. "Wait—traffic is blocked! Two cars! Feds! They're Feds!"

I crouched down, crawled to the edge of the roof. Special Agent Dailey—or maybe it was Special Agent Coursey—walked directly under my line of sight, heading for the front of the RV.

I played out the upcoming scene in my head. Coursey/Dailey would produce a warrant, because neither of them took a leak without first going through proper channels, Harry would stonewall for a minute or two, then the Feds would search the Winnebago, find the open roof panel, discover me and Phin. Then we'd be chased and eventually arrested, Lance would die, Alex would continue her reign of terror, and Phin would go to jail for a very long time.

Now was a pretty good time to run like hell.

I glanced over at Phin, still motioning for me to jump. On my best day, on dry ground, I couldn't make it. On a slippery roof, twelve feet above the street, I'd break bones for sure.

I heard Harry say, "How do I know this is a real warrant, and not something you printed on the Internet?" and decided that was my cue to give myself up. Phin could escape on his own, and we could contact him later. Depending on their evidence, maybe I wouldn't have to spend all night at FBI headquarters answering questions. I pointed at the street, mouthed the word *run* at Phin.

"He's on top of the bus!"

I glanced down. A Feebie had his gun out, bringing it up. Phin backpedaled out of range, shrugging off his backpack. He jerked down the zipper and reached inside.

There were Berettas in the backpack.

Bank robbery was one thing. Shooting a federal agent was another. I couldn't let Phin do that, not even to save himself.

I fumbled for my purse, yanking out my Colt, cop mode on autopilot. Without hesitating I pointed my gun at the man I'd been making out with only a few minutes ago.

Phin tugged something small and black out of the bag, I yelled "No!", and my finger reflexively tightened on the trigger, the hammer drawing back.

Walkie-talkie. He was holding a radio.

He cocked back his arm to toss it to me, and hesitated when he saw my gun out and trained on his chest. It was tough to see his expression in the drizzle and the darkness, but I imagined it was a combination of shock and disappointment. We both got over it quick enough, and I tucked my gun under my armpit just as he threw the radio across the gap. I caught it, and then he disappeared over the other side of the bus.

"On the RV!"

My shouting had done more than give away my position. It also confirmed that I was aiding and abetting a federal criminal. I was in deep. I shoved the radio and the gun into my purse and wondered what the hell I should do next.

"We followed you to the pool establishment, Lieutenant. You're under arrest."

I turned, saw Dailey or Coursey peeking over the rear of the RV, climbing the aluminum ladder attached to the back. His gun wasn't out. He probably figured I was trapped. A quick look at the street around me confirmed this: The Feds had the Crimebago surrounded.

"Give up, Lieutenant. There's nowhere for you to go."

But he was wrong. The bus was still there. I didn't think I'd make it, but I didn't have a choice. In less than seven hours, Lance would be dead, and it didn't matter to him whether I was in Cook County Jail or Cook County Hospital.

I set my jaw, sprinted for the edge, and jumped.

CHAPTER 20

ALEX PUSHES THE PATROL CAR up past 120, sirens screaming and lights flashing, flying over the state line. It's a rush. She can see what drew Jack to a career in law enforcement. No wonder so many cops are dicks. How easy it is to power trip when you have a car, a badge, and a gun.

Unfortunately, she can't keep it. The car will be reported missing, if it hasn't been already, and it probably has a GPS locator in it somewhere. The sooner she can ditch it, the better.

Luckily, getting another vehicle is as easy as pulling one over.

Alex chooses a Hyundai, dark blue, which is having some trouble staying in a single lane. Alex parks behind it and approaches the driver. He's older, a gray beard, looking guilty and confused and pretty plowed.

"Is there a problem, Officer?" he slurs.

Alex orders him out of his car, over to a ditch by the side of the road, and puts two in his head. Twenty bucks in his wallet. More goddamn SEE ID credit cards—why were people so damn paranoid? And a silver flask in his jacket. Alex unscrews the cap. Gin. Not her favorite, but it will serve her purpose.

She rips off the man's shirt, then hikes back to the squad car. Sprinkling alcohol on the cloth, she spends a few minutes wiping down the door handles, wheel, radio handset, and anything else she might have touched. Then she grabs what she needs and climbs into her new Hyundai, already focusing on her next victim.

Her original plan involved a time bomb, perhaps some plastic explosive wedged inside an orifice. Alex has killed a lot of people in a lot of different ways, but that would be a new one. Jack would enjoy a close-up pic of that, especially since it is someone she knows so well.

But a quick search of the police car had revealed something even better. An AED. Alex will have a great deal of fun with that. The role-playing possibilities are limitless.

The Hyundai conveniently has a GPS, which directs her off the expressway and into town. She reaches her target twenty minutes later.

It's a nice area, single-family homes each with neatly trimmed trees in their fenced-in backyards. Quiet, peaceful, but the streetlights are bright enough to read a book under. Probably a very low crime rate.

"Until now," Alex says, half her face curling into a grin.

She finds the right address and pulls up to the correct driveway. The house is completely dark, no lights inside or out. Sleeping? Possibly. It's not a stretch that he forgot to turn on the exterior lights. Or maybe there's no one home.

Alex pulls past, thinking it out. She can call, confirm if he's home. That might also let her know if anyone else is in the house too. But all she has is her cell phone, and she didn't bring her laptop along so she can't spoof the caller ID. A pay phone is a possibility, but there aren't many of those left, and Alex doesn't know where to look for one.

Better to just knock on the door. She should be able to assess and secure the situation easily. Especially in her new uniform. That's why she went through all the trouble to get it in the first place.

Alex drives out of the development, then finds a nice, dark stretch of road. She parks and quickly dresses in Officer Stark's discarded clothing. It's a little loose in the rear, and tight across the chest, but a good length. She fingers the badge on the leather jacket and buckles the utility belt. Alex can't find a band for her hair, so she tucks it under her collar for a more professional look. The cap fits fine. Then it's back in the car, and back to the house.

When Alex walks up the driveway, she does it with a swagger.

Wearing the uniform is an even bigger kick than driving the car. The stun gun is in her jacket pocket, the Maglite in her left hand, Stark's pistol on her belt. She presses the doorbell.

Twenty seconds pass. No sounds from inside the house. She presses it again.

Nothing.

There's a chance Jack knew she'd pick this target, and warned him away. A good chance. But if he went away, where would he go?

No way to know, standing out here.

Alex examines the door. It's heavy, painted aluminum, a dead bolt. She grabs the knob and tugs. The jamb is solid, the lock tight. She searches around the door for any signs or stickers warning of a burglar alarm. There aren't any.

Alex walks across the lawn, around the side of the house, over to the gate for the backyard. It's open. Unlike the street side, the back of the house is dark, so she flips on the Maglite. If a nosy neighbor sees her, they'll see a cop. It's doubtful they'll call the police when the police are already here.

She automatically searches the backyard for bones, poop, toys, bowls, or anything else that would indicate a dog. There wasn't any barking when Alex knocked, but a well-trained mutt might keep silent. She finds nothing.

First Alex tries the sliding glass patio door. Locked. She knocks again, waits, then switches her grip on the Maglite and hits the door with everything she has.

As expected, the window splinters but doesn't fall to pieces. Safety glass, like an auto windshield. Alex strikes it three more times in the same spot, breaking through the plastic coating, until she can stick her hand into the hole and unlock the door.

She steps inside, sweeping the flashlight beam across a sofa and a TV. It's the living room. Alex locates a wall switch, flips on the lights.

In a perfect world, there would be a vacation brochure sitting on the table, or an open phone book with a hotel name circled. Alex finds neither, but isn't discouraged. She sees a cordless phone next to the sofa and hits redial.

"Marino's Pizza."

Alex hesitates, thinks about ordering some food, then dismisses the idea and hangs up. A quick search of the living room provides no clues as to where he went. If he even went anywhere. Maybe Jack didn't warn him, and he just stepped out to get a six-pack.

Alex heads into the kitchen. She begins to search for a calendar, address book, Day-Timer, anything that might list friends, family, schedule. There's another phone, and she presses redial while rifling through a junk drawer.

"Thank you for calling the Holiday Inn. Press one for reservations."

Alex presses one, gets the front desk.

"Can I leave a message for a guest?"

"What's the guest's name?"

"Alan Daniels."

"Just a moment."

Alex gets put on hold, music comes on. She recognizes the tune as MC Ice Koffee. What the hell is wrong with the world when someone like that is popular?

"Would you like me to connect you?"

"Actually, I think I'll just drop by. What room is he in?"

"We can't give out that information, ma'am."

"No problem. Can you connect me to the restaurant?"

"Just a moment."

Alex endures more hip-hop before a woman answers.

"I believe you had a guest there tonight, single man, in his forties, blond hair. His name is Alan Daniels. Can I speak to his server?"

"That's me. I waited on him."

"I promised to buy him dinner. Can you check to see if he put it on my room number?"

"Let me check. Here's his ticket. He charged it to room 212."

"Thank you." Alex disconnects. "Thank you very much."

CHAPTER 21

SOME URBAN LEGENDS are too good to be false. There's the one about the crazed man, high on PCP and adrenaline, who displays superhuman strength and snaps police handcuffs in half while being arrested. And there's the oft-repeated tale of the desperate mother who lifts up a car to save her child trapped beneath it.

So there was a precedent, however slim, that I could leap from the RV to the bus solely fueled by fear, determination, and adrenaline.

My footing was good, and I measured my steps perfectly, launching myself into the air at the very edge of the roof, my new Nikes gripping despite the drizzle, my aim true and sure.

Halfway there I knew I wasn't going to make it, and three-quarters of the way there I knew it was going to hurt, bad.

I held my hands out in front of me, slapping palms onto the top of the bus while my ribs slammed into the side. The wind rushed out of me like I'd been, well, hit by a bus. Bright motes punctuated red and black splotches in my vision, swirling around and adding a shot of disorientation to the pain cocktail. My jaw connected with the roof, reminding me of the last time Alex hit me in the face, which then reminded me that this wasn't Alex, it was a bus, and I was twelve feet above the unforgiving blacktop and going to break something—probably several somethings—when I fell in a second or two.

As anticipated, my palms found no purchase on the slick bus top, and my ribs contracted and expanded, giving my body a springboard push off the side, and then I was falling backward through the cool Chicago night, wondering if the twinkling skyscrapers above me were the last things I'd ever see.

I may have shrieked a little.

But, incredibly, when I hit, I didn't hit hard, and I managed to remain lucid enough to wonder why. Rather than cold wet asphalt and hot sticky blood, I felt something semi-soft envelop me, wrapping itself around my legs and shoulders.

There was an "uumph," which didn't come from me, and then another small drop, and I stopped flailing long enough to see I was sitting in someone's lap.

Phin.

No time for thanks, or apparently even a tender glance, because he roughly shoved me off and then just as roughly grabbed my armpit and yanked me to my feet.

I sort of remember running through cars, people yelling, horns blaring, and someone blasting Motorhead. When my wits partially returned Phin and I were beating feet down the sidewalk, each of my steps less wobbly than the last.

Two blocks later Phin jerked me into an alley. We pressed our backs against the wet brick of an office building, the scent of old garbage mingling with the ever-present car exhaust. I was breathing like an asthmatic on a hayride, and Phin was bent in half, hands on his thighs, sucking just as much wind as I was.

I inventoried my aches and pains. Jaw hurt, but a quick tongue probe proved I still had all of my choppers. Ribs hurt, but nothing seemed broken. Left palm hurt, and I squinted in the darkness and saw I'd scraped it trying to keep hold of the bus's roof.

Amazingly, I still had my purse. Even more amazingly, I wasn't dead. I stared at Phin.

"You saved my life."

Between breaths he said, "I knew you were going to go after me, fig-ured you wouldn't make it, so I ran around to play catch."

"My hero." I coughed. "Except that's bullshit. You didn't think I'd go after you. I practically shot you."

He grinned, shrugged.

"The Feds chased me around the bus, and I just happened to be there when you fell."

That made more sense. "Well, thanks."

"My pleasure. Thanks for not shooting me."

He stared at me hard again, and I didn't mind as much this time. But when he moved in for the kiss I forced my elbow between us and gave him a less-than-delicate jab. The exhilaration of being alive was soured by the fact that I was now a federal criminal.

"They'll question Harry, but I don't know how long they can detain him for. He'll deny knowing you were wanted, lawyer up, and probably be on the street again tomorrow."

Phin gave me some space, rubbing his sternum.

"So what's our next move?"

"We need to go through Alex's files, see if there's a mention of a cop named Lance in her past."

"Your partner have the files?"

"No. They're probably with the lead detective. Guy named Man-kowski."

I searched through my cell phone numbers, found the right one. Mankowski was a good cop—smart, honest, sort of looked like Thomas Jefferson.

"Got my files in the trunk, Lieut. Figured I'd get some reading in on the road."

"I need to see them, Detective."

"Might take a while. I'm in Indiana. Gary. Was following up with some of Alex's hometown friends. Sorry I missed the funeral."

I glossed over the sentiment.

"We can come to you, Tom."

"Might not help. Car is in the shop. Radiator blew. If it's locked in the garage I can't get it until morning."

"You up to speed?"

"Sergeant Benedict filled me in. I know we only have a few hours left. I could maybe find the mechanic, get him to let me in, but there are three boxes of files. A lot to read."

"You go through them yet?

"Just enough to know that Alexandra Kork is a serious wack-job. But I haven't seen the name Lance mentioned anywhere."

I crunched the numbers. Three-hour round trip to Indiana, and several more hours to read through that stack—if Tom could even locate the mechanic. Maybe he could fax them, but there were hundreds of papers, and faxes weren't exactly lightning quick.

"See what you can do."

"I will, Lieut. You can also try that Crime Lab cop. He had the files checked out before me. Really into her case. I heard he was writing a book about it."

"Which cop?"

"Weaselly little guy named Hajek. He might know who Lance is."

Hajek had told me he read the files for research. It was for a book? Now I wondered if he'd actually been hitting on me, or simply wanting an interview.

I thanked Mankowski and hung up. I could call Hajek, even though he'd been less than receptive to my previous plea for help. News of my retreat from the Feds would be all over the airwaves by now, and once Hajek heard about it he'd never give up the information. Assuming he even had any information.

I stared at Phin, saw him looking at me with concern. I didn't return the sentiment. I had so many conflicting feelings about Phin right now that remaining neutral was my best course of action.

I called Herb.

"Talking to me is an aiding and abetting charge." I explained the situation.

"I'm hoping you thought all of this through, Jack. Is this guy worth it? Can you even trust him?"

I thought about having Phin in my gun sights, almost pulling the trigger, and didn't have an answer.

"I need a cop's address. Scott Hajek. CSU guy, lives near the Crime Lab. If I call Dispatch it'll throw up red flags."

"Call you back in two."

I looked past Phin, down the alley, trying to keep my mind on Lance. Save him first. Then deal with everything else.

Herb called back in seventy seconds.

"He lives in an apartment on Halsted." He gave me the address, then said, "Shit, Jack. Feebies calling on my other line."

"It's my career, my life. Not yours. Cover your ass, Herb."

"With both hands. Don't forget my Turduckinlux."

Herb disconnected. I wouldn't be calling him again, no matter how hot things got.

"Lieutenant Daniels? This is Special Agent Coursey, FBI."

The voice came from my purse. The walkie-talkie.

"You need to come in, Lieutenant, before this escalates."

Phin and I stared at each other. I had an irrational urge to drop my purse and run away from it. Or maybe it wasn't so irrational.

"Lieutenant Daniels, you have to remember that you're a professional. We understand you've been through a rough patch, but you're still a police officer."

"Let me talk to her." Harry. *"Carmalita, honey, that wasn't Immigration. You didn't need to run. Those ten men don't want to take you back to El Salvador, chicita. Now you need to bring back my walkie-talkie. It has a ten-block radius, and is very expensive."*

"May I have the radio, Mr. McGlade?"

"I got two words for you, Special Agent Pinhead: Carmichael and Levine. They're my lawyers, and they're going to sue the bone marrow out of you. They'll make you wish you never came aboard the Crimebago."

"We need to move." I switched off the radio. "Feebies have ten men. Figure two are with Harry, that's four teams of two out there."

Phin nodded. "Searching a ten-block radius. Harry isn't as stupid as he seems."

"No one is as stupid as Harry seems. Including the Feds. They'll add more teams, widen the perimeter. How far away is your truck?"

"Maybe four blocks."

"Could the Feebies know about it?"

Phin shrugged. "No registration. Stolen plates. But everything leaves a trail."

"It's still our best shot," I decided out loud. "Let's move."

We moved.

CHAPTER 22

LEX CALLS ALAN'S ROOM from the house phone in the hotel lobby. Jack's ex-husband doesn't pick up. She sets the receiver next to the phone without disconnecting and crosses the lobby to the stairs. Alex takes them three at a time, orients herself on the second floor, and quickly finds room 212. Placing an ear to the door, she hears the phone ringing inside.

"Mr. Daniels?" Alex makes a fist and raps hard.

No answer.

He might be a sound sleeper, assisted by pills or alcohol. But the smarter bet is he's not in his room.

Alex adjusts her bangs, finger-combing them over the scars while considering her next move. Alan might be elsewhere in the hotel, maybe the bar or the gym. She knows his face from his Web site. Alan Daniels is a freelancer and all freelancers have homepages. But people might see her approaching him, recall the police uniform she's wearing. Better to wait until he returns to his room.

Alex doesn't like waiting. She likes action. Always has. She remembers being a child in Indiana, when a bully picked on Charles during the walk to school. She kicked the bully between the legs, hard as any eight-year-old ever kicked anyone. They ran away, but the bully promised he'd take care of both of them once school let out.

Alex didn't even make it through the first hour of classes. The waiting was excruciating. So she asked for a pass to go to the toilet, snuck through the halls until she found the bully's room, and rammed a sharpened pencil in his eye when he looked up from the math book he'd been leaning over. Well worth the expulsion.

She hurt him bad, but knew from experience that a wounded dog was more dangerous than a healthy one. So later that night, after the police released her, she and Charles rode their bikes to the hospital and used a pen knife on the bully's other eye.

Good times.

The bully didn't die. Not then. He grew up, coped with his loss of sight, became some sort of minister. A few years ago Alex followed him home after church, and they had a thoughtful conversation about the nature of good and evil before Alex skinned him.

Alex has lost track of the number of people she's killed. While in Heathrow, her shrink made some half-assed attempts to get her to talk about previous murders. Alex played it coy. The truth is, she has no idea how many have died at her hands. It's like counting the number of times you've had sex. Maybe you can remember the first fifty. After that, everything becomes a blur.

If there's a secret to being a good killer, it's not finding anything wrong with killing someone. Enjoying it can be a plus, but some people with the thirst—like Charles—enjoyed it too much and got sloppy. The best way to treat murder is with apathy. Sometimes it's necessary, often it's fun, but it shouldn't be a compulsion.

Alex thinks back to the bully minister's death. He begged, like they all do. For fun, she made him renounce the God he'd spent more than half of his life serving. But she didn't consider her act evil, any more than a shark killing a seal is evil. Pain and death are part of life. And everyone knows it's better to give than to receive.

Speaking of giving . . .

Alex looks down the hallway, at all the closed doors. Like a giant box of Valentine's Day candy, offering the potential for limitless fun. Fun, but necessity as well. Alex can't check into the hotel—they'll ask for ID and credit cards, which she doesn't have. But she needs a room in order to deal with Alan properly.

She approaches the door next to Alan's, raps twice, turns her head so her good profile and police officer cap are viewable through the peephole.

"Who's there?"

A child's voice. Alex can't tell if it's a boy or a girl.

"It's the police. Is your mom or dad there?"

"They went to eat. I'm playing video games. I'm not supposed to open the door."

"That's very smart. But police officers are your friends. Push a chair to the peephole in the door and stand on it so you can see me."

Alex takes a step back so the child can take in her full uniform.

"I see you."

"Here's my badge." Alex holds it up. "When a police officer asks you to open up, you have to. It's the law."

"I still can't let you in unless you know the code word."

Half of Alex's face twists into a smirk. She considers pushing it, maybe telling the child that his or her parents are hurt. But this seems like a well-trained kid. One cell phone call to Mom and things could get complicated. Better to find easier prey.

"I understand. I'll come back later when your parents finish with dinner. Have a nice night."

Alex tips her cap, then moves on to the next door. Knocks. No answer. Moves another door down.

"Yes?" A woman's voice.

"Police. Can I ask you a few questions?"

This time the door opens. The woman is at least a decade younger than Alex, short, a bit plump. She's got the security latch on and is peering through the three-inch gap. Alex could break in with a single strike of hip, shoulder, or foot, but the finesse is more satisfying. She likes it when victims torment themselves with *why did I let her in?* thoughts.

"Have you been a guest here for long, ma'am?"

"Two days. Is everything okay?"

"There was an altercation earlier. We're interviewing witnesses."

"I didn't see anything."

"Actually, you were named as a participant."

"Me? I've been out all day."

"Then you have nothing to worry about. I just need to verify your whereabouts."

The door closes. Alex listens to the latch being removed. The door opens again.

Alex enters the room. It's dark, the bed unmade, the TV with the picture paused. Open suitcase in the corner, some clothing scattered on the floor. Room service dishes sit on the desk, fish bones and squeezed lemons. The woman is wearing red sweatpants and a T-shirt, no makeup, no bra. Her hair has unnatural red highlights. She's attractive, in a Gen-X kind of way.

A moment after she closes the door behind her, Alex lashes out with the knife edge of her hand, catching the woman on the bridge of her nose. The woman collapses. Alex gets on top, pressing her face into the carpeting, tearing at her cotton top for use in binding her hands. The scream is still building up in the woman's throat when Alex muffles it with a cloth napkin. Legs are tied using some discarded panty hose, and Alex hoists the woman up to the bed.

"Don't move, don't make a sound, and I won't hurt you."

The woman freezes, stock-still, eyes wide with fear.

"Now I want to ask you a question, and I need you to answer honestly. Nod your head if the room service fish was good."

There's a slow, unsure nod.

"Are you positive? Because I saw the restaurant menu downstairs and they have a prime rib special. I like prime rib, but I'll try the fish if you think it was worthwhile."

Another nod, more emphatic. Alex has learned not to trust people who fear for their lives, so she picks up the phone and orders both the fish and the prime rib. Just to be safe.

"So what's on?" Alex asks. She flops onto the bed next to the woman, gently strokes her hair, and hits the pause button on the remote.

CHAPTER 23

SCOTT HAJEK'S EYES bugged out when he saw me, and they practically escaped his skull when he noticed Phin. He tried to slam his apartment door, but my new Nikes were faster and I blocked the attempt.

"You can't be here." Hajek's face pinched. "The Feds are after you both."

"You found that out pretty fast." I pushed my way in. "Do you listen to your police scanner on your nights off?"

Hajek folded his arms. "Yes. I do."

The apartment was furnished in 1980s male fanboy, science fiction posters and paraphernalia of the *Star Wars* and *Battlestar Galactica* variety everywhere I looked. Phin followed me in and closed the door. I briefly wondered what his apartment looked like, and would have bet some serious money he didn't own a single collectible figurine.

Hajek reached for a *Buffy the Vampire Slayer* phone, and Phin stepped in front of him, fists raised.

"You're a fugitive. I'm calling the police."

"You are the police," Phin said. "You want to read me my rights?"

Hajek persisted in his quest for the phone. "I'm calling for backup."

Phin caught his wrist. "No, you're not."

"Or else, what? You'll beat me up?"

"That sounds about right."

Hajek thrust his lower jaw at Phin.

"You're not going to lay a finger on me with the lieutenant watching."

"Jack," Phin said. "Close your eyes for a second."

I turned away, heard the fist connect with Hajek's face. Not the way I wanted to play it, but I didn't want Scott to get into trouble for helping us. If he had a black eye, that was proof we'd forced him. Not a shining moment in my career, but we only had a little less than six hours to find and save Lance.

"Want me to turn away again?" I asked.

Hajek had his palm pressed to his right eye. The defiance had drained out of him.

"What is it you two want?"

I walked over. "You're writing a book about Alexandra Kork."

"I'm compiling notes, mostly. Haven't written much yet. Did he have to hit me?"

Phin picked up a replica *Death Star* bookend and whacked Hajek across the knuckles.

"Jesus! What the hell is wrong with you!" Hajek took the hand away from his eye to cradle the new injury.

"We made you give us information," Phin said, "but you fought back like a tiger."

Hajek looked at the blood on his fingers and grinned.

"Yeah, I did. Could you smack my other hand too? Make it look like I went all Charles Bronson on you?"

"Maybe later," Phin said.

"We should get some of your blood on my carpet. Maybe on my shirt too. For the DNA match. It will look like I really kicked your ass before you subdued me. I think I've got a syringe someplace."

"That's not going to happen."

"Okay. Can you spit on me, maybe? We can get DNA from that. Or when you're working me over, I can spit on you. Get in your face and be all *You can't make me talk*."

"No one is spitting on anyone," I said. "We need your help, Scott."

Scott held out his hand. "I should put some Neosporin on this." He eyed Phin. "You think Bronson used Neosporin?"

"Sure," Phin said. "Those punks he beat up were probably lousy with germs."

"Do you have germs? I mean, I don't want to imply that you're germy or anything. You're not germy, are you?"

I tapped his shoulder. "Scott, focus for a minute. I know more about Kork than anyone else. I could tell you things not in any files or newspaper stories. That's why you wanted to have dinner with me, right?"

He squinted at me with his good eye. "Partly. I also used to find you attractive, until you started bullying me around."

I took out the cell phone, showed him the picture of Lance on the bed, along with the text message.

"Ever see this guy in any of your research?"

"No." He rubbed his chin. "But that's a pigstick. They use them on bomb squads."

"We think he's an EOD cop. He's only got a few hours left to live. We need to save him."

I reached out, touched Hajek on the shoulder. He flinched a little.

"He might be from Alex's past, Scott. You've read the files. Did she know anyone named Lance?"

"I dunno. I can't remember."

"Can we see your notes?" Phin asked.

"Sure. They're in the study. I should get my Neosporin first."

"Notes first."

"That works too."

We filed into the study. Scott rubbed his knuckles on his computer screen, and across the top of his keyboard, but the bleeding had already stopped so I doubted the CSU would pick up anything.

"Can I have a few hairs at least?" he asked Phin.

Phin sighed, then bent down, allowing Hajek to pluck out a few blond strands and sprinkle them across the desk.

"Scott? The clock is ticking. We need those notes."

"Okay. I've scanned in a lot of Alex's files and used an OCR to turn the text into a Word document."

His screen saver, predictably, was Xena, but his computer desktop background surprised me.

"Sorry," he mumbled. "Didn't mean for you to see that."

Phin gave me a small nudge. "That's a good picture of you."

It was candid shot, at a crime scene. A close-up of my face. I was talking to someone out of frame. The detail was very good, and I looked closer and saw he'd used some computer program to airbrush out my crow's-feet.

"I took it a while ago," Scott said. "I think it captures the lieutenant's professionalism while also showing a softer side. She was breaking the news to the victim's mother here. If you look closely, at her left eye, you can see the underlying sadness, even though the face is all business."

Phin leaned in closer.

"Yeah. I see it. You see the sadness there, Jack?"

"The notes," I repeated.

Hajek pressed some keys, opened a word processing program. I wondered how many other candid shots of me were on the computer, and whether I should be flattered or paranoid.

"I'm searching for *Lance.* And here we are."

We all read the sentence. In some notes taken by Alex's court-appointed psychiatrist, she'd mentioned a relationship with a man while still in the marines and stationed at Ft. Geiger. But Lance wasn't his name. His name was David Strang, and he was a lance corporal.

"Can you find out anything about him?" I asked.

"I'm crawling the search engines now. Okay, here's a newspaper article. He's a cop in Milwaukee. Bomb Squad. No picture, but let me look for images."

Hajek found Strang's police ID photo. He was late thirties, mustached. I held up the picture on the cell phone and we compared the two.

"Same ears," Hajek said. "It's him."

We could be in Milwaukee in about ninety minutes. That left about four hours to find Detective David Lance Strang before the shotgun shell in the pigstick blew his head off.

"Thanks, Scott." I tugged Phin's arm. "We have to go."

"Wait!" Scott said, so loud I stopped in my tracks. "I, uh, maybe I should have a few strands of your hair too, Lieutenant. So they believe the story."

"You're not touching my hair, Officer Hajek."

Phin nudged me again. "Other ways to leave some DNA evidence, Jack. Give the little guy a break." He puckered his lips and made a kissing sound.

I sighed, then plucked out a few strands of my hair, offering them to Hajek. His eyes lit up like he'd just been handed the Holy Grail.

Phin led us out of the apartment. I could have told Hajek to contact the Milwaukee PD, but I knew he was on the phone before the door even closed.

"I think he likes you, Jack."

I followed Phin into the stairwell. "Do you know the quickest route to Milwaukee?"

"Did you know he was pining for you like that?"

"He's not pining."

"He looks at you every time he turns his computer on. That's either pining or stalking."

"He admires the job I do."

"He admires more than that. I think you came close to giving him a heart attack when you gave him some of your hair. I bet he's building a shrine to it right now."

We exited at the lobby, and I nodded at the doorman who'd let us in.

"So far, Alex isn't lying to us. She was telling the truth about being in Milwaukee, and the cop's name isn't Lance, but I bet the nickname has stuck with him."

We hit the sidewalk. The rain had started up again, even colder than before.

"You're shivering. Anything I can do to warm you up?"

I frowned at him.

"Phin, you and me, it's not going to happen. I almost shot you on the bus."

"But you didn't."

"It doesn't matter. There are some trust issues here. I'm flattered you're interested, but I'm a mess right now. Christ, I just buried my fiancé. My career is probably over. And we're chasing a psychopath who is sending me pictures of people she's going to kill. This isn't a good time to start a relationship."

My opinion apparently didn't matter much to Phin, because he tugged me close, his arms snaking around my waist and holding me so tight I could feel his heartbeat, and kissed me. For a few seconds everything wrong with the world vanished, and we existed only to feed our senses. The cold rain on my cheeks, Phin's warm tongue on my lips, his strong hands pressing into the small of my back, the sounds of our breathing lost in a thunderclap overhead, the taste of the cinnamon gum he'd been chewing, the ache in my jaw from when I hit the bus and a much different kind of ache building up between my legs.

"We'll take I-94," he said, breaking the kiss.

I was a little weak in the knees, and a little out of breath, and I hated him for that but didn't trust myself to say so. Like everything else that happened that day I'd have to file it away and figure it out later, when I had time.

I followed Phin to his Ford Bronco, climbed into the passenger seat, and didn't look at him until we reached the expressway.

CHAPTER 24

"GOOD CALL ON THE FISH, CYNTHIA. The prime rib was too well done for my taste. Sure you don't want any?"

Cynthia shakes her head, the napkin flapping in her mouth like a flag.

According to her driver's license, her full name is Cynthia Paulino, and she lives in Illinois. After the movie—a cute romantic comedy with Matthew McConaughey—Alex searched the room while asking Cynthia questions about her life. She didn't remove the gag, so the questions were all yes or no. But Alex was still able to determine that Cynthia was single, had a boyfriend who didn't want to commit, worked for a company that sold polymers—which are plastics—and was in town to run a trade show booth. The booth gig was boring, and resulted in very few sales, but Cyn liked it because it got her out of the office and the company picked up expenses.

Alex shared as well, talking about what she had done to Lance, what her big plan was, and how she might be obsessing a tad about Jack Daniels.

"She killed the man I loved, I killed the man she loved, so we should be even. But I still can't stop thinking about her, Cyn. Maybe part of the problem is that I like her. I mean, her sense of morality is really, *really* infantile. But she's a good dresser, good with a gun, good with her fists. Kind of like an older sister. You know, before she figured out I was a serial killer, we got along pretty good. Do you have any enemies, Cyn?"

Cyn nods.

"Someone at work?"

Another nod.

"If you want to talk about it, I'll take your gag out. But a warning first: If you start begging for your life, or try to scream for help, I'll cut you from your crotch to your breastbone. Got it?"

Cyn bobs her head up and down, then spits out the napkin.

"Can I have some water?" she asks, voice horse.

"No. I like your voice that way. Kind of sexy. Now tell me about this enemy."

"Her . . . her name is Gina. Works in Accounting. Has been a real bitch ever since I started there."

Alex flips onto her stomach, gathering a pillow under her to keep her head propped up.

"What did she do to you?"

"Little things at first. Like asking me really rudely if this is my natural hair color. I mean, of course it isn't. But she waits until there are people around to try to get a laugh."

Alex nods. "I hate her already. What else?"

Cyn's lower lip quivers, but she manages to work through it. "Every time I do one of these trade shows, she acts like a Nazi with the expense account. I mean, if I skip lunch and get a bigger dinner to compensate, she won't allow it."

"I bet she's tough with booze too."

"No liquor at all, even if I'm taking customers out. They want me to get sales, but they don't want me to buy a round of beers first? That's stupid."

Alex agrees. "Bitch. What else?"

"I can't be sure, but I think she started a rumor . . . a rumor . . ."

Alex reaches out, wipes a tear off Cyn's face. "Don't cry. It's okay. Everywhere I go, people talk about me in whispers. Right in front of me, like I'm blind and deaf as well as scarred. Words can hurt, Cyn. Sometimes they can hurt worse than anything."

"Please . . . oh God . . . please . . . I don't want to die . . ."

Alex frowns, only half of her face responding to the command her brain sends to her mouth.

"Cynthia, we're having a nice conversation here. Don't ruin it."

"Gina . . . G-Gina doesn't matter. None of it matters. Nothing matters. It's all . . . all bullshit. I still want to get married, have kids. I don't wanna—"

Alex sighs, stuffs the napkin back into Cynthia's mouth. She wonders if Jack's ex-husband is in his room yet, and uses the phone to try him. It rings and rings. Earlier, Alex had called from the lobby phone and let it ring, so she should have gotten a busy signal. Does that mean Alan is in his room and answered the phone earlier? Or that someone in the lobby found a phone off the hook and hung up?

After five more rings, Alex hangs up. She yawns, exhaustion washing over her. A few hours of sleep would be a smart idea. Especially since she wants to tune in and watch Lance during his last moments, which will happen in less than five hours.

Alex looks at Cynthia.

"I'm bushed. How about you, Cyn? Must have been a long day for you. Want to get some shut-eye?"

Cyn looks uncertain, but she nods.

"You should probably go to the bathroom first. If I untie your legs will you walk to the bathroom without giving me trouble?"

A nod. Alex uses the steak knife to cut the nylons binding Cyn's legs. Cynthia stumbles when she tries to stand, but Alex catches her under the arm and helps her keep her footing.

Cyn looks at the toilet, then looks at Alex. Alex laughs.

"No, I don't want to watch, Cyn. I'm not a pervert. Let me help you with your pants."

Alex reaches down and shoves Cyn backward, into the shower. Less mess there.

With her hands tied Cyn lands hard on her butt. As she starts to scream Alex forces the steak knife between her ribs, the blade twitching in her grip as Cyn's heart tries to keep beating.

Alex checks her uniform, happy that she managed to keep it blood-free. As Cyn dies, feebly trying to remove the knife—impossible because suction is keeping it in—Alex drops her pants and urinates in the toilet.

"Now who's the pervert?" she says, closing the shower curtain to block Cynthia's staring. Then she wanders back to bed, undresses, orders a wake-up call for five a.m., and sends Jack the latest picture of Lance, along with another text message. She falls asleep to a pay-per-view slasher movie, amused because the writer got the violence all wrong.

CHAPTER 25

THE PHONE WOKE ME UP. In the darkness of the Bronco's front seat, I fumbled around for my purse and located it by my feet. On the third ring I fished it out and flipped the top open, hearing several beeps.

Alex. Sending me another picture. Phin glanced over at me while I accessed it.

Lance appeared even worse than before, his face contorted with pain and blurred by motion. The lighting was a little better this time, the burn marks on his chest darker and more pronounced. I held it up for Phin, who divided his attention between the photo and the road.

"Are those letters?"

"Where?"

"His wounds," Phin said. "Connect the dots."

I traced my fingernail over the burns, and the letters seemed to pop out at me.

zd

There was also a text message.

FOUR HOURS LEFT.

"What the hell is Zd?" I asked.

"One of the elements? Zirconium?"

"That's Zr."

"Maybe an abbreviation. Or initials."

I closed my eyes, tried to think. Zd meant absolutely nothing to me. Maybe something in connection with Lance? Bomb squads? Some kind of explosives or equipment? Or something to do with Milwaukee?

"Where are we?" I asked.

"Just across the Wisconsin border. Got about forty minutes left."

I wanted to call Herb, but I promised myself I wouldn't bother him again. Harry was probably still occupied with the Feds. Hajek was almost certainly occupied with the authorities as well, and I had no delusions that a few strands of hair turned him from adversary into ally. That left Detective Tom Mankowski, still in Indiana. I fished out my personal cell and found his number.

"Lieutenant? I haven't been able to get in my car yet. Did you talk to Hajek?"

"Yeah. Cop's name is David Strang, out of Milwaukee. Look, Tom, things have gotten complicated, and I'm persona non grata with both the CPD and the Feds. Alex just sent me another picture. It's Lance again, but this time the burns on his chest look like letters. Capital Z, small d. Mean anything to you?"

"Not a thing. You sure it's a Z and not the number 2?"

"Could be a 2. Does 2d mean anything to you?"

"Two-dimensional, obviously, but I don't see how that's a clue. Alex did this as some kind of hint, right?"

"Probably."

"I read her shrink report. She has a genius IQ."

I sighed. Why did all the serial killers I chased have to be brilliant criminal masterminds? Where were all the psychos with average intelligence?

"I'm forwarding the photo and a text message to you. Pass it along. If the Milwaukee PD finds Lance, let us know. We're going to keep searching until we hear news."

Hopefully the news would be "he's safe" instead of "he's dead."

"Happy hunting, Lieut."

Mankowski hung up. I spent a few minutes fiddling with the cell phone, sending him the info.

"We're also low on gas."

I nodded, my mind attacking the Zd problem. What the hell was Alex trying to tell me? Zee dee. Two dee. Zee dee. Two dee . . .

"Wasn't she one of the girls on *The Facts of Life?*" Phin said. "Tootie?"

"Did I say that out loud?"

"Six or ten times."

I rubbed my eyes. "I'm pretty sure Alex isn't pointing us to an old sitcom."

"Apartment number?"

"Two dee. That works."

"Something to do with the Marines? Squad 2d?"

"I'm drawing blanks."

Alex's phone rang. I steeled myself, answered.

"What do you want, Alex?"

"Not Alex. It's Harry. I called on that phone because they're tracing and tracking your other one. Stay off of it."

Stupid. Now they knew Mankowski was helping me. How was I supposed to catch Alex when I was making rookie mistakes?

"Aren't you in federal custody, McGlade?"

"Hell, no. I cut a deal."

I didn't like the sound of that. "What kind of deal?"

"Jesus, Jack. Don't be so paranoid. I'm not going to betray my own flesh and blood."

"It's Phin?" I asked. "I thought you two were friends."

"It's not like he's an innocent bystander, Jackie. He robbed a bank. You do the crime, you do the time. Point is, now I've got some breathing room, and I've been looking at that photo of Lance."

"His name is David Strang." I gave Harry the blow-by-blow.

"Good. Send me the new pic and text. And don't bother with residential. He's in a hotel or motel, maybe a bed and breakfast."

"How do you know?"

"In the upper right-hand corner of the picture, on the nightstand, under the pigstick. Looks like the edge a red piece of paper. I enhanced the detail."

"What is it?"

"It's when I use a computer program to tighten the pixel pattern by adjusting contrast and color."

He did that on purpose. I kept my voice even.

"What did the enhancement show you, McGlade?"

"It's part of a Do Not Disturb sign. So she's holding him in a room somewhere."

"How many hotels in Milwaukee?"

"Lemme check." I heard fingers on a keyboard. "According to the Yellow Pages, only about six hundred. But that might include some overlaps."

"Search for Zd and 2d."

"Searching. A million hits on Zd. Wine. Digital cameras. Nothing pops out. For 2d, got two hundred million hits. Looks like a lot of computer tech stuff. Lemme try to cross-ref with Lance's name, motels, Milwaukee, and so on. Maybe a combination of terms will give us something. I'll call you back."

Harry hung up. My stomach rumbled, and I couldn't remember the last time I'd eaten anything. That made me remember the steaks I owed Herb. While waiting for Harry I put in a call to 1-800-MEATS4U and their twenty-four-hour customer service representative suggested the Meat Lover's Package, which included assorted steaks, burgers, chicken filets, and a Turduckinlux. I opted for the BBQ flavor over the savory garlic and rosemary.

Phin pulled into an oasis, up to the station. He parked, switched off the truck, and unbuckled his belt. But rather than get out and pump gas he sat there, staring straight ahead, fingers drumming the steering wheel.

"Harry going to turn me in?"

I nodded. "I'm surprised. I thought you guys had that macho code of honor thing. Death before betrayal and all that."

"McGlade doesn't owe me anything."

"So you would betray him too?"

"If I had to."

"Would you betray me?"

Phin stared at me, his blue eyes hard.

"No."

Which made me feel even worse about almost shooting him. He opened his mouth to say something more, probably to explain himself, and I didn't want to hear it so I put my finger over his lips to silence him. His mouth parted slightly, my fingertip brushing against the top of his teeth, and I pulled away and got out of the car before I gave in to all the dirty things I was thinking.

"Fill it up, I'll pay inside."

I walked into the mini-mart, and was assaulted by the cloying smell of hot dogs cooked way too long. It made my stomach rumble again. I'm proud to say that I'd never indulged in gas station cuisine, but I was almost hungry enough to start.

First things first, though. There was something weighing on my mind more than food. Something that had been troubling me for hours.

I wandered the short aisles, found the one with birth control. The store had the average assortment of jellies, foams, and condoms. I found what I needed and took it to the counter, breaking down and also getting a bag of tortilla chips and a jar of salsa. I grabbed a twelve-pack of bottled water, a box of granola bars, and a handful of beef jerky as well.

"This and whatever is on pump five," I told the attendant. He was young, scruffy, wearing a greasy baseball cap with an unnaturally curved rim that he must have spent some serious time shaping. He smirked at me when he saw my purchases, and then looked out the window at Phin and smirked again. I had an urge to slap him.

"Might want to check the expiration date," he said. "Those things expire."

He wasn't referring to the chips. And embarrassing as it was, he had a point. I turned over the package, found the date on the side panel. Still good for another six months.

Phin was still pumping, so I asked Smirking Boy where the bathroom was, and took the box with me.

As expected, the bathroom looked like a swamp creature blew up in there while engaging in every possible bodily function. I triple-plied the toilet paper on the seat, dropped my sweatpants, and sat down, staring at the three letters on the box.

EPT.

Latham and I practiced safe sex. I was in my late forties, but still a fertile Myrtle, and we weren't sure having a kid in college while we zeroed in on seventy was the way we wanted to spend our golden years.

But condoms were only 98 percent effective, and by my math, that meant condom use resulted in pregnancy one out of fifty times.

Latham and I had sex more than fifty times.

Still, it was virtually impossible. There hadn't been any breaks. Hadn't been any *oops*. My late period was the result of stress, not pregnancy.

It had to be.

I put a hand to my belly, overwhelmed by feelings. Fear, anxiety, depression, anger, worry, and something else. Something I wasn't expecting.

Hope.

Jesus, part of me was hoping I was pregnant.

I read the box.

Opened the package.

Peed on the stick.

Waited.

Waited.

Waited.

Looked.

Read the box again.

Cried. Cried so hard I couldn't catch my breath.

I must have been in there too long, because someone began to knock on the bathroom door.

"I'll be right out," I said, but through the sobs it sounded more like "Abeeioooud."

"Jack?"

Phin.

I unrolled some toilet paper, swabbed my face.

"Jack? You okay?"

I wrapped the pregnancy test in paper, held it over the toilet, and stopped. I realized I didn't want to throw it away. Instead I stuffed it into my purse.

"Jack? I'm coming in."

"I'm fine," I said, more in control now. "I'll be right out."

I washed my hands, avoided looking in the mirror because it wouldn't have improved my mood, and unlocked the door to Phin standing there, all sympathetic and concerned.

This annoyed me. I wondered if the real reason he'd never betray me was because I had two X chromosomes, and the little woman needed to be protected by the big strong man, which was BS because I've beaten up bigger guys than him.

"I'm fine," I repeated, pushing past him.

I threw some money at Smirking Boy, who hadn't bothered bagging anything. I tucked beef jerky into my pockets, and shoved the granola bars under my armpit.

Phin grabbed the water.

"I got it," I told him.

He spread out his hands and backed up. As he should have. I didn't need him. I didn't need anyone. I was perfectly capable of carrying a few lousy items. I crammed the bag of chips under my other arm, grabbed the salsa in one hand, the water in the other, and gave Phin a look that said he better not try to hold open the goddamn door for me. He didn't, giving me a wide berth, and I shuffled past and bumped the door with my hip, and the salsa slipped and broke on the floor like a gunshot, splattering red.

Phin didn't say anything. Neither did Smirking Boy. I continued out the door, piled everything onto the hood of the Bronco, and began stuffing it into the backseat. Then I sat down and waited for Phin.

He climbed into the driver's seat without comment and we got back on the expressway, and I tried to focus on the case instead of my personal life.

Big *Z*, small *d*. Big *Z*, small *d*. What the hell did that mean? Why did Alex burn that into David Strang's chest?

No ideas came. And the harder I tried to think, the more my mind kept drifting back to the pregnancy test in my purse, which I clutched in both hands like a life preserver on a sinking ship.

CHAPTER 26

A LEX DREAMS.

She's ten years old, in a cornfield in Indiana, in the center of a wide circle that she made with Charles. They stomped down all of the dry stalks around them and are sitting Indian style, face-to-face, knees touching. The corn is taller than they are, so no one can see them from the road or from the farmhouse. This is their private spot. Their special spot. No one can hurt them here. Not bullies. Not Father. Not anyone.

A wind blows through the corn, making a rustling sound. All around them, the corn ripples like a golden sea. Alex smells fresh earth and clean air. The sun is shining, bright overhead, and she turns up to feel it on her face.

But she doesn't feel it. All she feels is cold.

She looks at Charles, wondering if he's cold too. His eyes are closed.

"I love you," she says.

He doesn't answer. She reaches up, touches him. It's like touching ice. He's dead. Charles is dead.

Then his jaw falls open.

"You're ugly, Alex," Charles says. "Scarred and ugly."

It's isn't his voice. It's Jack's.

Charles becomes Jack, his features cracking and twisting, and then she's standing over Alex with angry black eyes, pointing down at her like a vengeful god.

Alex reaches up, feels her own face, feels the scars.

And she's afraid.

The pleasant field smell sours, becoming the acrid odor of sweat and fear. The gentle breeze goes rotten. The sun shines black.

Alex runs. Into the corn.

The corn grabs at her, tries to stop her. But Alex has a knife, and she cuts and slashes, and the corn cries out and bleeds, bright red arterial jets that sting like acid. Stalks morph into severed arms and legs, and Alex climbs up the bodies of the slaughtered, climbs up an ever-growing pile of people she has killed.

At the top of the mound is a face. Her face. Unscarred. It beckons her on.

Behind her, Jack grows to monstrous proportions, reaching out an enormous hand to pluck Alex away from her goal. Alex dodges, stabs at Jack's huge thumb, then launches herself upward, hands outstretched and yearning.

Alex's face is atop a pedestal, and she snatches it up and presses the perfect mask of flesh against her scars. It glows warm, then burning hot, shooting out rays that blind the Jack creature and cause her to tumble down the mountain.

And Alex smiles. Not a half smile. A full smile, all the muscles working, lips doing what they are supposed to, wide and bright and beautiful.

Then Alex begins to grow. Bigger than Jack. Bigger and stronger and almighty. She crushes the squealing lieutenant underfoot, her rib cage cracking like a bird's nest.

For miles around Alex, the corn trembles and begs for mercy.

Alex's blade stretches and curves, becoming a scythe.

As the world screams, Alex reaps.

CHAPTER 27

"I GOT NOTHING, SIS."

I rubbed my eyes, which felt like I had sand under the lids. We were parked in an all-night diner lot, which was half-full even at five in the morning. I'd gone in earlier, not to eat but to borrow a phone book. Now I wished I'd eaten. The salsa-less tortilla chips and five sticks of jerky hadn't done much to satisfy my hunger.

"Try searching for *motel* plus *Zd* plus *Wisconsin*," I told Harry.

"I tried that. I've tried every possible Boolean search combination, and I don't even know what *Boolean* means. Plus I'm exhausted. The only thing keeping me awake is this case of SuperMax Energy Drink I got at the discount store. What the hell is taurine anyway?"

"We're all tired, McGlade. Try pinching yourself."

"Does that work?"

"No. But it will amuse me."

"Funny, Jackie. We've got half an hour left. Maybe the Milwaukee PD has found him already."

"Milwaukee cops find him?" I asked Phin.

Phin shook his head. Naturally, Phin owned a police scanner. He was using an earpiece to listen in so the radio chatter didn't interfere with my phone call. I was using Alex's cell, because it was pretty much trace-proof. No doubt the Feebies were tracking my personal cell.

I yawned. "Did you try another search engine?"

"I'm using an aggregator that searches all the top search engines, including foreign ones. I've found some pretty horrible things, Jackie. Do you know what a brass clown is?"

"No. And have no desire to find out."

"It's this sex thing. But it isn't really sexual, unless you're some sort of sicko nutjob. You take a cup. Guess what you do with the cup?"

"I don't want to know what you do with the cup, and if you try to tell me I'll hang up on you."

"I wish I could do a system restore on my brain and go back to a time before I saw it. There are certain foods I can no longer eat."

For the fiftieth time I fought the temptation to drive to the nearest motel and start randomly searching rooms. With several hundred hotels within ten square miles, the odds weren't with us. Much better to stay centrally located and be ready to move when we got some information.

The problem was, we had no information. And I held out little hope that Alex would call back with a last-minute hint. The next time she called, it would be to send pictures of David Strang with his head blown off.

"Think Alex fucked him?" Harry asked.

"Not sure if it matters, McGlade."

"Maybe it does. What if there was some sixty-nine action going on?"

"What the hell does that have to do with anything?"

"A lot. If she was on top, she could have written the letters upside-down."

I accessed the picture on the cell phone, then rotated it one hundred and eighty degrees.

How about that?

"I bow to your deviant mind, Harry. Try all the searches again using PZ."

"Way ahead of you, Jackie. Got twenty-seven million hits. Some scientist named PZ. A punjabi site. An ID3 tag editor."

"What's that?"

"It helps you catalog your music collection if you appropriate MP3 files on the Internet."

"Appropriate? You mean stealing."

"File sharing isn't stealing. If I stole your bike, you lost property. That's theft. But if I copied your bike, you still have the bike."

"Then I've lost my right to sell the bike. How can I sell the bike if everyone is copying it?"

I bet myself twenty bucks McGlade was rolling his eyes.

"What if I already have the music on vinyl? Can't I download an MP3 of a song I already own?"

"Downloading music for free is illegal, Harry."

"No it isn't. Ask Phin."

"I'm not asking Phin."

"Ask Phin what?" Phin asked.

I sighed. "This really isn't something we need to discuss right now. Or ever."

I hit the button for speaker phone anyway and repeated Harry's question.

"It's illegal," Phin said. "You're taking money away from the artist. That's what intellectual property laws are for."

"So downloading an out-of-print album is bad, but it's okay to rob a bank?"

"That's illegal too," Phin said.

"We need to stick to finding Lance," I said.

"Phin, you ever see that brass clown video?"

"Yeah. It was horrible."

"Lance," I said, holding up the picture. "He's going to die soon. Remember him?"

"Remember that cup scene?" Harry said.

"Yeah."

"I can't eat corn anymore because of that."

"I had to give up Greek food for a while."

"Why Greek? Oh . . . oh yeah. You know, the last Greek I ate was a sorority girl."

I was going to tell them, more forcibly this time, to stay on task, but the word *Greek* stuck in my head and bounced around like a pinball. I looked at the PZ again.

"Harry, do a search for *Greek alphabet*."

"She was a physical therapy major, Phin. Had an incredibly strong grip. I used to fake injuries."

"Harry! The search!"

"Okay! Sure! Greek alphabet! Done! You happy?"

"What do *P* and *Z* stand for?"

"*P* is *rho*. *Z* is *zeta*. Rho zeta?"

"Row zayta. Row zeta. Rosetta?"

I flipped the Yellow Pages open to *Motels* and searched the Rs. No Rosetta Motel, or anything even close.

Harry chuckled softly. "Damn, Alex is smart."

"You got something?"

"I did a search for *Rosetta* plus *Milwaukee* plus *lodging*. First hit is for the Rosetta Stone—that old rock with all the languages on it. But farther down the page is the Old Stone Inn. If PZ is Greek for Rosetta, the Rosetta Stone was certainly an old stone. And the Old Stone Inn is near the Milwaukee airport."

I checked my watch. Lance had less than fifteen minutes to live. The clues fit, but that might have been because we were tired and hopeless and wanted them to fit.

"Where's the address?" I asked Harry.

"It's on Whitnall."

Phin started the truck. "Ten minutes, if we push it."

I didn't see we had any choice.

"Push it," I told him.

We peeled out of the parking lot.

CHAPTER 28

LEX WAKES to the ringing of the hotel phone and the homey smell of copper pennies. She gives the receiver a quick up and down, stretches, and pads over to the bathroom. Apparently Cyn had more life left in her than Alex thought, because she managed to pull herself out of the bathtub to curl up and die under the sink. There's a good amount of blood browning on the floor, and Alex watches where she steps—it's not wise leaving bloody footprints up and down the hotel hallway.

After using the facilities, Alex puts on a pair of fresh panties from Cyn's suitcase, and also liberates some sweatpants and a Hootie and the Blowfish tee. Cyn's shoes are too small, and the cop's black leather shoes look stupid with sweats, so Alex heads out the door in only socks.

Sunrise is still over an hour away, and outside it's cool and crisp with a wind that threatens winter. Alex digs her laptop out of the Hyundai and takes it back to the lobby, where complimentary continental breakfast is being served. Even this early there are three people milling about, reading papers, drinking coffee, pouring milk into bowls of cereal. Alex keeps her head down, bangs covering her face, and snatches a bagel and a small container of cream cheese without being acknowledged.

Back in the room she sets up at the desk and accesses the hotel's WiFi, charging it to Cyn's account. Then she activates the cell phone program and enlarges the window to the size of the laptop screen, which shows a live view of Lance at the Old Stone Inn.

Poor Lance is sleeping. He's made quite a mess of the bed—even in the close-up Alex can see the mattress is off-kilter and the sheets under him have twisted around. She zooms the camera out, and sees the duct tape is still holding him tight, but it has bunched up on itself so it looks like gnarled gray rope. The secret to binding someone with tape is to make it as tight as possible; it stretches, and sweat and blood work against the adhesive. Lance has more than a little blood around his wrists. He fought hard. Alex feels strangely proud of him.

She zooms out farther, and sees that the rest of Lance hasn't held up so well.

"Ouch."

The rubber band has transformed Lance's once proud manhood into something resembling a rotten banana, all brown and droopy. If Jack arrives in time, it's unlikely that part of him can be saved.

Alex smiles with half of her face, using her finger to apply cream cheese to half the bagel, imagining macho Lance living out the rest of his days as a chaste monk in some Tibetan monastery. Certainly his wife wouldn't keep him around. Infidelity can be forgiven. Having no dick would put an unrealistic strain on even the healthiest of marriages.

She zooms in, getting a close-up of the Greek letters burned into Lance's chest, and uses her screen capture to save a JPG. Then she checks the time. Twenty minutes after five. Lance has thirteen minutes to live.

Alex transfers the picture to her cell, then sends it to Jack Daniels. At this late stage in the game, it's unlikely Jack knows where Lance is. But there's one clue left to give, and Alex wants to make sure Jack has every possible opportunity to figure it out and save him, so she feels even worse when she fails. Alex texts:

STAIRWAY TO HEAVEN.

Simple. Clever. Elegant. After entering the message she tucks her legs under her in the desk chair, licks cream cheese off her fingers, and waits for the big bang.

CHAPTER 29

"HOW'S OUR TIME?" Phin asked.

I checked my watch. The pigstick was set to go off at 5:33 a.m. It was 5:24.

"Not good. How close are we?"

"I'm not sure. A few miles."

My eyes locked on the speedometer. We were already doing sixty mph in a thirty mph zone, and I stopped counting all the red lights we'd blown through.

"Go faster."

Phin nodded. The veins on the backs of his hands bulged out from holding the wheel so hard, and I noticed my legs were braced and my fingers had death grips on the armrests. As if that would help if we crashed.

The cell phone rang, and I pried off a hand long enough to answer it. Another picture of Lance, apparently asleep. The burns on his chest had scabbed over, becoming almost black. A message accompanied the photo.

"Got another text. *Stairway to heaven.*" I wrinkled my nose. "What does that mean?"

"That Lance is about to die."

The truck crept closer to seventy, which seemed a lot faster on the narrow street we were on. Each pothole we hit felt like a thunderclap.

"No . . . I mean—yes—that's part of it. But I think it's a clue. She's telling us something about his location."

"What does Led Zeppelin have to do with rho and zeta?"

I chewed the inside of my cheek. An earlier call to the Old Stone Inn hadn't given us much to work with. The front desk had confirmed the motel was full, all twenty-six rooms occupied. This was one of those single-floor, park next to your room motels. I asked about a woman with scars checking in, or anything out of the ordinary, but English wasn't the clerk's first language, or at least he pretended it wasn't, and I couldn't get anything out of him.

I had also dialed 911, explaining the situation and telling them a kidnapping and murder of one of their own was being committed there. I was sure they'd send a car, but had no idea of their response time or their procedure. Even if they got there before us, it's unlikely they'd get any more help from the clerk than I did. And no cop I ever met would kick in twenty-six doors without a warrant. *Exigent circumstances* and *probable cause* were weighty terms, but not as weighty as *lawsuit* and *disciplinary action*.

"What were the band members' names?" I asked Phin.

He took a corner so fast the tires cried out. "Robert Plant . . . John Paul Jones . . . Jimmy Page . . ."

"Which one died?"

"The drummer. John Bonham. Died in his sleep. Choked on vomit."

My heart rate jumped up even higher. "Did he die in a motel room?"

"Page's house. Drank too much."

Phin tapped the brakes and just missed clipping a Volvo, who laid on the horn to show his disapproval. I tried to swallow, but had no spit left.

"How about something in the lyrics?" I forced myself to focus, not the easiest thing to do when I predicted a car accident in the immediate future. "Any mention of rooms or motels?"

"It's about a woman who thinks she can get whatever she wants."

Phin swerved and climbed the curb, causing my body to rise up against the seat belt. I readied myself for the passenger-side air bag, but it didn't deploy.

"We're on the sidewalk." I tried to sound calm, but my voice came out squeaky.

"Motel," Phin said, eyes glancing right. I followed his gaze, saw the large Old Stone Inn sign a block ahead. A light illuminated its *$49.95 a Night* rates, but the *i* in *Night* was missing.

We came upon the parking lot fast—too fast—and Phin hit the brakes and still slammed into the rear of a parked SUV. Still no airbag. I wondered if the truck even had them.

I checked my watch. Five thirty.

The motel was laid out in an L shape, ground-level rooms stretching off in two perpendicular directions. Thirteen on each arm. With three minutes left, not enough time to check them all.

Phin and I ran for the lobby, at the center of the L. There was a Milwaukee police cruiser parked in front, and through the window I saw two uniforms talking to the desk clerk, who was shrugging and shaking his head.

"Four!" Phin yelled at me.

I looked at him, wondering if he had a golf club.

" 'Stairway to Heaven' is on the album *Led Zeppelin IV*!"

Was it that easy? Was Lance in room four? I didn't question it, I acted, yanking the gun out of my bouncing purse, running down the arm past rooms ten . . . nine . . . eight . . . seven . . .

Phin outpaced me, getting there first, slamming his shoulder into the door. It popped inward, Phin stumbling into the room, me coming in right after him, dropping to a knee, gun out, eyes and ears open.

The room was bright, every light on, someone in bed.

Lance.

He was naked, eyes wide, terrified. He screamed at me through his duct tape gag.

The pigstick was set up on the nightstand next to him, the shotgun shell held in place by a metal arm. I followed the wire to a timing device, realized I had no expertise at all to disarm it, and chose instead to simply point the contraption away from Lance.

Two seconds after I grabbed it, the charge went off.

The explosion was deafening, and the shock—coupled with the powerful vibration of the shot—made me drop the pigstick. I cast fearful eyes at the bed, expecting to see blood and guts and carnage.

The mattress had an ugly, ragged hole in it. Lance did not.

Phin said something that sounded like "Jesus," but my ears were ringing, so I couldn't be sure. I spun around, gun sweeping the room, then did a quick search, tugging open the closet and bathroom doors. No Alex.

"Please . . ."

Phin had removed the duct tape from Lance's mouth, and stared down at him, frowning. I glanced between Lance's legs and had to look away.

"Freeze! Police! Drop your weapons!"

The two Milwaukee cops were at the door, their guns drawn, their faces bright with urgency. I moved slow, deliberate, not wanting to spook them.

"We're putting down our guns," I said. "I'm the cop who called earlier. Lieutenant Jack Daniels, Chicago PD. My ID is in my purse. This man on the bed is David Strang. One of yours."

I crouched, setting my gun on the floor, putting my hands up. Phin did the same. The cops moved in, putting Phin against the wall, frisking him, taking his gun. As I watched, I noticed something taped to the motel wall. A cell phone.

Alex was watching.

"This man needs an ambulance," I said.

Neither cop said anything, but the taller one took his handcuffs out of his case.

"There's no need to restrain him. He's with me."

"There's a federal warrant out for his arrest," the tall one said. "There's one on you as well, Miss Daniels."

A sound from Phin, either a soft snort or a loud sigh. "We just saved your man's life."

"I'm sure you'll get all of this straightened out. Orders are orders. You understand. "

Phin tried to spin around, got a rabbit punch in the kidney by the shorter one. He dropped to his knees. So did I, picking up my Beretta. Just as Shorty pulled back for a second punch I fired into the ceiling.

"Hit him again," I said through my teeth. "See what I do to you."

Shorty opened up his fist and backed away from Phin.

"Guns. Drop them."

The cops looked at each other, then complied.

"Now get on the goddamn radio and call a goddamn ambulance for your man."

The taller one used his lapel mike. Phin stuck their guns in his waistband, retrieved his own, and jammed it into the neck of the cop who socked him.

I almost warned Phin not to do anything stupid, then remembered that I trusted him.

"I got a question," Phin said. "Is it just you, or do all short guys hit like sissies?"

Shorty didn't answer, which was probably wise.

I kept them covered and made my way to the cell phone, feeling for it on the wall and tugging it off. Held it to my ear.

"Alex?"

No answer. I powered it off and stuck it in my purse, then motioned for Phin to come over to the door.

"Your guns will be in one of the Dumpsters outside," I told the cops, "which is more professional courtesy than you've shown me."

"You sure you want to do this, lady?" Shorty said.

I frowned. Then in one fluid motion I tugged their guns out of Phin's belt, stuck my fingers in the trigger guards, and whipped them around butt-first while smoothly pressing both ejector buttons. The full clips sailed out the bottom ports and bounced off each cop's chest as they flinched.

"It's not *miss*, and it's not *lady*," I said. "It's *Lieutenant*."

"She outranks you guys because you suck," Phin offered.

I really couldn't blame them too much for trying to arrest us—the order probably came from the top—but I did pass up two relatively clean Dumpsters before finding one stinky enough to ditch their pieces, buried under a pile of rotten food.

Then I crashed. Big-time. The adrenaline that had been keeping me going had vacated the premises, leaving me an empty shell. Sleep had always been a problem for me, but I probably could have gotten forty winks right there, curled up on the garbage pile.

Phin didn't look much better. Long damn night.

"You okay?" I asked when we got back to the Bronco.

He nodded, but I noticed he was favoring his left arm.

"Elbow?"

"Yeah. One of them twisted it. I'll be okay."

Phin tried to start the truck using his left hand. I should have offered to drive, but I was lapsing into zombie mode and didn't trust myself. My phone rang. Mine, not the one Alex gave me.

"Hiya, sis." Long yawn from Harry, who must have been really concerned about us. "You save the day?"

"Lance lived. The police tried to arrest us. We disarmed them. Now Phin can't turn the ignition."

"Good, that's good." I don't think he heard a word I said. "I'm in Deer Park. I'm going to catch some Zs, then look for the last cell phone in the daisy chain. I've got a tracking device that pinpoints RF frequencies. But even better, these cells are Bluetooth enabled, and Alex never disabled it. I've got a computer program that can scan for Bluetooth devices. When it finds one, I can have it download SIM card info. So I don't even have to find the physical phone. I just have to get close enough to it."

Turnabout was fair play, because I didn't process a single thing Harry said either. I yawned, then reached over and helped Phin start the truck. His hand covered mine, held it. He continued to hold it as we pulled out of the parking lot. I was too tired to protest, and his grip was warm on my cold fingers. Warm, and strangely comfortable.

"Jackie? You still there?"

"I'll call you later, Harry. We're going to crash someplace too. Find a motel on the edge of town."

"One bed or two? Not that it's my business."

"You're right. It's not your business."

"I agree. So one bed or two?"

"Good night, Harry."

I hung up, cutting off his reply.

We drove for twenty minutes, silent, exhausted, and I felt every second of every minute of every hour I'd been awake—over thirty hours total. Phin found a chain hotel, dropped me off to check in while he parked the Bronco someplace inconspicuous. When he pulled away, my hand felt empty.

The employee at the front desk looked pert and freshly scrubbed, greeting me with a smile so wide it bared gums.

"Good morning." Her voice was full of annoying morning cheer.

"Two rooms," I muttered.

"Sorry." Smile. "We're all booked up." She leaned closer, conspiratorially. "Wisconsin Mom of the Year Awards." Smile. "It's our best turnout yet."

I yawned again, so big it hurt my jaw. "That's fine. We'll sleep in your lobby, on the sofa. My friend likes sleeping naked. I talk in my sleep, and since I work for a phone sex hotline I tend to use the word *cock* a lot. If you hear me yelling about how much I love big cock, or how I love to watch you play with your big cock, just give me a nudge."

Her smile drooped below the gum line.

"Let me double-check and see if there were any recent cancellations."

She stuck her nose into her computer, tapped a few keys. I dug around in my purse for my wad of Latham's cash.

"A single is recently available. King-sized bed." Smile. "Will that be okay?"

"That will be fine," I slurred, my eyes shutting briefly.

"Our rate is one hundred and thirty dollars a night."

"Cash okay?"

"Cash is fine, but I need a credit card for incidentals."

I always wondered why they called room service and pay-per-view porno incidentals. Weren't those the main reasons people stayed in hotels?

"Wallet was stolen," I told her. "No credit cards."

"That's terrible."

Perhaps, but she kept smiling.

"Cash deposit okay?"

She nodded; money, receipts, and key cards changed hands, and Phin came in. We managed to find our room, the key worked on the third try, and I stumbled to the bed and kicked off my shoes. Phin stood and stared.

"I can call down to the lobby, have them bring in a cot for me."

"Don't worry about it," I said, yawning. "Just try to control yourself."

He smiled, sheepish.

"What if I try really hard and fail?"

"I'll be sleeping. Try not to wake me up."

I tugged off my sweatpants, too tired to feel awkward or embarrassed. Then I noticed I was still wearing those lacy red panties, and I felt both awkward and embarrassed and not nearly as tired anymore. In fact, I was all of a sudden pretty awake.

Phin watched me, waiting to see what I did next. I looked down at my sweatshirt. Take it off, or keep it on? I had a sports bra on under it. Not sexy at all, flattening my boobs. But why should I care how I looked? We were just going to sleep. And seeing me in my underwear was the same thing as seeing me in a swimsuit.

Of course, it took me three hours to put on a swimsuit.

The hell with it. We were adults. I was tired and wanted to be comfortable.

The sweatshirt came off.

I met Phin's eyes and didn't feel comfortable at all. I felt awkward and vulnerable and nervous and also a little excited, like a teenager right before her first time. Phin's eyes had that purple hue again, and his expression was intense.

I levered myself between the sheets.

Go to sleep, I told myself.

But instead of closing my eyes, I watched Phin take his shirt off. His body was different than Latham's. Latham's body was decent. Lithe, strong, distinguished. But comfortable and familiar. Sort of like a Lincoln Town Car.

Phin had a Ferarri. Fast and sharp and sculpted. And dangerous.

Quit it. You just buried Latham. He hasn't even been dead for three weeks.

When Phin began taking off his sweatpants I used all of my self-control to kill the bedside lamp so I couldn't see anything else.

The bed bounced lightly when he climbed in, and then he turned off his light and we were both lying there in the dark and I was getting warm. Really warm.

Hot, actually.

If he tries something, I'll roll with it, I decided.

I closed my eyes, waiting for him to touch me. Wanting him to touch me. I knew it was wrong, for a hundred different reasons. But I wanted sex. I wanted to feel something other than pain. With all the death and horror of the past weeks, I needed something life-affirming.

I no longer had love. Love died with my fiancé.

But I didn't expect love from Phin.

However, an orgasm or two would be a good temporary placeholder.

The bed springs creaked, and I sensed him shifting. Moving closer to me.

Maybe my breath quickened a little bit. Maybe I shifted a little bit toward him as well.

I waited. Pictured his hands on my body. My breasts. Between my thighs. I remembered his kiss, how good it was, and imagined how his mouth would feel on other parts of me.

But nothing happened. He didn't make a move.

I'd been rebuffing him all night, and he hadn't been put off. Now, when I finally want him to try something, he decides to listen to me?

Didn't guys understand women at all?

I sighed, loudly, hoping he'd take the hint.

Nothing.

I sighed again, this time putting a bit of slut into the tone. More of a moan than a sigh.

Nada. Zip. Zilch.

I realized I couldn't back down at this point. I was turned on. All I had to do was reach for him, and I would make sure he was turned on as well.

My hand crept under the covers, toward Phin. I aimed low, for a part I was sure would get his attention. The king-sized bed seemed huge, the distance between us enormous, and I really did feel like a virginal school-girl, so much so that I almost giggled, and giggling is not something I'm known for.

And then I heard it. A sound. A horrible, libido-killing sound.

Phin was snoring.

My hand stopped, flattening out like someone had stomped on it. I shrunk back, turned and faced the other way, the luxurious heat of arousal transforming into the sting of rejection. Giggly and turned on to red-faced humiliation in less than three seconds. It had to be some kind of record.

I closed my eyes and swore that if he ever tried to touch me again I'd break off his fingers. Then I tried to sleep.

Exhausted as I was, sleep didn't come.

CHAPTER 30

L UCKY BITCH.

It had a December 31 vibe, like counting down the seconds until the new year, and Alex had been looking forward to seeing the monochromatic fireworks of poor Lance's head blowing up. But lucky Jack stormed in at the last possible second and saved his miserable life.

How anticlimactic.

Things became interesting again when the two cops arrived, but Jack killed the live feed in the middle of that little drama. Cue commercial. Switch channels.

Alex considers her next move. It's still too early to pay Jack's ex a visit, so she spends some time on the Internet, reading up on defibrillators, replying to an e-mail in her anonymous account, learning about bulletproofing a vehicle. Boring stuff, but necessary. Then she logs on to the homepage of her pay-as-you-go cell phone service provider. The phones are impossible to trace, but they do keep track of minutes and numbers called. Because Alex is spoofing caller ID, most of the numbers listed are 555-5555.

But there are a few real numbers. The numbers Jack has called from the phone Alex gave her.

One of them is interesting. An 800 number. Alex makes a mental note to call it later.

At a little after seven a.m. she dresses in the police uniform and goes for a ride, finding a twenty-four-hour convenience store and picking up two rolls of duct tape and some quick energy foods: chips, beef jerky, candy bars. She also gets a six-pack of bottled water.

It's going to be a thirsty day.

Back at the hotel she checks her appearance and then knocks on Alan's door.

"Yeah?" he answers.

Alex steps away from the peephole, letting him see her good profile and her cop clothes.

"Mr. Daniels? It's about your ex-wife."

She resists a smile when she hears the lock turn, the Cheetah stun gun palmed in her right hand.

Two seconds after the door opens, Alan is on his knees. Two seconds after that, he's facedown on the carpeting.

Alex checks the hallway for witnesses, and seeing none, drags Jack's husband to bed.

CHAPTER 31

I FELT LATHAM'S ARM slip around my waist and I sighed, happy it had all been some horrible dream.

But it didn't feel like Latham's arm—it felt like a stranger's—and everything came back at once and I jolted, then went rigid.

"You okay?" Phin, his voice sleepy.

"Yeah. Just forgot where I was."

Phin's hand was still on my hip, burning there like an iron. I nudged it off.

"I wasn't trying anything."

"I know." My tone had more regret in it than I might have liked.

Sunlight peeked in through a crack in the drapes. I looked at the clock radio. A little past ten a.m. I'd managed about four hours of sleep. Not too bad. I've been able to function on less.

I rubbed my eyes, felt some crud in the corners, and immediately wondered how my hair looked. My breath was probably awful as well. I wanted to get up, dress in the bathroom, but didn't want Phin to see me in my underwear. Earlier it seemed daring. Now it was just plain embarrassing.

"I'm not used to waking up next to cops," Phin said. "Especially pretty ones."

I felt his finger trail up my spine. I flinched away.

"Jesus, Jack. We're both adults."

I faced him, hugging the sheet to my chest.

"You're a good-looking guy, Phin. I'm sure you'll rebound quickly."

He smiled and locked his hands behind his head, triceps bulging.

"Do you like being miserable? Is that your thing?"

His pillow talk needed some work.

"No, Phin. Like most other people in the world, I actually try to be happy. And sometimes I actually achieve it for brief periods of time. But to me, being an adult means having responsibilities."

I was lecturing, but Phin appeared more amused than chastised.

"I used to be like that. Feeling like the only thing holding the world together was my self-discipline."

"There's a difference between taking care of business and being a control freak."

"I know that. Do you?"

And to think I almost slept with this guy.

"I try to do my best. Sometimes it doesn't work out, but I keep trying. It's all I can do."

Phin adopted a pensive look as if he was considering what to say next. I waited, feeling dorkier and dorkier in my sports bra and red panties.

Finally, he spoke.

"Let me tell you a story, Jack. Young man. Had a decent paying job in an office. Was in love with a girl who loved him back. They even had the wedding date set."

"This is you, I'm guessing."

"It was me. Living the American dream, on my way to two-point-five kids and a thirty-year fixed mortgage."

"So what happened? One day you just decided a life of crime was sexier?"

His eyes went somewhere else. "I was diagnosed with pancreatic cancer. Told I had eight months to live. Maria—Maria Kilborn, my bride to be—she and I were . . . *right*. Like we were supposed to be together. You know? When someone is just perfect for you?"

I nodded, a lump forming in my throat. "I know."

Phin focused, smiled sadly. "But she wasn't strong, Jack. She was strong in some ways. But not emotionally. She cared about people. A lot. Maybe too much. I remember driving home from the doctor's office, thinking about how I was going to tell her, seeing it in my head. And I couldn't do it. I couldn't hurt her like that. Not only the telling her, but thinking about her watching me die . . ."

Phin cleared his throat, then scratched the back of his neck.

"So I didn't go home. I rented a hotel room, called an escort service, and fucked my brains out while Maria was going crazy wondering where I was. She tracked down our credit card usage, came to my room, saw me with the whore. There was screaming, crying. She told me she never wanted to see me again. And she kept the promise."

I made a face. "Do you think that was noble, what you did? Breaking up with her instead of being honest?"

His gaze was intense. "You tell me, Jack. Is it easier to hate someone, or to miss them after they die?"

I thought about Alan, who left me, and Latham, who left me in a different way.

Phin was right. Losing Latham hurt more.

So was he a coward, or was he being strong?

When I met Phin, on the Job, I'd immediately liked him. He'd been involved in a gang fight, three against one. They were armed. Phin wasn't. All three wound up in the hospital.

During the arrest Phin was compliant, polite, even jovial. Like he didn't have a care in the world. I bumped into him accidentally sometime later, at a local pool hall, and we began playing eight ball on a somewhat regular basis. He was attractive, sure, but I think the thing that drew me to him was his attitude. He seemed free. Even bald from the chemo, taking breaks between games to go throw up, he seemed more at ease with himself than anyone I'd ever met.

I wondered what it would be like to live in the moment like that. To not worry about anything other than the now. Was it liberating? Or empty? Brave or weak?

"This was a few years ago." Phin turned on his side, propping his head up on his hand. "I had surgery. Had treatments. Still kept getting worse. Nine to five didn't really seem that important anymore, so I quit. Eventually I ran out of money, lost my insurance. Lived on the street, day by day, getting by. But something funny happened. I didn't die."

"Remission."

He shook his head. "Not really. Cancer's still there. Pain is still there. I'm going to die from it. But it isn't killing me as fast as the doctors have hoped. I thought I'd rob a few gangbangers, hustle a little pool, spend a few weeks partying like a rock star and then die in a gutter somewhere. But here I am. Still alive. Here. With you."

He touched my back again, and this time I didn't flinch. But since I'm cursed with the burden of overanalyzing everything, I ruined what could have been a romantic moment by asking, "Why are you here, Phin? Why are you helping me? This isn't your fight. Am I a diversion? Any port in the storm? A way to kill some time so you don't have to think about your life?"

Damn my big mouth. If he walked out the door right then, I couldn't have blamed him.

But he didn't walk out. He just stared at me. Not angry. But patient. Understanding. And I filled in the blanks. He wasn't with me because he wanted a little action, or because I helped him take his mind off his death sentence. He actually cared about me. I saw it in his face. Here was a guy who divorced himself from life, packing his feelings away like winter clothes in the summertime. He worked to keep people out.

And he let me in.

And the least I could do in return was live in the now.

In one quick motion I billowed up the sheets and cast them off the bed, exposing Phin in his red boxer briefs. His body was long and lean and cut, and I wasn't sure where I wanted to touch him first. I chose his abs, running my hand along his six-pack while sliding alongside him and hooking my leg up over his thigh.

The kiss could have been morning breath bad, but all I tasted was heat. Heat and passion and possibilities that I promised myself would be explored.

His arms encircled me, fingers of one hand running through my hair and tingling my scalp, the other wandering over the back of my sports bra.

I smiled while his tongue probed mine, then pulled slightly away.

"Sports bra," I said, "no clasps."

I dug under the elastic, stretched it up over my arms, and he helped me pull the bra over my head and arms. I paused, letting him look at me, drinking in how much he seemed to like the view. Then I grabbed his wrists and put his hands on my breasts.

He rubbed the flat of his palm over my nipples, rolled one between his fingers, tugging on it gently, making it stiffen. Then his arm was around the small of my back and he tugged me next to him, urgent, his mouth on mine.

His lips trailed down past my jaw to my neck, and I locked my legs around the side of his thigh and ground against it, feeling my first jolt of full-on arousal, building inside me like a wave.

Right then I was ready to go at it. I wanted him in me. Wanted to wrap my legs around his hips and ride him until I made him moan.

Phin had other ideas.

He kissed his way along my neck, sliding his body down next to mine, breaking my leg-lock on him. His arms encircled my hips, hands grasping my ass, and his mouth found my nipples. He caught one in his teeth, held it between them while bathing it with his tongue. I tried to open my legs but he held them together, which drove me a little crazy as he switched from one breast to the other. He was too low for me to touch anything other than his head and back, so I locked my fingers in his blond hair and held on.

His head moved lower, licking my rib cage, my navel, and then slowly, maddeningly, to the top of my red panties. He rested his mouth there, letting me feel his hot breath through the fabric, and then began to kiss.

I moved my arms down, trying to help him tug my panties off, but he held my wrists and wouldn't let me, continuing to move his mouth and jaw over my pubic mound, up and down and in small circles until it felt ready to catch fire.

I tried to fight him, wanted to end the foreplay and flip him over and straddle his face and let him devour me. I pressed up against his mouth, but he moved his face away each time I did.

Even though the panties stayed on, even though he deliberately avoided hitting the right spots, I felt the orgasm welling up. And then I understood what he was doing, other than teasing me.

It was okay to not be in control.

I moaned, turned my head to the side, took a corner of the pillow in my mouth, and let him have his way.

His way was torture. He licked my thighs, all around my panty line, his tongue slow and lazy, his hands cupping my bottom and raising me up to meet his mouth. Then, like it was tissue paper, he tore my underwear off, his warm wet lips directly on me.

Again I tried to open my legs. Again he held them together.

"Please," I said.

But there was only more teasing, to the point where I couldn't endure it anymore, and I was going to come even without any direct stimulation. My hips began to pump, moving without my control, and my hands clutched the mattress and a scream welled up in my throat and then . . . *oh my God* . . . then he finally opened my legs and his tongue found me and the tiny orgasm became a monster, pleasure so intense it almost hurt, building up and multiplying until I was nothing but pure sensation. I grabbed his head and ground against him as my whole body shook, captured and helpless in his beautiful mouth.

But it didn't end with one. After the first, his fingers came into play, and he coaxed another orgasm out of me, and by that time I was pleading with him to enter me, promising him nonsensical things, begging to the point where I was near hysterical, and *then he did.*

Holy Mary mother of God.

Half an hour later, arms and legs tangled up, sweaty and glowing and wonderfully sore, I realized I could get really used to living in the now. For a guy dying of cancer, Phin's refractory period was impressive. We'd done it twice, and might have gone for thirds when my cell phone rang.

Harry.

"I should get this," I told Phin, pulling away.

His hand stayed on my ass, his finger making lazy circles. I slapped it away. I didn't want to talk to Harry McGlade while in any stage of arousal.

"Morning, Jackie. I found the first phone. Guess where it was? Go on. Guess."

"I have no idea, Harry. A supermarket." Postcoital glow left me a little scattershot.

"A supermarket? Why would she hide the phone in a supermarket?"

"You said guess, I guessed."

"You sound funny. Did you just get laid?"

"Where was the goddamn phone, McGlade?"

"It was a supermarket. She plugged it into one of the outlets behind the fresh produce. According to the SIM, the second phone is in Gurnee. I'm on my way now."

"We should meet you," I said. "We still need the rifles."

While fleeing from the Feebies, we'd left our long guns in the RV.

"I should be there in about an hour. And I've got someone for you to meet."

There was a screech in the background.

"What was that?"

"That's who I'm talking about. I've recruited some extra help on the case."

Another screech. It sounded like a parrot.

"Did you buy a parrot? You had that Baretta fetish when we were partners."

"That was Columbo, not Baretta. I liked him for his trenchcoat. And Slappy is not a parrot."

"Slappy?"

"You'll meet him soon. I'll call when I'm close. And make sure Phin wears a rubber."

He hung up. I turned to Phin, wondering if I could make him beg like he had made me, but he was unfortunately putting on his jeans.

"Starving. I'll pick up some food. You want coffee and donuts?"

"I'm a cop. Of course I want coffee and donuts. There's money in my purse."

I trusted him, I reminded myself. As he fished out a wad of bills, I reminded myself of it again.

"I'll be back soon."

"I'll be waiting." I grinned.

He left, and my grin became a crushing feeling of despair. What was up with that?

I didn't regret the sex. The sex was great. I needed it. Phin was a fun partner, and lived up to the fantasies about him I'd never admitted to myself I had.

Latham? Of course I still missed Latham. Of course I still blamed myself for his death. But I wasn't being disloyal, wasn't cheating.

Alex wasn't on my mind at that exact moment—we couldn't do anything until she contacted us again anyway—so she wasn't the cause of my emotional pain.

It was the pregnancy test. That's why I wanted to weep.

I touched my belly, letting the tears come, feeling so interminably alone.

CHAPTER 32

LAN ISN'T A BAD-LOOKING GUY. Not as muscular as Lance, but wiry and well proportioned, and easier to lift onto the bed. He's dirty blond, and has a few days' growth of beard that is salted with gray. Alex let him keep his underwear on for the time being; she has some questions to ask before they get to the fun stuff.

"Stay still and keep quiet, or I'll juice you again," she warns. "Just one more leg to secure."

Alan stays still. He seems more dazed than scared. A combination of stun gun zaps and slaps to the side of the head make for a pretty disorienting cocktail. She tapes his ankle to the last foot of the bed, then gives the bottom of his foot a little tickle.

In the bathroom, she pours half a glass of water. On the marble sink top she crushes one of the egg-shaped tadalafil tablets she took from the coffee shop Lothario under her thumb, then scoops the powder into the water and stirs with her finger until it mostly dissolves. She brings the water back to Alan and holds up his head while he drinks.

"Do you know who I am?"

Alan swallows. He has a large Adam's apple, which Alex finds sexy.

"You're Alexandra Kork. You're a serial killer. You escaped from a maximum security prison."

"So Jack has mentioned me."

Alan shakes his head. "Heard about you on CNN. Jack and I don't talk."

Alex runs her hand across his chest, squeezing his pecs.

"You must talk sometimes. Because here you are, hiding out in a hotel. Hiding from me."

Alan's face creases, what Alex takes to be his serious look.

"Jack and I are over. We're divorced. We're not even friends. Hurting me won't hurt her."

Half a smile forms on her face. "Oh, I think it will. But we have time for that later. First I want to show you something."

Alex collects the AED from the floor. She brought it in from the Hyundai. It's the size of a laptop computer, in a rugged plastic clamshell case, bright yellow with a red and white medical cross on it. Alex places the device on the bed, opens it up.

"Originally, I was going to do something creative to you with plastic explosives. But I'm going to use this instead. It's an automatic external defibrillator. Just like on all those TV doctor shows. I put the pads on your chest like this—"

Alex places one high up to the right of his sternum, and one low down on his left side.

"—and press this big red button, and it delivers a nice thousand-volt shock across your heart, resetting its normal electrical rhythm. But if I stick the pads here—"

She removes the protective backings, exposing the adhesive, and places both pads on the left side of his heart.

"—then it will induce a fatal arrhythmia, or stop the heart altogether, or fry your organs. Or it might just hurt like hell. I've never done this before, so it's all theory."

Alex fingers the button, stroking it sensually while Alan's eyes get wide.

"What do you want?" Alan finally asks.

"Tell me about your first time. With Jack."

"You want to know about the first time we had sex?"

Alex nods.

"That's sick."

"I'm a psychopath, remember? If you don't want to talk about it, we can play *press the button* instead."

She gives the AED a soft caress. Alan's mouth becomes a tight, thin line.

"It was in a bar. In the men's bathroom."

"How many dates?"

"Second date."

"Second date? Jack moves pretty fast. So what made her drag you into the bathroom? Were you kissing first? Having some chicken wings, feeling each other up under the table?"

"We were standing at the bar, drinking beer, and she dared me to go into the bathroom with her."

Alex unbuttons her uniform shirt. The bra underneath is black, lacy, tight. True to male form, Alan stares at her tits.

"What did she do to you in the bathroom, Alan?"

"We kissed, then she put my hands up her shirt."

"Like this?"

Alex brings her hand up her stomach, fingers going up under the underwire of the bra. Alan still looks nervous, but the initial repulsion on his face is replaced by fascination, perhaps even interest. Her other hand unbuttons her pants and unzips the fly, letting the pants fall around her ankles.

"Keep going, Alan. What happened next?"

"We got into a stall. She . . . she put her hand on me."

Alex steps out of the slacks and sits on the bed next to him. She traces a lazy finger down Alan's chest, slipping it under the waistband of his underwear. It's too early for the tadalafil to be working, but it doesn't look like Alan needed it after all.

"Jack sounds aggressive. You like aggressive women, don't you Alan?"

"What are you doing?"

Alex pumps her hand up and down.

"What happened next, Alan?"

"We had . . . we had sex."

Alan closes his eyes, and Alex feels his hips rise. She leans toward his ear and whispers, "Would you like to have sex with me, Alan?"

He shakes his head.

"You can keep your eyes closed, pretend I'm Jack."

Alan softly answers, "No. You're a killer."

She grips him hard, digging her nails in. Alan yelps, his face contorting with pain and fear.

"Good," Alex breathes. "Sex is so much more fun when it isn't consensual."

She slaps him across the face, then grabs the duct tape to make a gag.

Things are about to get loud.

CHAPTER 33

H OW LONG DOES IT TAKE to get donuts?

My watch read a quarter to twelve. Phin had been gone for over an hour. I'm naturally paranoid, something my chosen profession compounds, so I was conjuring up scenarios to explain why he was so late, like being grabbed by Alex, or hit by a bus, or caught by the Feds, or killed by Milwaukee cops, or the most frightening of all: ditching me because he thought the sex was a mistake.

I tried the walkie-talkie, but he either wasn't answering or he had it turned off. I counted and recounted the cash left in my purse, and calculated he either took twenty dollars or a thousand and twenty dollars—I couldn't remember how much I'd taken from the bank, and couldn't find the withdrawal slip.

While waiting I spent a good half an hour wondering about Alex, and how we were going to find her. I wound up coming to the obvious conclusion: We couldn't. Not unless she let us, or she made a mistake, and she hadn't done either yet.

So I spent the next half an hour wondering if I should put on makeup or not. Just because I'd gone to bed with Phin didn't mean our relationship had really changed, and the last few times I'd seen him I hadn't worried if I was wearing makeup. Putting on makeup now would mean I cared about how I looked, which meant his opinion of me mattered, which meant our relationship actually had changed. I didn't know if I wanted to acknowledge that, or if he wanted to acknowledge that, or how he would act if I acknowledged it and he didn't, and vice versa.

Basically, I just shouldn't have sex. But it was too late for that, so I was stuck dwelling on it.

"If he wasn't here, would I wear makeup?" I asked myself honestly.

Maybe. Maybe today would be a makeup day.

Which was a dishonest answer.

So I didn't put on makeup, and stopped obsessing over it, and went back to obsessing over where the hell he was.

My ringing cell phone dragged me back into reality.

"Hello? Jacqueline?"

My mother. Mom had met Phin, and I think she liked him. But that didn't mean I needed to blab to her that I slept with him.

"I slept with Phin," I told her.

"I'm so happy for you," she said in a way that sounded like she was so happy for me, "but I've got a real big problem right now."

I remembered Mom's Alaskan cruise.

"Flight delayed? Or is it TSA? Mom, you didn't try to bring your brass knuckles on the flight, did you? I told you not to buy those."

"I didn't bring the brass knuckles. I'm already on the ship. And I just saw *him*."

"Saw who?"

"Your father."

I remembered Dad's Alaskan cruise, and the astronomically high improbability that they'd both be on the same boat.

Fate's a funny bitch.

"Are you sure it's him?" I asked, knowing it was. "It's been forty years."

"I'll remember that deceitful face until a thousand years after I die. He's still got that smarmy, cocksure look, and that dishonest little smile. But he's lost the little Hitler mustache. I distinctly remember the little Hitler mustache."

"He never had a Hitler mustache. You're projecting."

"You were too young to remember it, and how he used to goose-step around the house, planning to invade France."

I sighed. "Look, Mom, you're both adults. This will give you a chance to work things out."

"Work things out? Never! He left us, for no good reason."

"He had a good reason," I said, "but you made me promise never to mention him again."

"And I insist you keep that promise. I don't want to hear about the lies he told you. The fact that you even want to have a relationship with that horrible man makes me think I should have named you Ilsa."

"He's actually a nice guy, Mom. You'd like him."

"I'm going to kill him."

"Mom!"

"I'll wait until he's near one of the railings and I'll push him overboard. Hopefully the sharks will get him before he drowns."

"Mom," I couldn't believe I had to say it, "please don't kill Dad."

"Maybe I won't have to. There was a welcome brunch, and the food was horrible. Maybe salmonella or E. coli will do the job for me."

I looked at the front door. It didn't open, and Phin didn't walk in. I checked my watch again.

"You need to have a few drinks, relax, and stop plotting murders."

"It's too early to drink."

"It's never too early to drink. Have a whiskey sour. Or a bloody Mary."

"Don't want one."

"Then a rusty nail. You used to drink those."

"That's too strong. I'll be passed out by dinner."

"Get a foo-foo drink then. Try a fuzzy navel."

"What's in it?"

"Orange juice and peach schnapps."

"That's too foo-foo. I'd have to drink ten of them to feel anything. Maybe I'll have a dirty martini."

"Good," I said. "I was running out of drink names."

"I'm telling you, Jacqueline, I don't think I can handle ten days of being trapped on a boat with that man."

"I'm sure it's a big boat. You probably won't even see him again."

"If I do, I'm going to grab a lifeboat oar and knock his teeth down his throat, I swear to God."

My call waiting beeped.

"I got someone on the other line, Mom. Have a nice cruise. Call me if you get arrested."

I switched over just as Mom was yelling at some ship employee for vodka.

"Jacqueline? It's Wilbur. I'm on the ship and I think I saw your mother."

I sighed again. "You did. It's her. Imagine the odds."

"The expression on her face . . . well, let's say she didn't seem pleased."

"You're both adults," I said. "This will give you a chance to work things out."

"I don't know if that's possible. I mean, I'm willing to try, but Mary looked like she was going to come after me with a wooden stake and a mallet."

Or a lifeboat oar, I thought. I glanced at the door again. Still no Phin.

"You don't think she'd actually try to hurt me, do you?"

"Stay away from railings," I suggested.

"This is horrible. I'll have to spend the whole cruise in my cabin, with a chair wedged against the door. There was a thousand-dollar cash prize for bingo tonight too. I hate to miss that."

"I'm sure it's a big ship," I said, wishing I'd taped my earlier conversation so I didn't have to have it twice. "Maybe you won't even see her again."

"Does your mother like bingo?"

What was it with older people and bingo? Maybe it was something in the genes, and once you turned sixty some kind of internal switch was flipped.

"I have no idea."

"Maybe I'll go. I could wear a disguise."

"As long as it's not a tiny mustache."

"Think she'd accept a peace offering? Flowers, maybe? There's a florist on board. She used to love roses."

I pictured Dad dead in his bingo chair, two dozen roses crammed down his throat.

"Hiding is probably smarter."

"I need a drink," Wilbur said.

"I gotta go, Dad." I didn't want to play bartender again. "Call me if she kills you."

I considered calling Mom back, warning her not to play bingo, but stopped myself. I shouldn't be using my cell—the Feds could trace it. Besides, they'd thank me for it later, after they worked things out. What child didn't want to see their parents back together again? Of course, they wouldn't actually be together. But maybe they could resolve their differencs and pick up guys together.

Or maybe Mom would be serving twenty to life.

I decided to call her back, but the motel door opened mid-dial.

"Sorry I took so long. Had to run an errand first."

Phin had a bag of donuts and a cardboard container holding two coffees. I had an urge to press the issue, and another urge to do him right there in the doorway. I fought both urges and kept cool, waiting to see how he played it.

"I didn't know if you took cream or sugar." He shrugged. "I guess there's a lot I don't know about you."

He handed me a cup. I took it. There was some awkward staring. What was he thinking? Was he thinking what I was thinking? What was I thinking?

I was thinking I should have put on makeup.

"Black," I said, breaking the silence. "I take it black."

"Me too. Why dilute the caffeine with all of that other crap?"

I took a sip. Lukewarm. He'd bought this a while ago. Where had he been all this time?

"Didn't know what donuts you liked either. Got assorted."

He sat down on the bed, dug into the bag, his foot tapping. Was he avoiding talking about us, or didn't feel the need to?

Well, dammit, I felt the need to. We couldn't work together until we figured out where we stood with each other. One of us needed to act like a grown-up.

I sat next to him, hip to hip. He didn't look at me. Not a good sign. I reached up a hand to touch his face, and he flinched. An even worse sign.

"You've got some powdered sugar on your lip," I said, rubbing it off with my thumb, automatically putting the thumb in my mouth to taste the sweetness.

It was bitter, and made my tongue tingle.

That wasn't powdered sugar.

I recalled our earlier conversation, in the bar, when Phin told me he needed to stop back at his apartment to pick up some things.

Drugs? Had he wanted to pick up some coke?

And if that was cocaine on his lip, had he bought it with my money?

Phin seemed oblivious to my reaction, tugging out a cruller, eating a third of it with one bite. His foot kept tapping, and there were sweat beads on his forehead.

Years ago, I worked Vice. I knew narcotics. Phin was high.

I didn't want to get involved with a drug addict. I didn't want to get involved with a bank robber either. But I was more than involved— besides sleeping with him, I'd enlisted him to help me find Alex. To back me up. I was entrusting him with my life.

And he was offering to help me. Willing to risk his own life, and asking for nothing in return.

Except, possibly, free sex and money for coke.

I wondered why I couldn't fall for a normal guy, then remembered I had, and just went to his funeral yesterday.

Jesus, what a mess.

"You like chocolate?" Phin asked.

I managed a nod. He handed me a chocolate frosted. I took a token bite, but my appetite was gone. The right thing to do was tell him I appreciated everything, but I didn't need him anymore. I wasn't even sure if that was the truth.

"Phin—"

The phone cut me off. Alex's phone. But it wasn't her—no 555 number. It was Harry again.

"Hiya, sis. I'm in Gurnee. When can you meet me?"

I stared at Phin. Was this the time and the place to make a big scene? Phin had the car. Would he drop me off in Gurnee after I told him to take a hike? Should I ask Harry to pick me up here? Could Harry and I handle Alex on our own? And was I willing to lose one of my closest friends just because he had some issues? A close friend who was great in the sack?

"An hour," I told Harry.

"Call me when you're close."

I hung up. Phin was working on his second donut.

"We're meeting Harry in Gurnee," I said.

He nodded, stood up, grabbed the backpack, and stopped at the door. The moment stretched.

"You okay?"

A ridiculous thing to ask, considering everything.

"Look, Jack, you've probably figured out I'm not good with this intimacy thing. I'm out of practice. Hell, when I was in practice, I wasn't very good at it."

He paused. I waited.

"I want to tell you . . . I don't think this morning was a mistake. And I'd like to know if you feel the same way."

He's giving you an out, Jack. Tell him it was a mistake.

"It wasn't a mistake," I heard myself say.

"I'm glad to hear that. And there's something on my mind. If it's okay we're talking."

"It's fine," I said to his back. "Say what you need to say."

"When I took the money from your purse . . ."

Here we go. He was going to open up about the drugs. About stealing from me. How should I react? Ask him to rob another bank to pay me back? Offer to pay him to help me with Alex? Lecture him about the dangers of drug abuse?

"I know it's none of my business," he said, "but I saw it."

"Saw what?"

"The pregnancy test." He turned around, his face serious. "You want to tell me what's up?"

CHAPTER 34

ALEX CLIMBS OFF THE BED. Naked. Satisfied. Bloody.

The blood isn't hers.

Jack's husband held up pretty well. The erection pills probably helped, but twice in an hour was more than Lance ever managed.

"Not bad, loverboy. If you enjoyed yourself, don't say anything."

Alan stays quiet. The duct tape gag has a lot to do with it, but it makes Alex feel good just the same.

In the shower, she lathers up and plans her next few moves. Alex is good at planning. Thinking things through. Anticipating problems. It's one of the reasons she's been such a successful killer, caught just one time in a career lasting well over two decades. Being careful doesn't just happen. It requires deliberation. One must consider every possible contingency, and then predict probable outcomes.

Though genetically she's a predator—something she got from Father—she can also thank him for her plotting capabilities. Growing up in a household ruled by fear and abuse can turn the most innocent child into a cold, calculating machine. Alex never learned how to play chess, but guesses she'd be good at it.

She playfully swishes a toe through the blood-streaked suds swirling down the drain, and decides to find some time in her busy schedule today to paint her toenails. She likes how the red looks.

The hair dryer is even worse than the one at the Old Stone Inn—

Alex bets her hair is growing faster than it's drying. She gives up after a few minutes, putting it into a ponytail while still damp. Makeup is a chore. She's going out in public, so that means caking on the thick scar cover. The product comes with a tiny spatula, and it goes on like flesh-colored Spackle. Alex fusses with her bangs, letting them hang down over the bad half of her face, and then chooses to walk away before she starts to get angry again.

Back into the bedroom, naked. No real room for any serious exercise. But then, she probably got enough exercise in the last hour. She dresses in the cop uniform again, pleased that Alan is watching her. He's gone from looking scared to looking devastated. Like a kicked dog.

"I'll be back soon, dear. Don't wait up for me."

He doesn't answer. She spends ten minutes online, giving Alan's credit card a little workout. She remembers his e-mail address from his Web site, but she does have to give him a few gentle slaps to get him to spill his preferred Internet password. It gives her tremendous pleasure to hear his password is *Jacqueline*. What a sap.

When she's finished with the computer, she sits on the bed and opens up the defibrillator, pretending to press a few buttons.

"I've activated the automatic motion sensor. So if you struggle, or try to scream, it will give you a nasty jolt. Plus, it will make me really angry. Trust me, I'm much easier to get along with when you're on my good side."

She runs a finger along his forehead, wipes the blood off on a pillowcase, and leaves the hotel room, making sure to put the Do Not Disturb sign on the door.

It's a bright day, bright and painfully sunny, a sharp contrast to the cool wind chilling her scalp. Alex stands in the parking lot, pretending to search her pockets for her keys but actually getting the lay of the land. No one loitering. No parked cars with tinted windows or with the engines running. She knows that the authorities have by now found the Hyundai's owner, dead in the ditch, and are looking for his car and his murderer.

She heads on to the car, climbs in, and drives twice around the parking lot. No tails.

Using the onboard GPS, she searches department stores in the area, and heads for the closest. She finds the superglue, the floss, the half-inch screw eyes, the inkjet printer and specialty paper, the socket set, the road flares, and the five-gallon gas canister easily enough, but has to walk up and down several aisles before finding the outlet timer. In the cosmetics department, she chooses a fire engine red nail polish. Standing in the checkout line, Alex notes that people are avoiding looking in her direction. She's used to that—people tend to be repulsed by deformities, and after one glance they turn away. But in this case, people aren't even giving her that first look.

It's the uniform. People naturally distrust cops. In a weird way, it's almost like being invisible. Alex watches a mother in line ahead of her, repeating over and over that she isn't going to buy her son the toy he's clutching and whining about. It reminds Alex of Samantha, the stripper with the little girl from yesterday, and Alex digs out her cell.

"Sammy? It's Gracie."

"Gracie?" Samantha sounds groggy. It's lunchtime, but dancers work late hours.

"We met yesterday at the bookstore. You offered to take me clothes shopping."

"Oh, hi! Glad you called."

Alex's eyes flick to a woman, Caucasian, mid-fifties, wearing jeans and a sweatshirt that she probably bought at this store. Short hair, brown with blond streaks. Gym shoes. Strangely, no purse. She's beelining in this direction, face frantic, arms pumping.

"I'm free tonight," Alex says. "What's your schedule look like?"

"I have off. I can call my neighbor, have her watch Melinda."

The woman is a few steps away now, so close Alex can see the trickle of blood leaking from her nose.

"Officer!" the woman calls.

"That would be so cool," Alex says into the phone. "You've got my number, right?"

"Yeah. I'll call you. Awesome!"

"See you later."

She hangs up just as the woman is tugging on her arm.

"He hit me and took my purse!" The woman's voice is high-pitched, tinged with hysteria. Her cheeks glisten with tears.

"I'm off duty, ma'am." Alex points at her cart with her chin. "You should call 911."

"You have to help me! Please! There he is!"

Alex follows the woman's finger in the direction of a teenager sporting gang colors, heading for the exit. He's about forty yards away, young, moving fast. He'll be out the door in a matter of seconds. A challenging target.

The holster on Alex's hip has an unfamiliar snap holding the gun in place, and she loses half a second fumbling with it. But the draw is smooth, her aim is sure, and the kid flops to the ground minus his right knee.

There's a moment of shocked silence, then pandemonium, people diving and ducking and screaming and shouting. Alex drinks in the reaction.

"I can't see from here, but it doesn't look like he has your purse." Alex talks louder than normal; her ears are ringing, and so are everyone else's. "But he probably has your cash and credit cards on him. I'm guessing he ditched your purse someplace in the store."

The woman's jaw is hanging open. Alex tips her cap, holsters her gun, and pushes her cart toward the exit.

The gangbanger is on the floor, clutching his knee, face wrenched with pain. Early teens, peach fuzz on his chin. His running days are over. And from the amount of blood on the floor, his walking days might be over as well. He sees Alex approach and fumbles for something in his loose-fitting jeans. Alex draws again, pointing the barrel at his groin.

"I blew off your kneecap from over a hundred feet away," she says. "You want to see what kind of damage I can do this close to you?"

He shakes his head, his whole body twitching, and slowly raises his empty hands. Alex digs into his pocket, takes out a battered .22. She tucks it into her belt.

"Do yourself a favor, kid, and quit crime. You suck at it."

She walks out of the store with a cop swagger and a cart full of merchandise she didn't pay for.

CHAPTER 35

PHIN AND I STARED AT EACH OTHER for a little bit. I put on my cop face to keep my emotions hidden. But instead of Phin wearing his tough-guy face, he looked like the last kid picked for kickball.

"I'm not going to be around for long," he said.

I folded my arms. "I'm not forcing you to help me, Phin. You can leave whenever you want to."

"I meant being alive. I'm dying of cancer, Jack. I might not make it through winter."

"Oh." I was trying to be strong, not be an asshole. "Sorry."

"It's just—women carry pregnancy tests for two reasons. Because they think they're pregnant . . ."

"I'm not pregnant."

". . . or because they want to get pregnant."

"I don't want to get pregnant. And you had no right to search my purse."

"I wasn't searching your purse. You told me to take money for donuts."

"And you saw something wrapped in toilet paper and decided to take a look?"

"It wasn't wrapped in toilet paper. It was sitting on top of your wallet."

I wasn't buying. I reached into my purse, pulled out the wad of toilet paper I'd used to wrap up the EPT, and waved it like a surrender flag.

"Are you saying this isn't toilet paper?"

"Yes, Lieutenant, that's toilet paper. But it wasn't wrapped around anything."

"Why else would I have toilet paper in my purse?"

Phin shrugged. "Emergencies? Afraid of being caught without it? How should I know? I'm not a chick, I don't own a purse. I don't know why you women keep half that stuff in there."

"I only keep essentials in my purse."

"You've got a wind-up plastic nun in there."

"That's Nunzilla. She shoots sparks out of her mouth."

"That's essential?"

"It was . . . a gift."

Latham gave it to me, on our first-year anniversary.

"Look, I know you're hurting. I know you miss him a lot. But if you're trying to get pregnant to fill a void in your life, you should find a father who will be around for a while."

I wasn't sure what rankled more, Phin thinking I slept with him to get pregnant, or Phin thinking I needed a child to fill some void in my life.

"It's not any of your business, but since you brought it up, I missed my last period and thought I might be pregnant, so I bought a pregnancy test when we were at the gas station last night. If you'd bothered to look closer, you'd see there was only one blue line, not two. I'm not pregnant, so this conversation is over."

Phin shifted his weight from one foot to the other, then cupped his elbow and rubbed the back of his neck.

"I believe you," he said.

"Good. Because I'm telling the truth."

"But if it's negative, why did you save it?"

I opened my mouth to answer, but nothing came out. What was I supposed to tell him? That part of me wanted to be pregnant, so I could always have part of Latham with me? That maybe I did have a void that needed to be filled? That keeping a negative pregnancy test was one more way I could punish myself, as a reminder of what never would be?

I wasn't ready to tell him that. Especially when he was high on coke.

"If you think I slept with you because I wanted a sperm donor—"

He raised his palms. "I'm just trying to understand you a little better."

"Why? Why the hell do you need to understand me?"

"Because . . ."

He gave me that look again and I knew that he was going to say the L word, and I did not need to deal with that right now.

"Never mind," I interrupted. "We need to get to Gurnee and meet Harry. You want to drive, or rifle through my purse some more?"

He went from lovey-dovey to wounded, which I preferred.

"I'll drive."

I followed Phin out to the Bronco. The day was gray, overcast, and matched my mood. We got in the truck and didn't say anything to each other for the first half hour of the drive. I finally got hungry and picked out one of the donuts he bought.

"Sprinkles," I said, after swallowing a bite.

"Excuse me?"

"I like donuts with sprinkles."

"Oh. Good to know. Anything you want to know about me?"

He sniffled, rubbed his nose. I resisted the temptation to ask which coke he preferred, Colombian or Panamanian. I also resisted asking him about criminal acts he'd committed in his past. I was curious how bad this bad boy really was, but I was also a cop and might feel compelled to act on the information. Sometimes ignorance makes things easier.

"Does it hurt?" I asked instead.

"The cancer?"

I nodded.

"Only some of the time."

"When doesn't it hurt?"

"When I'm asleep."

"The pain is bad?"

He nodded, took one hand off the wheel to rub his elbow again. I reached out, touched his injury.

"Jesus, Phin! It feels like you have a beanbag in your elbow."

"It's pieces of cartilage. I'm supposed to keep it immobile."

"You should have it in a sling. You don't want permanent damage."

"It won't be permanent," he said.

He didn't say it with regret, or self-pity. He said it matter-of-factly, like he was talking about the weather.

I'd met some tough guys. Cops. Military. Bikers. Mobsters. Killers. With one sentence, Phin took the tough-guy crown. Which made me want to kiss him.

Jesus, this was messed up.

The phone rang. I cringed, thinking it was Alex, but it was Harry again.

"Where you at, sis?"

"We're taking the Gurnee exit now."

"I'm on the north side of the mall. Knock three times."

"What about that deal you made?" I asked, referring to him selling out Phin to the Feds. I didn't want to walk into a Feebie party.

"Not until we catch Alex. Trust me."

Gurnee Mills was one of the largest malls in America, but the Crimebago was easy to find, even in the packed parking lot. Phin pulled up behind it, and I knocked three times like Harry instructed.

"Door's open!" he called from inside.

Upon opening the door, I was greeted by a nasty smell. Not the normal nasty smell I associated with Harry. Something far worse.

"Jesus, Harry, it stinks in here."

"I'm working on that."

Harry was in a rumpled suit, stained with wet spots of various colors. He was holding a handful of those cardboard pine-scented car fresheners shaped like Christmas trees. But I wasn't smelling pine. I was smelling zoo on a hot day.

There was a scream to our left, and I dropped to one knee and struggled to dig my gun out of my purse. When I got it in my hand Harry grabbed my wrist.

"Sis, don't shoot Slappy!"

Another screech. I followed the sound to a large wire cage. Inside the cage was a monkey. It was light brown, perhaps eight or nine pounds, with large brown eyes and the cutest little monkey face.

I put my gun away.

"This is the extra help you recruited?" I asked.

He nodded, grinning. "He's a pig-tailed macaque." Harry said it *mack-a-cue.*

"I think it's pronounced *ma-kak,*" Phin said.

Harry scratched his stubble. "That's not what Al told me."

"Al?"

"Al at Al's Exotic Pets, in Deer Park. He sold him to me this morning."

"He's adorable," I said, meaning it. "Why'd you name him Slappy?"

On cue, the monkey slapped himself on the side of the head. He did this over and over, increasing in speed and force. The sound wasn't unlike applause.

Harry frowned. "There wasn't much of a selection down at Al's. It was either him or another primate I would have named Gassy. He also had some sort of gibbon, missing an arm and both legs."

"Stumpy?" Phin said.

"More like Sitty. I've seen turtles that moved faster. I wonder if he was dead."

"I think you chose perfectly," I said.

Slappy screeched again, baring sharp yellow teeth.

"You sure he's tame?"

"Most of the time. But don't put your fingers near the cage."

I knelt down on the carpet to get a closer look. Monkeys always fascinated me, ever since I was a little girl. Blame Curious George.

"Hello, Slappy. I'm Jack."

Something wet hit me in the cheek. Something wet and brown and horribly stinky.

"Your monkey threw poop at me."

"He does that. There are baby wipes next to his cage."

I reached for one, and Slappy managed to pitch another slider, which hit me in the nose.

"I think he's aiming for my mouth," I said, mopping my face with baby wipes.

"Are you wearing makeup? He was rescued from a research lab. They tested cosmetics on him. Don't let him see your lipstick—he gets a little agitated."

"I'm not wearing—" I dodged left, a monkey turd zinging by my face. He was definitely aiming for my mouth.

"I like him," Phin said. "He's spunky."

Slappy aimed and Phin ducked, dung splattering on the wall.

"Remind me again why you bought this thing," I said to McGlade.

"I wanted to train him to get me beer and watch sports. But all he does is throw feces, hit himself in the face, and scream. He's kind of a downer."

Slappy screamed in agreement. Then he pressed his pelvis against the side of the cage and urinated on the floor. The smell was pee times a hundred, and made me cover my nose.

"He does that too," McGlade said. "A lot. Al said he knows how to use the toilet."

The stream arced through the air, landing on Harry's sofa. Harry picked up a coffee mug that said *Don't Worry Be Happy* and tried to catch the stream. I stepped away.

"I think maybe Al lied to you."

Slappy screeched, then began banging his little monkey head into the side of his cage.

"You should buy him a helmet," Phin said.

"He came with one. I took it off because I thought it was cruel. Now I'm afraid to get close enough to put it back on."

I crouched down again, wary of another salvo but determined to make friends.

"I think you just need to learn some manners, and then you'll be fine," I told Slappy, keeping my voice soft. "You're probably just scared. I would be too, living with Harry. But I bet with a few days of training, you'll be a perfect gentleman."

Slappy stopped banging his head and made an adorable cooing sound. Then he grabbed his little monkey ding-dong and began to beat off with frightening intensity, keeping his eyes on me the whole time.

Never saw Curious George do that.

I got out of range and busied myself looking for the rifles. They were in the bedroom closet. I checked to make sure they were loaded, safeties on.

"What does he eat?" Phin asked.

"It's called monkey chow. It's not that bad. Sort of tastes like meat-flavored charcoal briquettes."

"You tried it?"

"Yeah. Want some?"

"I'm gonna pass on that one."

"Slappy hates them. See?"

I carried the rifles back to the main room just as McGlade was bending down, handing Slappy a tan square object the size of a mini candy bar. Slappy took it, screeched, and bounced the food off Harry's forehead.

"Well, it's been fun," I told Harry. "But we've got to get going."

Harry frowned. "But I want to tell you how I found the second phone. It was in the mall, hidden behind a flat-screen TV at Sears. I used my Bluetooth receiver and . . ."

I kept one eye on Slappy as Harry droned on. The macaque seemed to be temporarily out of bodily fluids, but I didn't know what his refractory period was.

"That's brilliant," I interrupted, "but we really have to hit the road."

"How about lunch? We can grab some lunch together. Sis?"

"Not hungry," I said. "Might never be hungry again."

"Phin?"

"No thanks."

"Please don't leave me alone with Slappy," Harry said.

"Maybe a beer will calm him down."

"You think?"

"Can't hurt."

"How about whiskey? Think a shot of whiskey is too strong?"

"I'd give him a different kind of shot," Phin said. "One in the head, then a quick funeral wrapped in newspaper."

Harry stared at Slappy, as if considering it.

"Harry, you can't kill your monkey."

That was how my day was going, cautioning people against murder.

"Maybe Al will trade him for the amputee one," Phin suggested.

"How can a no-legged monkey fetch me beer? Roll it to me?"

"You can tie a little cord to his neck, and he can tug it behind him." Phin mimed a one-armed primate dragging itself across the floor.

McGlade winced. "That's not fun. That's depressing. I wanted a fun pet."

"You're right. A pet that throws shit at you is a lot more fun."

"Maybe a glass cage? Then he couldn't throw anything."

"He still could," Phin said. "It would just cling to the inside walls. You'd have a big brown box."

"How about some sort of restraining device. Do they make little macaque-size handcuffs?"

Monkey bondage was our cue to leave.

"We gotta go, Harry. I'll call you later."

I herded Phin past the monkey cage, giving Slappy a wide berth. He was sitting down, looking vaguely superior, like a king on a throne.

We got out of there before the king threw anything else at us.

"Where to?" Phin asked after we climbed into the truck.

"The woods. Someplace secluded."

"Got something in mind?" He grinned at me.

"In fact I do. But it's not what you're thinking."

"Want to clue me in?"

I closed my eyes, thought it through, then said, "Just drive to a place where no one will be bothered by gunfire."

CHAPTER 36

THE COP UNIFORM has gone from asset to liability. Showing off at the department store was a mistake, though an amusing one. Alex needs to ditch the Hyundai and the uniform, and find suitable replacements for both. She was planning to do it today anyway, but shooting a teenager in front of a dozen witnesses made it a little more pressing.

Clothing is the easier of the two. She finds a local mall, hits Neiman Marcus, and buys a Joan Vass striped tunic with matching beige boot-cut pants. The Ferragamo loafers are overpriced but cute, and that purchase leaves her with thirty dollars in cash. Not enough to even pay the taxes on a handbag, and they have a Marc Jacobs satchel that would go perfectly with the outfit.

Alex changes clothes in the mall restroom. The gun, holster, and accessory belt gets put into one of the Neiman Marcus bags. The pants from the police uniform get stuffed into the garbage. The shirt gets a nice long soak in the sink and then placed into the other Neiman bag—it's plastic, so it won't drip.

Then it's time to do a different kind of shopping.

Alex leaves the mall and hangs out next to the exit doors, scanning the parking lot as if waiting for a ride. What she's really waiting for is a single woman to come out. A single woman with some fashion sense.

It's a nice neighborhood, with a nice mall, and it doesn't take long for a chunky yuppie type with a four-hundred-dollar haircut and a Prada bag to stroll outside, one hand clutching some merchandise from Saks, the other fussing with the touch screen of her iPhone. Alex falls into step behind her.

Following her requires zero stealth—the woman is oblivious to everything but her electronic gadget. The parking lot is full. She stops twice to get her bearings, then eventually finds her car a row over from where she thought it was. Alex had been hoping for something sporty, maybe a BMW or a Lexus. Instead, the woman drives a white Prius.

Alex checks the parking lot, but there's no one nearby, and she reaches inside her shopping bag for the wet shirt. She wraps it around the gun, covering her entire hand. The chubby woman keeps playing with her iPhone up until the moment Alex jams the barrel into the back of her neck and fires.

The gun is loud, but the shirt muffles it somewhat. Alex doesn't stop to check if anyone is watching. She kneels down next to the body and opens up her new Prada bag.

Except it isn't Prada. It's a knockoff.

"Hell," Alex says.

All that work for a Prius and fake Prada.

She finds the car keys, hits the unlock button on the remote, and horses the dead body into the cramped backseat, keeping low and out of sight of the cars circling the lot looking for spaces. On a whim, she checks the Saks bags. Vera Wang pajamas. They're nice, but Alex doesn't wear pajamas, and she certainly doesn't wear a size fourteen. She arranges the pajamas and assorted bags over the body to cover it up, and locks the doors.

Another 360 check for witnesses. No one is paying attention to her.

Then Alex marches back into Neiman Marcus and buys the Marc Jacobs satchel. The cashier, a young blonde who probably went to a local community college and majored in giggles, asks Alex for an ID to match the dead woman's credit card.

Alex leans in close.

"It burned in the crash, along with half my face. I haven't gotten a new one yet, because I'm afraid to drive again. Would you like me to speak to your manager?"

Blondie declines. The fifteen-hundred-dollar charge goes through, and Alex heads back to the Prius. Once in the driver's seat she transfers the contents of the fake purse to the real purse, and tosses the fake one onto the corpse.

"You died too young. Should have treated yourself and bought the real thing."

Happily, there's more than two hundred bucks in the woman's wallet, along with half a pack of gum and a canister of pepper spray, which the woman should have been holding instead of her iPhone. Alex pops a stick of spearmint into her mouth and pulls out of the parking space. She heads back to the Hyundai, loads her previous purchases into the Prius, and drives until she finds a gas station.

She fills the five-gallon plastic canister she bought at the department store and retraces her steps.

Her previous stolen car blew up, and it's unlikely they'll link it to her. Plastic explosives do wonders for removing fingerprints.

Multiple witnesses saw her shoot the gangbanger, including the gangbanger, but it could take a few days before her name gets pulled into it. If ever. She left no evidence; the brass belonged to the cop and Alex wiped off the cart handle. There were security cameras, but Alex always keeps her head down in public places, a habit from before the disfigurement.

The Feds are no doubt looking for her. As is Jack, and all of Jack's department. But they have no reason yet to think she's in Iowa.

Unless they get lucky. Alex can't discount that. Luck is how she got caught. Luck is how Jack got away last time. Which means it's time to get the hell out of Dodge.

If the authorities haven't gotten lucky yet, there's no reason to make it any easier for them.

Alex drives back to the Hyundai and double-parks behind it. All five gallons of gas get splashed around the interior. She considers tossing the body in there as well, but a homicide will get more attention than a vandalized car, so she lets her be for the moment.

The license plates are attached with nuts and bolts, and Alex removes them with the socket set she bought. She tosses the plates onto the body—something else to dispose of later—and lights up the car with a road flare. Then she climbs into the Prius and heads back to the Holiday Inn.

No squad cars in front. No men suspiciously lingering outside. Alex parks. The police band radio is attached to the cop's utility belt, in one of the bags. Alex switches it on, finds the local dispatch frequency, listens to chatter. It's all in code, which Alex doesn't know, but she does hear some talk about the car bombing at the mall.

She turns it off and lugs everything back into the hotel. It's with much amusement, and some disappointment, that she sees Alan is still tied to the bed. Unlike Lance, who butchered his wrists trying to get free, the duct tape securing Jack's husband still looks freshly applied. The poor dear must have actually believed that BS about the motion sensor. Maybe that's Jack's secret to finding men: She picks the really gullible ones.

"Did you miss me?" Alex asks.

He mumbles something around the gag that sounds like *bathroom*. Alex shakes her head.

"You don't want to go in there. Trust me. Single women can be sloppy." She holds up her new satchel, posing with it. "Do you like my new bag? Marc Jacobs. It was a steal."

His eyes are pained, tired. Alex sits next to him, gives him a gentle pat on the cheek. Then she examines the defibrillator. It has a battery pack and an AC cord. The back opens up, and Alex pulls out the battery. Since it isn't plugged in, the unit goes dead. She flips one of the switches to manual override, then presses the big green button with a hotel pen and squeezes on enough superglue for it to stay in the on position. Theoretically, once she plugs it into the wall, it will shock Alan. And will probably keep shocking him, over and over.

The outlet timer has settings that are pretty self-explanatory. It's made to turn on lights, or a coffee machine, or anything plugged into it, at a preset hour. Alex programs in the current time.

"How long should we give Jack to save you? Let's make this one exciting. She's probably in Wisconsin, but she'll assume you're still in Iowa, which gives her an advantage. It took me three hours to get here, but I was stopped by the police. Let's give her two."

Alex sets the gadget, allowing for extra time to run some necessary errands. When she calls Jack, the lieutenant will have 120 minutes before Alan gets a jump start.

She tapes an extra cell phone to the wall, switches on the camera, and checks her laptop to make sure the live feed is working. Then she uses her main cell phone to snap a picture of Alan. He looks suitably pathetic.

She gathers up her things, then plugs in the outlet timer and defibrillator.

"Thanks for the sex," she tells Alan. "For what it's worth, I won't mind too much if Jack saves your life. And if you do live, I wouldn't worry about the scars. I think they'll heal up nicely."

Before she leaves, Alex takes thirty seconds to jerry-rig the door latch. It's a standard privacy lock; on the door, at eye level, is a brass knob on a plate. It fits into a U-shaped bar, which is attached to the jamb. When the bar is swung over the knob, the knob slides into the groove, preventing the door from being opened more than an inch or two.

Alex twists a screw eye into the door just behind the brass plate. She feeds the floss through the eyelet and ties it to the U-bar. She plays out a few feet of floss—enough to open the door—and leaves the room, shutting the door behind her. The floss is still in her hand, caught between the door and the jamb. Alex pulls the floss, taking up the slack until she hears a soft clink: the sound of the U-bar swinging over the knob.

She uses the key card, tries to open the door. The latch prevents it. Alex tugs on the floss, snapping it off at the knot, and then closes the door.

The lock isn't really an effective deterrent, and won't stop a determined criminal, or in this case a determined cop. But it will stop a maid.

Alex takes the Do Not Disturb sign off the knob, places it on a room across the hall, and heads down to her new Prius to do some hotel hopping.

CHAPTER 37

"SQUEEZE IT," I told Phin. "But be soft and gentle."

He looked up and grinned at me. "You're turning me on talking like that."

"Focus on the target, not me. And squeeze the trigger until you feel it break."

"It's going to break?"

"That's what it's called when the trigger gives. The .377 is going to kick, hard, and sound like you stuck your head in a thundercloud. But don't hesitate with the second shot. Relax and fire another round as fast as you can."

Phin was in a sniping position, on his belly, legs splayed out behind him, the big H-S Precision rifle resting on a tree stump. We were in a fallow field, a few miles west of I-94. Phin had taken a dirt road to get here, and there wasn't another soul as far as the eye could see.

We'd spent twenty minutes attaching our scopes, configuring the crosshairs. Now we needed to zero them out, a task that had to be individually configured for each shooter. I'd already zeroed out my scope to about two hundred yards, and put four rounds into a target the size of a grape.

Phin had no experience with long arms. I set up his target—a Realtor's For Sale sign we'd liberated from the front of an old farmhouse—thirty yards away, its iron legs stuck in the dirt.

"Aim for the letter *O*." I'd shot through the *E*. "Line it up and squeeze. And do it after you exhale."

"Who taught you how to shoot?"

"My mother."

"My mom taught me how to make fried chicken."

"Focus. Soft and gentle."

"Soft and gentle." Phin blew out a breath, pulled the trigger.

The rifle crack was loud enough to scare crows two counties over. The target twitched back, then righted itself.

"Again!" I yelled over the ringing in my ears.

He pulled back the bolt, ejected the brass, and pushed another round into the chamber. Then he fired again, but Phin did what every newbie did when anticipating the sound and recoil: He flinched and jerked the trigger, missing the target completely.

Without prompting he loaded the final round from the internal magazine, aimed, and fired more carefully, getting another hit. I waited for him to eject the round, told him to leave the breach open, and went to check his target.

The two bullets that struck were an inch lower than the *E*, and slightly to the right. I'd given Phin a penny and instructed him to turn the scope's vertical and horizontal screws in the proper directions to adjust the crosshairs. He loaded three more rounds, rested the gun on the stump, and fired again.

This time the bullets all hit the *E*. I marched the sign back another fifty yards, wet dirt clinging to my new shoes, then got clear and yelled at him to try again. Phin put another three into the sign, faster this time. Only one hit the sign. He'd probably turned one of the screws too far.

My phone rang before I had a chance to tell him. I fished it out of my pocket, my mind blanking when I saw who the call was from.

555-5555.

Alex.

The text message came first.

THIS IS ALAN. HE'S YOUR HUSBAND.

Oh God. Oh no. She was lying. She had to be.

Please, be lying.

Then the picture. Alan, tied to a bed. His bare stomach sliced up, the blood dry, but the cuts on it forming unmistakable words:

TILL DEATH DO US PART

My legs stopped supporting me and I fell onto my ass. I kept staring at Alan—poor Alan—and thinking about that last awful argument I'd had with him. It was my fault he'd been grabbed by the monster. My fault he was in this mess. The very thing he'd been preaching at me all these years had come true.

Another text came. I opened it, trembling hands barely able to hold on to the phone.

HE DIES IN TWO HOURS.

Two? That wasn't right. That had to be a mistake. Alan lived in Iowa. A three-hour drive from here. Alex wasn't playing fair.

"That's not fair," I said, but it didn't sound like me. "Two hours isn't enough time. It's not fair."

"Jack?" Phin was standing over me, breathing hard, his hand on my head.

"Not fair."

"What's not fair?" He took the phone from me.

"I can't save him in two hours. It's not enough time."

Phin looked at the text, pressed a few buttons. I stared beyond him, past the For Sale sign, past the field, to the horizon—that faint line where the brown earth met the gray sky, the great divider between heaven and earth. Except that there was no heaven. No hell either. But there didn't need to be.

We were already in hell.

I had no spirituality. The little I was born with vacated the first time I saw a dead child, my second week on the Job. But I always had my morality. Always had my altruism. I was destined to be a Girl Scout, for-ever helping people cross the street, gaining whatever satisfaction I could from the meager act.

But my efforts weren't meager. They were worthless. Completely fucking worthless.

Life had no meaning. It had no point. I'd chosen a career to do good. To prevent cruelty, and death, and suffering. To right wrongs. To fight for something important.

But nothing I did mattered. I didn't change anything. And I'd brought upon myself the very things I'd tried to prevent.

There are no heroes. There are only losers.

"We have to go." Phin grabbed me under my armpit, pulled me to my feet. "Where does he live?"

"We can't make it."

"We can try."

What was Phin's problem? Didn't he know it was useless? Alex will just keep on doing this, over and over. And if not Alex, someone else will. You can't fight darkness. Darkness comes. You can turn on some lights, lie to yourself that it will all be okay. But it never is.

"Goddamn it, Jack. You can have your breakdown when we're in the car. Move your ass."

"I've been lying to myself," I whispered.

"No shit. You've been lying to yourself for your entire career. But this is a piss-poor moment to stop lying."

His words settled in, gave me something to latch on to. Because he was right. Being hopeless had never stopped me before.

Maybe I couldn't prevent tragedy. Maybe I couldn't make a differ-ence. Horrible things would keep happening, that was a guarantee, and maybe I'd never be able to stop them.

But I still had to try.

"Okay," I said, forcing my voice to be strong. "Let's save him."

I sprinted for the truck, the moist earth sucking at my shoes. Tripped.

Slid on my knees, banging into a rock. Scrambled on all fours until I was up and running again.

I beat Phin to the Bronco, wondering where he was, and then he was in the driver's seat and starting the engine.

"Do you know where we're going?"

"Iowa. I've got a GPS thing on my phone."

All four tires kicked up mud, and we headed west.

CHAPTER 38

ALEX HEADS EAST, wondering if she'll pass Jack on the road somewhere. It's an amusing thought. Two mortal enemies, their cars zipping by at high speed, perhaps even going too fast to recognize each other. Alex considers pulling over, waiting on the side of the road, shooting out her adversary's tires so they can have their final showdown.

No, it's best to wait. Now isn't the right time. Let Jack lose a few more people she cares about first.

Alex doesn't believe in destiny. Fate is a future you didn't try hard enough to change. If you want things to go your way, being smart and being strong are helpful, but you still have to work your ass off. Ways and means plus determination.

Jack is smart and strong and determined. She's also lucky. But she keeps making a key mistake. The same mistake that loses ball games, and fights, and wars. Jack is reacting rather than acting. And as long as she keeps doing that, she's not going to change fate.

Alex pulls off the highway to grab something to eat, and after a greasy fast-food meal that will probably go straight to her hips if she doesn't schedule a workout later, she wanders into a chain store and picks up a few supplies. Focusing on the next victim. Staying one step ahead of Jack. Calling the shots.

Back in the car, the Midwestern great plains blurring by on both sides mundanely, hypnotically, Alex lapses into a very old habit.

She daydreams.

"Daydreams aren't practical," Charles used to tell her. "Escaping reality is bullshit. Confront reality. Kick its ass. Make it what you want it to be."

Easier said than done, growing up with Father. A fantasy world offered a brief vacation from the horrors.

Alex never imagined she was a princess, or owned a unicorn, or any magical shit like that. Her imagination was closely tied to reality. The only difference was that in her daydreams, Alex had absolute control.

Daydreaming now, the endless miles of brown fields morphed into the farm where she grew up. She and Charles are children, and have placed a bushel basket on the hood of Father's truck, playing a makeshift game of basketball. Father comes out of the house. Normally he'd scream at them, preaching some biblical nonsense mixed with his own particular brand of paranoia, self-hatred, and psychosis. That might lead to Alex being punished, or almost as bad, Alex being forced to punish Father, wielding some of the awful implements he employed for the task.

But in the daydream, Alex is all-powerful. She prevents him from acting crazy. He stands there and watches, hands on his hips, his face neutral. Then, incredibly, he smiles, and asks to join the game.

A painfully obvious, incredibly pathetic scene. Alex knows this, but it pleases her anyway. In this insipid little fantasy, Alex has everything that was taken from her. Charles. Her face. Her childhood. In having total control, she can give up total control, and the feeling brings a real-life smile to her face.

Well, half a smile.

Which forces reality to return.

Alex then lapses into another childhood habit. When in pain, the best way to take your mind off it is to cause pain. She locates her cell phone on the passenger seat of the Prius and calls Jack.

"I hope you're close," she says. "By my watch, you've got less than a half an hour."

"Fuck you, Alex."

"That's probably what your husband is thinking about you right now. About how you fucked him by marrying him. I guess it doesn't pay to get close to you. If we were friends, I'd fear for my life."

Jack doesn't answer, but she doesn't hang up either. Maybe she's hoping Alex will give her something. Alex plans on it, but there's no rush.

"He still loves you, Jack. Did you know that? He even called out your name while we were making love. He likes it on the rough side. Ever try cutting him before? He screamed, but I think he enjoyed it."

"Is that Alex?" Phin, in the background. "Tell her to drop dead for me."

"I always liked Phin. What is it about bad boys, Jack? Not that you'd know. You like falling for wimps. Does it make you feel stronger, being with men that you can manipulate? Or does their neediness fill some maternal urge?"

"Are you going to get to the point, Alex?"

"No time for girl talk? I understand. You're on a tight schedule. Another man you love is going to die. Tough to concentrate on idle chitchat."

"I'm hanging up."

"No you're not. You'll listen for as long as I want you to, hoping for a precious clue. Well, here it is, Lieutenant. I'm sure you're heading to Iowa now, but you probably don't know where I've got your husband stashed. There are a few dozen hotels in Dubuque, and trust me, I've made it hard for you. So if you need a little hint, ask Jim Hardy. And here's some good advice, woman to woman. If you find Alan, and he's all lit up like a Christmas tree, keep your hands to yourself."

Alex hangs up, pleased. The hint is obscure—a lot harder than the "Stairway to Heaven" clue. But it's just cute enough that when Jack figures it out, she'll kick herself.

Having enemies is so much fun.

Alex pulls off the main highway, into the nearest town, looking for a coffee shop, bookstore, or Internet café. Something with WiFi access.

The next show is about to start.

CHAPTER 39

A S SOON AS I GOT off the phone with Alex I called Harry.
"How are you doing with Alan's credit cards?"

Phin, talking about his past while we were in the motel, reminded me that the easiest way to find someone is to track their
latest credit card purchases. If Alan listened to my warning and
checked into a hotel, he probably made the reservation using a card.
Harry, given the nature of his business, had sources with all the big
banks.

"It's not good, sis. Ah, Christ!"

"What? What is it?"

"Slappy just puked beer all over the place. He can puke farther than
he can piss. This is even messier than a brass clown. Good fucking suggestion, Phin."

"Focus, McGlade! Can you get his usage history?"

"I've got his complete history. But Alex must have known we'd do
this. I've got hotel charges for eight hotels in Dubuque, Iowa, all made
within the last twenty-four hours. She must have made the reservations
using his card."

Shit.

"Can't you tell which one came first? Or which is the most active?
Maybe he had room service, or watched a movie."

"Negativo. All I've got are pings, not actual charges. Billing doesn't happen until hours, sometimes days, after a card gets authorized. That's why it doesn't appear on your statement right away."

"Give them to me."

Harry read the list. I wrote the names and addresses down on the back of the donut bag.

"How far are we?" I asked Phin.

He had the accelerator pinned, and we were flying so fast that even seat belts and air bags wouldn't save our lives if he made a mistake.

"Ten minutes from Dubuque. What's the destination?"

Alan had eight minutes left. "We don't know yet."

"We're going to hit traffic when we reach the city. There will only be time to try one hotel."

"How about Jim Hardy?" I asked Harry. "Anything?"

"The main Google hits are for a pro golfer, an old-time newspaper comic, an NFL quarterback from the fifties. But the golfer gets the most."

"Those eight hotels. Do any of them have a golf course nearby?"

"I can check. Aw, Jesus!" Harry made a gagging noise. "Right in the mouth! Do I gotta buy a goddamn hockey mask to protect myself from flying monkey dung?"

My call waiting beeped. Tom Mankowski. "Call me back," I said, and clicked over to Tom. "Please give me some good news."

"The Dubuque cops are calling all the hotels, searching for an Alan Daniels, and so far they've found six reservations."

"Any check-ins?"

"All six. They're sending out teams, but they're not a big department. The town only has sixty thousand people in it, and there was some big shoot-out at a department store, so they can't spare many men."

"How about Jim Hardy?"

"I've been poring through Alex's files. So far, nothing. Lieut . . . there's something else you need to know."

"Spill it, Detective."

"The Feds have a warrant. Dubuque PD was ordered to arrest you on sight. They believe you're harboring a fugitive. Are you?"

"He's a bank robber. You want to talk to him?"

"Tell him I said hi," Phin said.

"Be careful, Lieutenant. I'll call when I hear something."

I hung up. Phin tapped the brakes, causing me to lurch forward in my seat.

"Exit, Jack. We have to make a decision."

I stared at the list of hotels. We had a one in six chance of picking the right one. And even if we did pick correctly, we might not make it in time. I hated these odds, almost as much as I hated my job, my life, myself. And Alex. God, did I hate Alex. For what she did to Latham, and now to Alan. Harry figured out from the picture that she'd hooked him up to a defibrillator. Which explained her "light him up like a Christmas tree" comment.

Or did it?

Alan wouldn't actually light up. He'd be electrocuted. She could have easily made a snide comment about him being shocked, or fried, or something to do with his heart. Why'd she mention Christmas?

I redialed Harry.

"Google *Jim Hardy* plus *Christmas*."

"Hold on, I'm brushing my teeth."

"Now, McGlade!"

"Fine! Aw, God. There are chunks of monkey chow on my keyboard. It smells awful. I'm starting to think this pet thing wasn't a good idea."

"Harry!"

"Okay! Jeez! First hit is . . . *Holiday Inn*. How about that? Jim Hardy is the character Bing Crosby played, sang 'White Christmas' in it. Slappy, no! One beer is enough!"

"Holiday Inn," I told Phin, squinting at the directions on my GPS-enabled cell phone.

Phin gave me a quick sideways glance.

"I thought you weren't supposed to use your cell. Feds could track it."

"No choice. Turn on Fourth Street, right on Main."

I called 911, told them there was a murder being committed at the hotel, just as we pulled into the parking lot, squealing tires.

"The cops know about you," I said to Phin. "You should stay in the car."

"Like hell."

We both got out and ran for the lobby.

"Alan Daniels," I yelled at the front desk, flashing my badge. "What room number?"

Wrong approach. The girl was flustered, scared, and kept screwing up her typing. Finally, after an eternity, she said, "Room 212."

We stormed up the stairs, less than two minutes to spare, and found Alan's room, a Do Not Disturb sign hanging from the lock. Phin unleashed a vicious kick. The door was strong, and held firm. But it couldn't hold up against three shots from a forty-caliber Beretta.

"Alan!" I cried, barreling into the room, eyes and gun swinging over to the bed.

Empty. The room was empty. The bed was empty. Sitting on top of the sheets was one of those tiny bottles of liquor from the hotel minibar.

A bottle of Jack Daniels.

I thought of Alan, of our wedding day, our vows to love, honor, and protect.

"Alex was here," I said. "Alan is still at the hotel. He has to be close. Check all the doors on this floor with Do Not Disturb signs on them. She wouldn't want the maid coming in."

In the hall Phin went left, I went right. I found a door with the sign, banged on it, got an annoyed response from inside. Not Alan. Moved farther down the hall, but there were no other signs.

Gunshots. Phin, bursting through a door.

I ran to him, praying to a God I didn't believe in.

Another empty room.

Think, Jack, think. Alex brought him somewhere. It had to be close, had to be on this floor, because she took him with force, dragging him or pointing a gun at him, not wanting to be seen, not wanting the maid to find him . . .

The maid.

I picked up the room phone, punched the button for Housekeeping.

"'Allo?"

A woman, foreign.

"Listen very carefully," I said. "I'm a police officer. I want to know what rooms on the second floor haven't been cleaned yet."

"I dunno. I ask Maria. She do second floor."

And she put me on hold. I felt like screaming. According to my watch, we were already a minute late.

"This is Maria."

"What rooms weren't cleaned on the second floor?"

"Lemme see. Room 212, I think. Room 203. And room 208. I knocked, no answer, but they had lock on."

"Two oh eight," I said to Phin, and we were flying out the door.

Found the room.

I shot the lock.

He put his shoulder to it, and then we were inside.

Alan was taped to the bed, jerking and twitching, eyes rolled up in his head, a terrifying buzzing noise filling the room. I launched myself at him, reaching for the pads on his chest, and as soon as I touched him my arms locked up and pain flared through my body, like being dropped in scalding oil, so hot I felt it in my muscles and bones. I couldn't let go. I couldn't move. I would have screamed, but my throat slammed shut.

Then I was on the floor, Phin's arm around my waist. I gasped for air, managed to get some in, while Phin tugged at an electrical cord plugged into the wall. I crawled back up to Alan, pulled those horrible pads from his chest, pulled up burned skin from where they were attached.

Touched the raw flesh, feeling his heart.

Nothing. No beat.

Hands shaking, I tore at his tape gag, trying not to look at his eyes, his dead eyes, wide open in agony and showing only the whites.

Put my ear to his mouth.

No breath. He wasn't breathing.

CPR. He needed CPR. I put my lips to his—when was the last time I kissed him?—then pulled away in horror.

He tasted . . . *cooked.*

I did it again, not hesitating, pinching his nose, blowing life into his lungs.

There was a wet, rumbling sound, and then brown blood frothed out of his mouth.

I straddled him, put my hands on his chest, began doing compressions.

Blood foamed out of his nose. Out of the corners of his eyes.

"Jack . . ."

Phin, touching my shoulder.

"The defibrillator," I said. "We can shock him again. Get his heart started."

Phin gave me a gentle tug. I shoved his hands away, went back to heart compressions.

"Jack, he's lost too much blood."

"Give me the goddamn defibrillator!"

Phin wrapped his arms around me, pulled me off Alan. I brought my heel down on his instep and he released me, then I spun around and punched him in the jaw, staggering him back. I scanned the floor for the defibrillator, found it, saw the button was glued down. No matter. I could put the pads on, plug it back in, it should work.

It had to work.

I picked up the pads, shakily placed them on Alan's chest, and then noticed that the mattress was soaked in blood.

Too much blood. Much too much.

I gasped, brought a hand to my mouth. Then I placed my palm on his chest, pressed down. More blood sluiced out from under him, between his legs.

"No. Oh no no no no . . ."

Phin put his arms around me again. I heard sirens in the distance.

"We should go, Jack."

I reached for Alan's face, touched his cheek. Then I used two fingers to close his tortured eyes.

"I'm sorry. I'm so sorry . . ."

The sirens got louder. Phin half pulled/half carried me away from the bed, past the bathroom, where I noticed something out of the corner of my eye. A person, hiding under the sink.

Alex.

I shoved Phin back, reaching for the gun in my belt. Except I didn't have a gun in my belt. It had somehow gotten in Phin's belt. I yanked it free, aimed, and fired three times as fast as I could pull the trigger.

Alex didn't move.

Phin wrestled the gun away from me. I let him, reaching for the bathroom light.

Blood, everywhere. From the woman on the ground. A woman who had a knife stuck in her chest, and who definitely wasn't Alex.

I crumpled to the floor. Again Phin supported me, holding me around my back with his hand under my armpit, maneuvering me down the hallway, to the stairwell, down the stairs, through the lobby, into the parking lot, while tears streaked down my face.

By the time I was in the truck I was wailing louder than the police cars that were surrounding us.

CHAPTER 40

NOW *THAT* WAS GREAT. The only thing missing was sound. It would have been wonderful to hear Jack's cries of anguish, Alan's muffled screams, the zap of electricity. But then, the other patrons in the coffee shop might have complained.

Alex closes her laptop, then closes her eyes, reliving the scene in her head. Her favorite part had to be when Jack began CPR, not knowing that each time she pressed Alan's chest, blood squirted out his ass. When she socked Phin—that was priceless too. The girl can hit hard. Jack was too self-absorbed to see Phin probe the inside of his mouth, pull out a tooth.

Yes, it worked much better than Alex could have hoped.

Now to concentrate on the next victim, the next phase of the plan.

Alex finishes her coffee, then gets back on the road. An hour later, she's standing on the street corner in Chicago, hood up, sunglasses on, hands jammed into her pockets.

Winter will be here soon. Alex won't miss it. Growing up in the Midwest, she has long outlived her fondness for snow and ice.

It will be so nice to go someplace where the only ice comes in drinks.

She stands there for twenty minutes before hearing a rumbling, up the street. Alex checks her watch as the truck passes by. Right on time. The first time she saw it, two weeks ago, was pure luck. Seeing it twice, same place, same time, isn't luck. It's a pattern.

It motors past, turning where it did before, and Alex jams her hands back into her pockets and heads for her car, parked in an alley a block away. She climbs in and heads north.

Ninety minutes later she's back in her hotel room in Milwaukee, using the Internet to instruct her in the finer points of using cell phones as radio transmitters. Then she calls Samantha to plan their date.

"Is your neighbor going to babysit?"

"She said sure. Do you have a car?"

Alex considers the Prius, the dead yuppie still in the backseat.

"No. Do you?"

"Sure. Want me to pick you up at your place?"

Alex isn't keen on letting Sam know where she's staying.

"I'm already downtown. Why don't we meet at a mall? Isn't there one called Bayshore?"

"Yeah. I'll meet you at J. Jill. Great store. You'll love it. When?"

"An hour?"

"Excellent!"

"Quick question. Have you ever done a bachelor party?"

"You mean like go to the guy's house, give them lap dances, pick up twenties out of the groom's mouth with my hoo-ha?"

"Yeah, like that."

"Once. Didn't pay too well, and the guys were assholes."

"Did you do it outlaw, no agency?"

"No, I went through a local place, called Laugh-O-Grams. They also send birthday party clowns and stuff. You thinking of trying that?"

"Just keeping my options open. Looking forward to seeing you."

And Alex is. Men are fine, but women have their own particular flavor, and in many ways are more fun. Alex can't wait to get into Samantha's pants. It will be the perfect end to a perfect day.

CHAPTER 41

"JACK! PUT ON YOUR DAMN SEAT BELT!"

The Bronco jumped a curb, clipped a mailbox, and then fishtailed back onto the street. We had three or four squad cars behind us, sirens blaring, hot pursuit. I had a bump on my forehead from whacking it against the dashboard. Not what I'd been hoping for. I wanted to get thrown through the front windshield and splattered on the pavement. Let it end already.

Phin reached over, his hand seeking my seat belt. Not the easiest thing to do while cruising fifty miles an hour down a heavily populated side street. I shoved his arm away. We were in a residential area, single-family homes with carefully manicured front lawns. A place where you'd get married and settle down.

Something I'd fucked up twice.

He stopped trying to save my life and instead fiddled with his police band. I caught the word *Staties*.

"They're calling in the state cops. We're screwed."

I didn't care. Getting arrested was the least of my worries.

"Come on, Jack. Give me a suggestion here."

"Ditch the car."

He made an aggressive lane change, my shoulder bouncing off the passenger door.

"And try to make it on foot? We have to lose them first."

"You can't lose them. Air support is next. They'll plot your route, take out your tires, follow you until you run out of gas. It's over."

"I say when it's over."

Typical macho bullshit. I wasn't surprised. But then Phin did do something that surprised me. He tapped the brakes, jerked the wheel, and cut across someone's driveway, the four-wheel drive digging trenches in the sod.

I flinched when we hit the backyard fence, popping onto someone else's property. We bounced across their front lawn, back onto the street, and then Phin did the same thing all over again.

"You're going to kill someone." I was clinging to the armrest.

We narrowly missed a swing set, Phin overcompensated, and we spun out, crunching through a doghouse that I sincerely hoped was empty. Phin hit the gas, the Bronco lurched forward, and we tore through another backyard, down an embankment, and into a cornfield. This was feed corn, beige and dry and standing over ten feet tall. Rows, acres, miles, an endless ocean.

Driving through it was agonizing, because we couldn't see any farther than the hood. At any moment it could have ended and we'd be in the middle of the street. Or in a school playground during recess.

Phin didn't let up. He pushed the accelerator, ears and husks banging against the windshield with a rhythmic *thump-thump-thump-thump-thump*. First came some stress fissures. Then bigger cracks. Then the glass became one giant spiderweb, impossible to see through.

Phin kept the engine gunned.

"Okay. That's enough."

Thump-thump-thump-thump-thump.

"Phin—" I warned.

He ignored me, his fate determined, his jaw set.

"Goddamn it, Phin!"

He swerved hard, knocking me into him, the truck doing a 180, 360, 720, before stalling to a stop.

"Finally start caring again?" he asked.

I pushed myself off him.

"Asshole."

Phin shifted in his seat, frowning at me. "I'm the asshole? You're the one who wanted to give up."

I turned on him, teeth bared, filling with rage.

"You've already given up. You aren't living. You're just existing. You don't care about anything."

"Keep telling yourself that, Jack. That I'm here with you because I don't care about anything."

Sure, he was here for me. And I just threw my career away to protect him. I didn't see him kissing my ass for that.

"You've got it easy," I said, low and mean. "Some of us have to deal with the consequences of our actions. Maybe I should just drop out of society. Start robbing banks. What's the current street price of coke, Phin? We can get stoned out of our minds and go knock over a liquor store. The hell with tomorrow, right?"

Phin went very cold. "I hurt," he said evenly.

"Welcome to the club."

"I physically hurt, Jack. It's like someone is stabbing me in the side. All day. Every day. The cocaine helps."

"I bet it does."

"You want to compare losing some loved ones to dying of cancer?"

"How would you know? You don't love anyone."

"You're wrong. I love—"

"Don't fucking say it," I warned. "Don't you dare fucking say it."

He stared at me, hard, then slowly nodded. "I get it."

I wanted to hit him. "You don't get shit. You think I'm afraid to get close to you because I'm afraid I'll lose you? Get over yourself. I don't want to get involved with a drug-sniffing loser."

"Then maybe you should stop calling me when you need help."

I was done with this conversation. I grabbed my stuff and got out of the damn truck. I was ten yards into the corn before remembering I left my rifle behind. Screw it. Let Phin keep the damn rifles. He could rob an old folks' home, or sell them for cocaine.

Noise, from behind. I increased my pace.

Then a tug on my arm.

I whipped around, jammed my palm into his chest. Phin staggered backward.

"The lady doesn't want to be touched," I said, teeth clenched.

"The lady is acting like an asshole. You're the only one in the world that hurts, is that it, Jack? And feeling sorry for yourself is the only way you can cope?"

"You don't seem to be coping too well either."

"I take it day by day. That's all anyone can do."

Day by day? What total crap.

"You're one sorry SOB, you know that, Phin? You told me the sex wasn't a mistake. You were wrong. It was a mistake. The latest in a long line of mistakes I've made. I'm through."

"What about Alex? She wins?"

"You're the big macho stud. You can handle her. I think you guys would make a really cute couple."

I turned, and appropriate for my environment, stalked away. Phin made the mistake of grabbing my arm again.

I spun, whipping around my right leg, aiming to knock his sanctimonious head off. But he anticipated the move, already had his arm up over his head, and caught my foot in his armpit.

And then he made the biggest mistake of his life. He dropped my leg, took a quick step forward, and slapped me in the face.

Slapped me. Open-handed.

I felt my face go red, and not just the cheek he smacked. The hitting I didn't mind. Hitting me meant he thought of me as an equal, that he could defend himself appropriately. But the fact that he actually pulled his punch—took it easy on me because I was a woman—that was infuriating. He didn't think we were fighting. He thought he was *handling* some hysterical little girl.

That showed no respect for me at all. And I slept with this guy?

"Not smart," I said. I dropped my gear.

"I'm sorry." He put his hands up and backpedaled. "Did I hurt you?"

Apparently, he wanted to make it even worse. A breeze blew through the corn, making a peaceful, rustling sound. The sense of tranquility was shattered when I clenched my fists so tight we both heard my knuckles pop.

"If you want to hit me back, that's fair."

Jesus, he was just digging his own grave. Phin was lean, muscular, and had a few inches and maybe forty pounds on me. He could fight. I'd seen it. But I was a black belt, and I was beating up kids bigger than me while he was still in diapers.

I moved in with two quick steps, feinted left, then hit him with a left-right combo to the body. Phin brought up his fists, taking the shots on his shoulders. I jerked forward, head butting him between his arms, connecting with his jaw.

Phin kept his footing, but he was unsteady. I got a leg behind his and pushed, flipping him over my hip. He went down, hard, and I dropped a knee on his chest, fist poised to slam into his naked throat. A killing blow.

Instead, I opened my hand and slapped him across the mouth.

"You're not worth a punch either," I said.

He stared at me, stunned. I got up, grabbed my stuff, and stormed off.

"You're mad because I slapped you and didn't punch you?" he called after me. "You're out of your goddamn mind!"

I didn't dignify that with an answer. The more corn I got between us, the better off I was.

"Dammit, Jack! I didn't punch you because I love you!"

I thought about yelling something back, but decided against it. I wanted the last words I ever said to Phineas Troutt to be the ones I'd already spoken. That's all he deserved.

But even though he was out of my life, permanently, I had to begrudgingly thank him. Because of Phin, I was back to being angry.

Alex was going to suffer for what she did. I would make sure of it.

CHAPTER 42

"OH MY GOD!" Samantha squeals. "Those boots are to die for!"

They're bright shiny red, just like Superman wears, except these have stiletto heels and red fringe around the top. Might as well write *I'm a stripper* across the tops.

"And they're only eighty bucks! I'm soooo buying these!"

"I think I'll get a pair too," Alex says, battling her reluctance and picking one up. She checks the insole. *Fabrique by Enrique Perez.* A nobody, with zero fashion sense.

"You'll look totally hot in those, Gracie."

Was Sammy just being friendly? Or flirting? "Thanks. So will you."

"I know I'm in shape, but I don't have definition like you do. You can see your leg muscles through your pants."

Sammy runs a finger along Alex's thigh. This is definitely flirting.

"I work out a lot."

"I knew you did. Pilates?"

Alex pictures her martial arts kata, kicking and striking to break imaginary boards and bones.

"Something like that," she answers.

"I've tried them all. Jazz-Kwon-Do. Swimmerobics. Tramp-O-Chi— that's tai chi on a trampoline, not with tramps, which would be gross. The local gym has a Spankercize class, but I don't think I want my personal trainer whacking my ass."

"Might be fun."

"Depends on the spanker," Sam says, winking.

The clerk comes by, and they request two pairs of Enrique's finest, in the same size. This naturally provokes a squeal of delight from Sam. How nice it must be to get excited over such trivial things. Half an hour ago, she practically died of pleasure because the mall sound system played a Muzak version of Nirvana.

"So where to next? We hit all boutiques in the mall. There's a Boston Store. I think they have a sale going on."

"I'm starving," Alex says. "How about food?"

"I know this groovy little Thai place. They've got this green curry to die for. I love spicy foods. They make me hot."

Alex smiles her half smile. "Then we have to try it. Can you drive?"

"Sure!"

Sam takes Alex's arm, and they walk out of the mall, Sam yapping and giggling, Alex genuinely amused by this woman's spirit and enthusiasm. The enthusiasm is dampened somewhat when they get to Sam's car.

A Prius.

"It gets sixty miles per gallon. It's so green. I'm all about the planet. People are destroying the earth. We all need to conserve, or there won't be enough left for everyone."

"Or we could just kill a lot of people."

Sam raises an eyebrow at Alex, then begins to laugh.

"God, you're so funny! I thought you were serious!"

Alex lets out a few chuckles, hoping they don't sound as forced as they feel. When they're in the car, Alex touches Sam's arm.

"Samantha, I'm having a good time, and I don't want to be reading you wrong. But you do like girls, right?"

"You mean sexually?"

Alex nods.

"Sure! I'm totally bi. I mean, guys are great, but most of them are really impatient, you know what I mean? Women know how to take their time. Don't you think?"

Alex nods, but the truth is, she's feeling pretty impatient right now too.

After dinner, she tells herself.

They hold hands as Sam pulls out of the parking lot.

CHAPTER 43

A FTER THREE HOURS of sitting next to a cornfield, hiding every time a police car cruised by, I was almost grateful when the Crime-bago pulled up.

Almost.

Harry parked alongside the street, and I entered cautiously, wincing at the noxious odor when I stepped inside. It smelled like Mighty Joe Young had run a marathon and then taken a bath in his own feces.

McGlade was standing next to the sofa, arms folded, frowning. I noticed Slappy's cage was empty.

"Did you get rid of the macaque?" I asked, hopeful.

"No. He kept screaming and hitting himself in the face, so I let him out until he calmed down. Not my brightest idea."

"Where is he?" I asked, casting nervous rapid-fire glances around the RV.

"In the corner there. He learned a new trick."

Slappy was propped against the wall, upside-down with his legs over his head. He was urinating, again, but this time he managed to catch most of it in his open mouth.

"That is one of the most disgusting things I've ever seen."

"It gets worse," McGlade said. "When he's all done, he tries to spit it on you."

Slappy began to make a gargling sound. For the first time ever, my cat Mr. Friskers didn't seem so bad.

"Did you call Al's Exotic Pets?"

"Al said all sales are final. Can't really blame him."

"Would he trade for anything else? Like maybe some feeder minnows? Or a chew toy?"

"No. But he offered to euthanize Slappy for fifty bucks." Slappy puffed out his cheeks and spit a stream of urine toward us. We jumped away. "I'm thinking about it."

"Don't you dare, Harry. You just need to take some time and train him."

"I tried. I don't think he likes me."

"What's not to like?" I did my best to say it without sounding sarcastic.

"He might be mad because of the stick. When he was in his cage, I kept showing him a picture of Alex, and then poking him with a stick. You know, so if he ever saw her, he'd attack. But he seems to be holding a grudge. See?"

Harry took a step toward his monkey. Slappy opened his mouth, baring yellow fangs, snarling like a pit bull.

"Maybe you should stop poking him with the stick," I said.

"No shit."

Keeping one eye on the primate, I walked to the sofa and sat down. I stood up again immediately, my butt damp.

"There's something wet on your couch."

Harry nodded. "Do yourself a favor and don't try to smell it. It's better to lie to yourself and pretend it's ginger ale."

"Did you spill ginger ale?"

"No. That's piss, shit, or monkey spooge."

I made a face.

"Might also be some combination of the three," Harry added. "Or vomit. Could be vomit."

I let out a slow breath and wondered how I'd get the ginger ale stain out.

Slappy made a screeching sound that eerily resembled laughter. He was still upside-down, but was no longer going to the bathroom. Instead, he was abusing himself with his little monkey fist, eyes locked on mine. The expression on his face was one of smug satisfaction.

"Al told me that macaques can live for thirty years," Harry said.

I actually felt a little sorry for him. I moved cautiously over to the computer, checked the chair for unpleasant surprises, then sat down.

"Did you find the latest cell phone?"

McGlade nodded. "It's in Milwaukee. Where's Phin?"

I felt myself go cold. "Phin won't be helping us anymore."

"How'd you scare him off? Did he see you naked?"

"I didn't scare him off. And fuck you."

"We need him."

"We don't need him. He's unreliable."

"Hasn't he saved your life a bunch of times?"

"He's a drug addict."

"You just figured that out now? Of course he's a drug addict. He's dying of cancer. If I had the big C I'd be snorting so much cocaine I'd need two crack whores to help me hold the heroin needle steady."

"There are prescription drugs."

"We're chasing a killer. You want him stoned on opiates? At least with coke he'll be alert."

"We'll be fine without him."

"Sure. Slappy can watch our backs. Right Slappy?"

We looked at Slappy, but he wasn't in the corner anymore. He was gone.

"Uh-oh," McGlade said. He grabbed something off the kitchen sink and tossed it to me. A Ping-Pong paddle. He also brandished one in his good hand.

"I'm not going to spank your monkey, McGlade."

"I hope not, sis. That's gross."

"You know what I mean."

"This is purely defensive, if he tries to—"

Something flew across my line of sight, and McGlade brought the paddle up to his face. A clump of monkey dung splattered onto it.

I quickly stood up and looked around the room, raising the paddle up over my mouth. About the only thing that could make my life worse was a faceful of Slappy crap, and I wasn't about to let that happen.

"Where is he?" I said, justifiably paranoid. "I don't see him."

"We should get back to back," Harry said. "Then he can't sneak up on us."

I nodded, backing into Harry, my eyes scanning the RV for any movement.

"Let's go up to the cab. We can close the door so he can't get us."

"Good call."

We walked cautiously over to the front of the Crimebago, my senses hyper-alert, like I was in a gunfight. I felt things squish underfoot but was afraid to look down and see what they were.

We were only two feet away from the cab when the monkey jumped off the refrigerator and leaped at me, howling, fangs bared and eyes wild. He caught my paddle, and his teeth latched on to my knuckle. I shook him free and then ran, with Harry, into the front of the RV and slammed the door behind me.

"Your monkey bit me!"

"Yeah, he does that."

Harry settled into the driver's seat. I stared at the blood running down my finger.

"Jesus, McGlade! Should I get this looked at?"

He shrugged. "I would. I can't even remember all the disgusting things he put in his mouth today. Plus, he probably has all sorts of monkey diseases." He started the engine. "Maybe you should just cut the finger off, before the germs get into your bloodstream."

I used my sweatshirt to swab away some of the blood.

"Do you have a first aid kit?"

"It's in the back."

We both stared at the closed door. Scary monkey sounds came from behind it.

"Want to use my gun?" Harry asked.

I declined, instead using some tissues from the glove compartment and half a bottle of water that was in the cup holder.

"I know what will make you feel better," Harry said.

He pressed a button on the dashboard, and the RV filled with Pink Floyd.

Amazingly, the screeching and pounding stopped.

"I guess Slappy is a fan of seventies psychedelic rock," I said.

"That or he found my Vicodin. He got into my medicine cabinet earlier. Are those little bottles monkey-proof?"

"Probably." I had no idea.

"You want to go check?"

"Hell no."

"Well, then. We'll assume it's the Floyd. Wisconsin, ho."

Harry put the RV into gear, and we headed east.

CHAPTER 44

A LEX HAS THE WINDOW CRANKED DOWN—a temporary solution for the smell coming from the body in the backseat. She'll deal with it soon. But she has other business first.

The wind is cold, harsh, and slaps at her cheeks. She only feels its sting on her right side. Alex brings up a hand, touches the rubbery scar tissue, feels a bit of stubble. One of the skin grafts was taken from her leg, and the hairs are sharp and pointy. She thinks about shaving again—an act that humiliates her almost as much as it angers her—and decides not to.

Samantha didn't seem to mind it.

Alex smiles privately. What a wonderful evening it turned out to be. Shopping was fun, even though the boots are hideous. A terrific dinner. Then back to Sam's apartment for a drink and whatever.

They never got around to the drink.

Alex closes her eyes for a moment, and can practically feel Sam's body lying next to hers. It's so pleasant, so right, that it makes her anger fade away.

The future is looking brighter and brighter.

This is the home stretch. Soon after Chicago, Alex will leave the country. She'll be gone for a while. A year at least. Sun and fun, rest and recuperation. And then, who knows? Once everything is taken care of, the whole world will be open to Alex. It will be like starting a whole new life.

"I think I can fall in love with you, Samantha," Alex says, half of her face grinning.

She reaches Chicago an hour later, never having to stop for gas. Maybe there's something to this Prius hype after all.

The neighborhood is dark, quiet. She got the address, and the idea, from an earlier phone call. Rather than park anywhere near the house, she finds a space next to a fire hydrant, one block over.

If Alex wanted to do this quick, she could burst into the house, guns blazing, and kill her intended victim. Well, maybe it wouldn't be so quick. He's armed, has a burglar alarm, and has most assuredly been on heightened alert since Alex has gotten out. She could set the building on fire, wait to shoot him when he came running out. Or use some of Lance's ordnance to send the house into the stratosphere. But those aren't nearly as fun as what she has planned.

Giving Jack a sporting chance to prevent this murder, and watching her fail, is simpler, and more satisfying. Plus the authorities, and the media, will be focused on events here while Alex is off doing other, more important things.

She grabs her duct tape and a fresh cell phone. With some difficulty—both with the climbing and the securing—the phone gets set up in a tree across the street from the house, some dead leaves packed around it to keep it hidden. Then she brushes off the bits of tree from her outfit and heads back to the car.

After all the text messages she's sent lately, Alex is becoming pretty adept at what is an awkward skill. Maybe she's not as fast as the average schoolkid, but the six words appear on the screen quickly and easily.

THIS IS HERB. HE'S YOUR PARTNER.

CHAPTER 45

NO PHOTO THIS TIME. But the first text message was followed up by:

HE DIES TOMORROW.

I was on the phone with Herb ten seconds later.

"Herb! It's Jack. I—"

"Jack, I'm absolutely starving," he interrupted, talking louder than normal. "Why don't we meet tonight at that sushi restaurant you liked? Remember how you went crazy for the maki roll?"

"Enough with the food, Herb. Alex just called me. You're her next target."

"Let's discuss it over raw fish."

"Did you hear me? I said Alex is coming after you."

"I'll be fine. Trust me. And I insist we grab a bite together. If not sushi, how about that seafood place on Halsted?"

"Herb—"

I stopped myself. Herb never met a food he didn't like, but I'd met several, sushi being one of the biggies. He took me to a place a few years back and the maki roll made me so ill I still can't eat fish. He knew that.

"Would dinner be just us?" I asked carefully. "Or would we have some friends along?"

"I'm pretty sure the Nicholas Brothers would be there too."

Cute. The Nicholas Brothers were tap dancers. Herb also could have mentioned drinking draft beer, which was another reference to *tap*.

The Feds. They were listening in.

"Sounds nice, but I can't make it. You need—"

"We can have a few draft beers afterward," Herb said.

"I got it already, Herb. Now listen closely. The message from Alex said that you'll die tomorrow. I need you to go away for a while. No credit cards, no relatives, don't tell anyone."

"I'm pretty sure I'll be safe here. I have angels watching me."

Herb isn't good at subtle.

"Don't put your faith in angels, buddy. She's smarter than they are."

"If we have a chance to catch her by making me bait—"

"No!" I yelled it loud enough that Harry jumped in his seat.

"It's not your call, Jack. You'd do the same thing."

"Dammit, Herb—"

"I'll come out of this okay. I'm not the one you need to worry about."

"Catching Alex isn't going to protect me, Herb. You need to protect yourself and your wife. Alex . . . she killed Alan."

There was an uncomfortable silence. I shut my eyes, saw Alan's face, opened them again.

"I'm sorry, Jack. But that's all the more reason I need to do this."

"Herb, please—"

"Looking forward to that Turduckinlux. We'll deep fry that baby when this is all over."

He hung up on me. I stared at the phone.

"We could kidnap him," Harry said. "Toss him in back with Slappy."

"Bad idea."

"Why? You think he'd eat my monkey?"

"The Feds." I rubbed my temples. "His phone is being tapped by the Feds. And now that they know Alex is after him, they'll camp on his front lawn. I won't be able to get within a mile of him."

"That's a good thing. If you can't get to him, neither can Alex."

"She has to know that. She told me Herb was the target, which means she has a way to get through them."

Harry gave me a sideways glance, then narrowed his eyes.

"You didn't call Fatso on your phone, did you?"

I still had my cell in my hand. Harry made a face.

"Christ, Jackie. I told you the Feds can trace that. Have you been using that a lot?"

"No." Then I remembered the long conversations with Mom and Dad earlier. "Not much."

Harry rubbed his eyes, then extended the motion downward, massaging his jaw.

"You need to keep your head in the game, sis. The bond between siblings may be one of the strongest in nature, but those Feebie pricks pretty much guaranteed I'd do time if I help you or Phin."

I folded my arms, anger creeping up my back and perching on my shoulders.

"So don't help me, McGlade. Let me out here."

He sighed. "Sis—"

"And stop calling me *sis*. There isn't any proof we're actually related."

Harry shook his head. "You don't know that. What about the DNA test thingy?"

"The lab hasn't called. But I don't need a lab to know that I share more DNA with Slappy than I do with you. Hell, McGlade, take a good look at yourself. You actually think we could have the same genes?"

"Mom says I look like my father."

"Mom has trouble remembering to take her arthritis medication every day. You think she can remember a one-night stand from fifty years ago?"

"You're just jealous she likes me more."

"Likes you? No one can stand you, Harry. You're an obnoxious, irritating, offensive, petty little man."

"You forgot *ugly*," Harry said.

"I'll also add *dirty* to the list. Lathering yourself with aftershave is not, nor has it ever been, a substitute for a shower."

"Wow. I really suck. You must have hated all of that time we were partners."

I nodded. "I did."

"And you must really resent that I still keep popping up in your life."

More nodding. "I do."

"And you must think I'm a total idiot that I never knew any of this before."

Really enthusiastic nodding. "You got it in one."

"Except I've known it all along."

"I—" I squinted at him. "Huh?"

"Remember the Grant Park case?"

Of course I remembered the Grant Park case. An unsolved rape/ murder, gone cold. I worked it in my free time, gathering evidence for over a year, building a case, sharing my findings with Harry. He made the collar without me and got all the credit.

"I'll never forget it, McGlade. You got the promotion, when you didn't do a damn thing."

He smiled, the bastard.

"You still think it's funny that you screwed me?"

"After all these years, you still think I screwed you? No one wanted to work with you, Jackie. You weren't a team player. All you cared about was proving to the world that you were a good cop. Guess what? Every- one thought you were a single-minded, self-righteous, ball-busting bitch. They respected you. But no one liked you. You think I got a higher rank because of one lousy arrest? I got it because I passed the damn tests, had been there longer than you, and I bowled with the captain on my days off. Maybe you should have been doing the same thing, then you would have gotten promoted sooner. Hell, you might even still be married."

I made a fist, wondering where I was going to hit him first.

"You stole the credit for that bust," I said through my teeth.

"Yes. Yes I did. And it was wrong. But maybe if you'd been the least bit cool, and not constantly acting like I was something you wanted to scrape off the bottom of your shoe, maybe I wouldn't have. But here we are, two decades later, and you still treat me like shit. You know something, Jackie? I've changed. But you haven't. You're still the same holier-than-thou supercop, chasing bad guys instead of having a life. Say whatever you want about me. I like myself. Do you like yourself?"

"Stop the car."

"It's not a car. It's a Crim—"

"Stop the fucking car, McGlade!"

He put on his turn signal, then coasted onto the shoulder of the highway.

"Jackie, we're in the middle of nowhere."

I needed my backpack, but it was in the motor home section, with Slappy the Psychotic Macaque. I opened the door anyway, ready for a fight.

The monkey was sitting on the sofa, chewing on a remote control. He eyed me when I entered.

"Don't fuck with me," I warned him.

He stayed where he was, watching as I grabbed my stuff and opened the side door.

"Jackie, you have to stop pushing away the people trying to help you."

"Go to hell, McGlade."

I stepped onto the side of the road.

"Come on. This is stupid." McGlade, poking his head out. "Come back."

I spotted a road sign, stating the next exit was two miles ahead. I started to hike.

"It's cold and dark, Jackie, and there are probably wild animals. I think Wisconsin has wolves and mountain lions. And mad cow disease. At least let me drive you someplace."

I picked up my pace.

"You can't take on the whole world by yourself, Jackie!" Harry called after me. "The world always wins!"

Not this time, I swore to myself. *This time, I'm going to win one.*

But my threat, and my conviction, got lost in the darkness as McGlade pulled away.

CHAPTER 46

A NOTHER DRIVE, BUT SHORTER THIS TIME.
Staying in Chicago isn't a smart idea. By now the authorities know she's here. Killing across state lines is a federal crime, so the FBI is going to be involved. Plus, the CPD won't take threatening one of their own lightly. Everyone will be looking for her, and hers isn't a face that's easily forgotten.

But just because Alex has to be in Chicago for one final crime doesn't mean she has to stay there. So instead she gets a room in nearby Rosemont, at a second-tier hotel near the airport. She dons the black veil and pretends to be a grieving widow as she checks in, the fake sniffles and sobs giving her an excuse to keep her hand on her face, over her scars.

When Alex gets to her room she collapses onto the bed, exhausted. She thinks about her upcoming sabbatical, and how nice it will be to take a break from killing for a while. After she kills the doctor, of course.

There's still Jack to deal with. And that asshole Harry. And Phin. But the need for revenge, pressing on Alex's every thought like a full bladder, isn't quite as pressing. Jack's not dead, but she's certainly suffering.

And it's going to get a lot worse, Alex thinks. After Herb dies, she's going after Jack next.

It's kind of sad, really. Alex has been fixated on Jack for so long that having her gone will leave kind of a gap. Perhaps it's best to savor the little time they have left.

Alex kicks off her shoes, wiggles her toes, and locates the nail polish she bought earlier. She dials, then begins painting the first little piggie.

The phone is answered on the third ring, but Jack doesn't say anything.

"What, no hello?" Alex asks. "Rude. Are you still mad at me for Alan? That was hours ago."

"I'm going to find you."

Jack sounds weak.

"I know. And I'm going to make it easy for you. Tomorrow, after your partner dies, I'm going to call you and we'll set up a meeting. Just me and you, Jack. That's what you want, right? Revenge?"

No answer.

"Are you still there? If you want, I can call up Harry instead."

"I'm here."

"And you want revenge, don't you?"

"Yes." Quiet and squeaky, like a mouse.

"I'm an expert in revenge, and let me tell you something. It doesn't bring back the dead. Sure, it's fun. I'm having a great time slaughtering everyone important to you. But Charles is still dead. And even if, by some miracle, you happen to kill me, Latham will still be dead. Herb will still be dead. Alan will still be dead."

"You're the next one to die, Alex."

Alex listens to the background sounds. Wind. A car passing at a high speed. She discerns Jack is on a highway.

"What happened to Phin? Were you too much of a downer so he took off?"

"Get to the point."

"I wanted to tell you that I watched you try to save your husband. Exciting stuff. You know, you were only about thirty seconds late. If you'd been just a little faster, he'd still be with us."

Another sound joins the wind and car noises. Alex is overjoyed to hear it.

"Lieutenant Daniels, are you crying?"

The sound becomes muted. Jack has put her hand over the mouthpiece. Not only is she devastated, she's also embarrassed.

How delicious.

"He's in a better place, Jack. If he lived, he'd just be pining for you. Did you know his Internet password was *Jacqueline*? I'm not making that up. And he still had a picture of you in his wallet. Poor sap. I bet he was the type who sent you poems. Did he write you a poem, after your first time? Something about how lovely you were, fucking him in that restaurant bathroom? What rhymes with *toilet*?"

"I'm . . . I'm going to—"

"Jack, woman to woman, threats don't really work when you're crying like a baby. It's pathetic. Now, fun as this little chat has been, I'm painting my toenails and it isn't easy holding the phone at the same time. So here's the deal. When I call tomorrow, with the clue to save your partner, you'll have to react fast. You won't have twelve hours, or two hours. You'll have less than a minute. Use it wisely."

Alex hangs up, pleased with how the call went, but not pleased with the job she's done on her first few toes.

Now isn't the time to be sloppy. Alex pads over to the bathroom, dumps some acetone on a hotel towel, and wipes off the nail polish to start again.

CHAPTER 47

B Y THE TIME I found a room for the night I was a mess. Mentally, physically, emotionally. I'd walked several miles, freezing my tail off, before finding a small mom-and-pop motel with carpeting older than I was. I ate out of the lobby vending machine, not tasting a damn thing, and drew a bath in a cracked tub with water tinted orange.

I crawled in and let the guilt overtake me, crying until my throat hurt. Mixed with the guilt was shame, for not being there for Herb when he needed me most, and anger, at Phin and Harry and Alex, but most of all at myself for allowing all of this to happen.

And hate. I felt hate so dark it scared me. I didn't just want to kill Alex. I wanted to burn her alive and watch her scream. I've lived—hell, I've *dedicated* my life to upholding the law, but I would trade every arrest I'd ever made, ever perp I ever put behind bars, for twenty minutes alone with Alex in a small cell, her handcuffed to a chair, me with a baseball bat.

What had I become?

A drip, from the lime-coated showerhead above me, dimpling the surface of the water between my feet. I stared up at it, and then the shower curtain, old and stained but on an aluminum rod that looked strong, sturdy. It would probably support my weight. I didn't have any rope, but there was a gas station on the corner.

Stupid. Cops don't hang themselves. They eat their guns.

I thought about the Beretta in my backpack. One bullet, and I'd stop feeling this awful. I'd let so many people down, myself included. One bullet would make it all go away.

You're being weak, Jack.

So? Can't I be weak for once?

Killing yourself is the coward's way out.

Okay, I'm a coward. One more reason to hate myself.

I stood up, walked naked into the bedroom. Stared at my backpack.

You're seriously considering this?

A sob caught in my throat. I blinked away some tears.

Yes. It's the best idea I've had all week.

I reached my hand inside, wrapped my hand around the butt of my gun. It felt solid. Reassuring.

Just do it.

I closed my eyes, tried to think of a reason to stop myself. Faces popped into my head.

Mom, begging me not to.

Sorry, not good enough.

Dad, tacking an article about my suicide onto the wall in his spare bedroom, to add to the dozens of other articles and pictures of me.

Take it all down, Wilbur. I'm not worthy of a shrine.

Harry, telling me I hated myself.

You nailed that one, bro.

Phin, saying he loved me.

Looks like you'll outlive me after all.

Alex, laughing at all the pain she's caused.

Not my problem anymore.

Latham, his kind, sad, beautiful face, telling me I had to be strong.

Why? Why do I have to be strong all the goddamn time? Where has it gotten me?

Alan, his eyes rolled up in his head . . .

Enough. I'm done.

I want out.

I opened my mouth, brought up the gun, my hand shaking so much I had problems getting the barrel between my lips.

Lieutenant Jacqueline Daniels vs. the world.

The world wins.

It always does.

I flicked off the safety, put my thumb on the trigger, and opened my eyes so I could watch myself do it in the bureau mirror. I wanted the last thing I ever saw to be how pathetic I looked.

Movement, peripherally, to my right.

My gun pointed reflexively, and I pulled the trigger on instinct.

Rat. Big one in the corner.

Deader than hell now, without a head.

I laughed, once, but it sounded more like a strangled cough.

In a way, that's all I was good for. Killing rats.

But I *was* good. I was very good.

And there was still one rat left to kill. The biggest one of all.

I put the gun back in the pack, got dressed, and called a cab to take me to a better motel, all thoughts of suicide momentarily replaced by thoughts of murder.

CHAPTER 48

THE MORNING AND EARLY AFTERNOON are going to be un-eventful. Alex orders room service and spends some time familiarizing herself with a M18A1 she's taken from Lance's boss, the bomb squad lieut. It's a serious piece of hardware, appropriate for the job, and comes with det wire and a spring trigger. On the green plastic cover are three words.

FRONT TOWARD ENEMY.

Alex runs her fingers over the embossed letters and smiles her half smile. God love the military.

Next she shapes a good-sized hunk of PENO into a cone and sets up the blasting cap, sun cord, and sparker.

Then it's a pay-per-view action film, charged to the room. A cop thriller, with a hard-nosed veteran chasing a wily serial killer. Alex liked it up until the end, when the cop predictably shot the villain down. Why can't there be a movie where the killer beats the cop and gets away? Wouldn't that be cool?

Alex blames the writers. None of them have the balls to let the bad guy win.

But the bad guys do win sometimes. People have to learn to accept that.

Lunch is room service, again, and the food is so bland and mediocre, and the room so run-down, that Alex wonders how this place can even stay open, especially since it isn't really cheap. Maybe they have a lot of conventions here.

The hotel has a tiny workout room with a dearth of decent equipment. Alex makes use of the StairMaster for an hour, a towel wrapped around her neck and hiding her face should anyone else come in. No one does. Then it's back to her room for a shower and another movie—this one a romantic comedy starring Sarah Jessica Parker, who is cute and dresses great but can't make up for a lackluster script.

Finally, the clock zeroes in on three p.m. She grabs her gear, fights awful traffic, and makes it to downtown Chicago and the corner she'd staked out yesterday. Alex parks in a pay lot, sets up her laptop, finds a free WiFi connection—Chicago abounds with hot spots—and accesses the phone taped to Herb's tree. She watches the live feed.

The house looks normal, no unusual activity, but Alex can guess that there are a bunch of cops inside, as well as throughout the neighborhood. All waiting for her.

Won't they be surprised when she doesn't show up?

Alex keeps her cell phone handy—when things happen, they'll happen fast. Then she settles in to watch the show.

CHAPTER 49

*I*T WAS ALL I COULD DO not to tear out my hair in frustration.

Two calls to Detective Tom Mankowski confirmed that Herb was being closely guarded. He was still home—something he insisted upon because he wanted to be bait—but he had three cops and two Feebies in there with him. In neighboring houses were ten more cops and just as many Feds. There were three SRT snipers on nearby rooftops. Air support was standing by. As Mankowski said, a squirrel couldn't fart within a block of the area without having six guns drawn on it.

But the waiting was still torture. Herb was my partner. I should be there. Instead, I was pacing in a Wisconsin hotel room, my fingernails chewed down to blood, waiting for something to happen. Hopefully, the something would be of the good variety, involving Alex getting gunned down. But I had a feeling that Herb wasn't as safe as everyone wanted to believe.

What were they missing? What was I missing? How do you get to a guy who is heavily protected?

A long-range weapon? That had been anticipated. A mail bomb? The mail for Herb's route had been checked out and cleared back at the post office, and FedEx, UPS, and DHL had nothing for Herb or for his address. Hidden explosives? Earlier in the day, two bomb-sniffing dogs had covered every inch of Herb's property.

He was safer than the Pope. But we had to be forgetting something. Unless Alex was lying. Unless Herb wasn't the target at all.

She couldn't get to my parents. Phin was unreachable. Harry?

I called him, using the hotel room phone.

"Hi, sis. I forgive you for acting like a jerk yesterday. I found the Milwaukee cell phone. Motel lobby, at the Old Stone Inn, behind the ice machine. Weren't you just there?"

"Where are you now?"

"On my way to Chicago. That's where the next one is. You wouldn't believe how much gas I've gone through the last few days. I think I'm getting about three hundred yards per gallon."

"Harry, Alex might have been lying about Herb. You might be the next target."

"Let her try for me. Slappy will take care of her."

"I'm being serious."

"I am too. After you left, I gave the monkey some pills, to calm him down."

I shook my head, amazed. "You gave the monkey Vicodin?"

"I thought it was. But the wrong pills were in the bottle. I actually gave him Viagra. He's been a little, uh, *aggressive* since then."

"I bet."

"I got him back in his cage by throwing in a cashmere sweater he's taken a serious liking to. He and the sweater have been going at it nonstop for about eight hours. But if I open the cage, he'll pounce on Alex like a starving man after a donut."

"Be careful, McGlade."

"I'll be okay. If he jumps on me, I'll be wearing earplugs and noseplugs and keep my mouth closed tight."

"I meant with Alex."

"Slappy and I are ready. Does Mom like cashmere?"

"That's disgusting."

"Not this sweater. A new sweater. I was going to give this one to Herb."

"Stay in touch," I told him.

"Does this mean we're partners again?"

"Just stay in touch."

I hung up, did some more pacing, tried to eat a room service turkey club, failed, did more pacing, tried to watch a movie, failed, called Tom again for an update when none was needed, did push-ups until my arms wouldn't work anymore, paced, and finally around four p.m. Alex's phone rang.

I picked up, expecting to see a text message. But instead I saw a photo, of Herb's house, a red car parked in the driveway.

No, it wasn't a photo. This picture moved, the car door opening.

This was a live feed.

I got on the phone, my phone, and hit the speed dial for Herb.

One ring.

A man was getting out of the car. Big, muscular, wearing a tight shirt.

Two rings.

The shirt had a logo on the back, large enough for me to read even on the small LCD phone screen.

1-800-MEATS4U.

Three rings.

But this couldn't be the meat I ordered for Herb. That was being sent UPS, and not for another few days.

Alex. Somehow Alex knew about it.

The man reached into the passenger seat, removed a large white foam box.

Why weren't the cops taking him down?

"Hello?"

"Bernice! It's Jack!"

The big guy walked up to the front door. Two figures with FBI on their jackets rushed at him from both sides.

"Jack, the Turduckinlux is here."

"I didn't send the—"

Herb's front door opened, and then an explosion shook the camera. I heard a shocking *BOOM* through the tiny speaker of my cell, so startling I dropped my phone.

My other hand clenched Alex's phone, the screen fuzzy and gray. I watched, horrified, as the smoke cleared.

Herb's front porch, and a large chunk of his house, were gone.

I picked up my cell, whispered into it, "Bernice."

She didn't answer. But in the background, I heard screaming.

CHAPTER 50

ERFECT. ABSOLUTELY PERFECT. The male stripper Laugh-O-Gram showed up with the package right at the scheduled time, and wore the meat shop T-shirt Alex had made for him, using the inkjet printer and an iron-on silk-screen design. She hopes the guy spent the five hundred bucks she paid him yesterday to make the trip from Milwaukee, because he certainly wouldn't be spending it now.

Quite a lot of damage a few pounds of plastic explosive can cause. The house is trashed, and Alex can see several dead bodies inside. It would be fun to sit and watch the ambulances come, the corpses removed, but Alex has business to take care of.

Big business. The original plan. The real reason she's in Chicago.

She tucks away her cell phone, checks her watch, then grabs her gear, which is resting on the dead body in the backseat. A few police cars whiz by, sirens blazing. Perfect. The authorities, and the media, will be going crazy over the bombing. Which means they'll pay less attention to what she's going to do in about sixty seconds.

Alex pulls up her hood, dons her movie star sunglasses, gets out of the car, and removes the M18A1. She holds it and the cord in one hand, the plastic trigger in the other, and waits for the truck to arrive.

It's a minute late. Understandable, given all of the police traffic. There are other cars on the road, but Alex doesn't give them any unneeded attention. She's got tunnel vision, focusing on one thing and one thing only: the armored money truck, heading her way.

When it's within twenty yards, Alex steps out in front of it, raising her hand up. The truck slows. Alex walks forward, waits for it to stop, then drops the M18A1 down onto the street and kicks it under the truck's front end, directly beneath the engine.

She backpedals, playing out line, and then hits the detonator while the truck is shifting into reverse.

The M18A1 Claymore mine does what it was made to do: fire seven hundred steel balls in a sixty-degree outward pattern at 1,200 meters per second.

Not enough to seriously damage the truck, or hurt its occupants. Not even enough to crack the engine block or sever the drive train. But enough to shred the armored vehicle's electronics under the hood.

It won't be going anywhere anytime soon.

Moving quickly without rushing, Alex heads to the rear of the truck, sticking her cone of PENO onto the back door lock. She unwinds some cord, stands clear, and hits the sparker.

The armor is thick, tough. But so is a Sherman tank's, and the plastic explosive makes easy work of the door, blowing it open so it hangs outward on its hinges. Alex waits alongside the truck, out of the line of sight, for the hopper to come out. A trained professional, one with enough experience to follow this training while in combat situations, would take cover and wait inside for Alex to enter. But an average guy with average training would want to get the hell out of there.

This guy is average. He fires twice, then comes jumping out of the cargo hold and racing down the street. Alex shoots him in the back. She approaches the truck low, on an angle, and makes sure there are no other guards. The driver wisely stays in the front cab. He's protected as long as he doesn't come out.

Alex isn't concerned about him for the time being. If he wants to try to be a hero, she'll deal with it. What has her attention are the canvas money bags on the floor of the cargo area. She has extra PENO and detonators with her, in case she had to deal with safes, and also an extra Claymore in case this truck turned out to be a bust and she needed to find another.

Alex uses her folder knife to cut open the first bag, and one look confirms that a second robbery won't be necessary. The bag is loaded with banded stacks of twenties. Maybe ten thousand dollars' worth.

And Alex counts twelve bags in the back of the truck.

She opens up the army duffel, begins stuffing in bags. She fits five, and can sling five more over her shoulders. The last two she has to leave behind—she doesn't have time to make two trips. The driver has already called it in, and even with all the commotion the bombing has caused, the cops will be here soon.

Alex heads for the alley, following it through to the parking garage, waddling up a flight of concrete steps, and loading everything into the Prius. Almost home.

As she pulls down the circular driveway, heading for the exit, she hears police sirens. She stops at the exit gate, lowers her window, and sticks the parking stub into the slot. The automatic machine flashes twelve dollars— a ridiculous amount to have to pay for parking less than an hour. Alex reaches for her purse, but it isn't on the passenger seat. She looks around the Prius, on the floor, in the back, and her purse is nowhere to be found.

The hotel. She left it back at the hotel.

"Is there a problem?"

The voice is coming through a speaker, attached to the gate machine. A parking lot attendant.

"No," Alex says. "Just looking for my cash."

Alex unclips her folder knife, cuts open the nearest bag of money. Something catches her eye, and she checks the rearview and sees the guard is coming up behind her, holding a walkie-talkie.

Alex considers killing the guard, but there's the possibility he has a partner, and has already called in her license plate number. That could get linked to the armored car robbery, less than a block over, and Alex will be pulled over by the first cop who sees her.

She fishes out a wad of fifties, breaks the seal. The guard is getting closer. If he looks in the car, he'll see the bags of money. If he looks really close, he'll see the body still in the backseat.

Alex shoves a crisp fifty into the slot. It sucks up the cash, then spits it out. Alex tries again, with similar results. Then she notices the sign on the machine.

Only accepts $1, $5, $10, and $20 bills.

The guard is almost at her back bumper. Alex practically laughs at the absurdity of it. She's got maybe a hundred grand in the car, but can't find twelve lousy bucks.

She slits open another bag, and fate smiles on her—it exposed a sheaf of twenties. Alex peels one off, sticks it into the machine, and the gate rises.

Alex waits for the road spikes to go down, then hits the gas, pulling out of the parking lot, swerving to avoid an oncoming police car, and tearing down the street, driving as fast as the Prius can handle.

CHAPTER 51

THE FEEBIES ARRESTED ME AT THE HOSPITAL.

"I'm sorry," I told Special Agent Dailey as he put on the cuffs. In front of me, not behind. Professional courtesy. "Coursey was a good man."

Dailey looked positively haggard, the neutral expression he constantly wore replaced by a drawn-out, faraway look.

"He's the one who answered the door. He told Sergeant Benedict to stay back."

"Where is Herb?"

"Intensive Care. He just got out of surgery."

"Can I see him?"

"I have orders to bring you in."

"Please," I said.

"I can't. The SAC wants you in custody."

"He's my partner. You know how important that is."

Dailey stared at me, then nodded. He took my elbow and escorted me down the hospital hallway. His grip was heavy, but I felt it had less to do with me running away, and more about giving him something to cling to.

There were guards in front of Herb's room. One of them was Tom Mankowski. He was in a rumpled, filthy suit, standing almost a head taller than me. His blue eyes appraised me kindly.

"I was at the neighbors'. When the car pulled up, we were ready to move in. But Sergeant Benedict told us to hold off. He thought it was some steaks you were sending him. Actually, that saved a lot of lives. We lost three, but it would have been four or five more if he didn't order us to stand down. Me included."

I nodded at him, turned my attention to the door.

"Ten minutes," Dailey told me.

I went inside.

Herb was under an oxygen tent, the clear plastic windows looking futuristic and strangely cheap. Bandages were swathed around his chest. Two tubes were taped to his face, one going up his nose and the other jammed down his throat. Another tube—I guessed it to be a drain— snaked out through his bandages, taped to the bed rail along with his IV. His eyes were closed, puffy. The steady *beep beep beep* of his vitals drilled into me, accusing, blaming.

Bernice was slumped in a chair next to him, some gauze on her forehead, her hand under the tent and clutching her husband's. When she saw me she stood up and threw her arms around my waist.

I couldn't hug her back because of the handcuffs, but I put my head on her shoulder.

"How's he doing?" I managed.

"Critical. His chest is all messed up. The bomb—it was packed with roofing nails."

"What did the doctors say?"

"They wouldn't give me a clear answer. I had to scream at the head surgeon. He told me . . ." Bernice sobbed, her body shuddering. "Jack, his chances are fifty-fifty."

Fifty-fifty. The toss of a coin.

"I'll find her," I said.

I expected her to tell me that's what she wanted. That I'd better.

I was wrong.

"No," she said. "You should let this go."

Bernice drew away from me, teary eyes staring back at her husband.

"We were talking about you earlier, Jack. The Job is killing you. It has been for years. Herb's seen it. He's watched you die, a little each day." She paused. "You need to quit."

"I have to finish this, Bernice."

She looked at me sadly. "Oh, Jack, there's always one more thing you have to finish. One more crime to solve. One more perp to catch. Someone hits, you hit back. You're always hitting back. Sometimes, the best thing—the sane thing—is to just walk away. That's what Herb wanted you to do."

"He wanted me to quit?"

"He wanted you to be happy. And you'll never be happy if you keep heading down this path. Happiness isn't having complete control, Jack. Happiness is realizing you don't have any control at all."

I stared at my partner, a lump in my throat, and everything everyone had told me over the last few days suddenly made perfect sense.

And I knew what I had to do.

I had to let it all go.

"I have to go, Bernice. But I understand. When he wakes up, tell him . . . tell him I . . . just . . . just give him this."

It wasn't easy fishing it out of my purse with my hands cuffed, but I managed, pressing it into Bernice's hands. She held it up.

"Your badge."

"Last night . . ." I took a big breath. "Bernice, last night, I almost . . . I thought it was the only way, you know, to stop the pain. But I don't need to die. Only part of me does. The cop part."

"You're resigning?"

"I'm done. It's over. Tell Herb I love him, and I quit, and I'll be over next week for Turduckinlux."

Bernice smiled sadly. "He'd be so proud of you right now, Jack."

"Take care of our boy, okay? I'll be back soon."

I heard yelling from the hallway. I gave Bernice another hug using just my head and neck, and then walked outside.

McGlade, pointing his prosthesis up at Mankowski.

"I told you she's my sister, and if you don't let me—Hey, Jackie, tell this very tall piece of shit who I am."

"It's okay," I said to Tom. He nodded, backed off.

"Sis, the last cell phone—it's *moving*."

"I don't care anymore, Harry." I turned to Dailey. "I'm ready."

"Can I have a private brother/sister moment, Special Agent?"

Dailey nodded. Harry whispered to me.

"You don't get it. If it's moving, that means Alex has it on her. It's the last phone. We can track it right to her."

"It's not my problem anymore. I just quit the force."

"You . . . *what?*"

I reached into my pocket, took out the cell phone Alex had given me. The leash she'd been using to lead me around.

"Here. Take it. I don't care what you do with it."

The act was so liberating I actually felt about fifty pounds lighter.

Special Agent Dailey led me down the hall, away from a bewildered Harry McGlade, and into the parking lot. I got into his car and we drove to the federal lockup for booking. The arrest papers were drawn up, I was printed, mug shots taken, and I was placed in a holding cell, all the while unable to get the serene smile off my face.

I should have given up years ago.

CHAPTER 52

ALEX YAWNS, STRETCHES, AND OPENS HER EYES. The hotel room is dark, but sunlight is peeking in through a crack in the drapes, illuminating the stacks of money laid out on the floor in thousand-dollar piles.

There are eighty-seven of them.

Alex smiles her half smile at the sight of it. She'd been hoping for at least forty thousand. That's the number quoted in the e-mail exchanges. The number she needs to start her new life.

Truth told, Alex had no idea how much money armored trucks carried around. Long gone are the days of cash payrolls, and bank transfers are made electronically with the press of a button. But she assumed with the constant stocking of ATMs and currency exchanges, and the cash flow generated by the shopping on Chicago's Magnificent Mile, money was probably being hauled every day.

She assumed right.

Alex rolls out of bed, uses the washroom, then flips on CNN. The Chicago bombing is still the main story. Alex's scarred mug shot is shown, her hair shorter and black. They also mention the armored car robbery, but her name isn't brought up in connection with that, just that the robber is tall, muscular, with dark red hair. The driver's description. He managed to ID her hair color beneath a hood, but for some reason didn't realize she was a woman. Fear does funny things to memory.

Alex changed her hair last night, stopping at a drugstore and buying some bleach. She's now a perky blonde.

Eighty-seven grand can make even a stone-cold killer downright perky.

Now it's time to get out of town, disappear. Yesterday, things had been too hot. Alex narrowly missed a roadblock before getting back to the hotel. It should be safer to move today. But first, one last thing to deal with.

Jack.

Alex dials, ready to offer the lieutenant her condolences. The victims' names haven't been released yet, but her fat partner is surely one of them. The roofing nails were a special touch, a nod to one of Jack's high-profile cases Alex read about while in Heathrow. Icing on the irony cake.

But Jack doesn't answer. A man does. A man Alex can't stand.

"Hiya, freak show. How's the psycho business?"

"Where's Jack, Harry?"

"She doesn't want to talk to you, because you're crazy and your face looks like a slice of country-style ham. If your nose was a side of hash browns you'd have a line of fat people chasing you with forks."

Alex frowns, uncomfortably aware that only half of the muscles are working. "Put Jack on."

"That's a negative, ham-face. She's done playing with you. But I'm not. I'm coming for your loony ass. In fact, I'm knocking on your door right . . . about . . . *now.*"

Against all common sense, Alex focuses on her hotel door.

"Gotcha, sucker."

Alex grits her teeth. "If you don't put Jack on—"

"Blow me. I'm walking up to your door right now. You ready? Here I come. Almost there. And *heeeeeere's* Harry!"

Again, Alex stares at her door, annoyed that she's buying into this stupid game.

"Gotcha again! Die paranoid, you bitch."

Harry hangs up. Alex fights the urge to open the door and check the hallway. It's ludicrous. Harry has no way to find her. She's in the hotel under a false name. There's no way to trace the cell phone daisy chain.

Right?

But Harry—goddamn Harry—sounded so sure of himself. When Alex first met him, she thought he was dumber than a crate of melons. And while she never really amended that initial impression, she doesn't want to underestimate the irritating little bastard. Her plan was to lure Jack to a secluded location and grab her. But now Alex just feels the need to get the hell out of Chicago. The sooner, the better.

She starts stuffing everything into her duffel bag, including the empty canvas money satchels. It's heavy, unwieldy, the zipper threatening to burst. Alex slings it onto her shoulder, heads for the door, remembers that her face is exposed, and creates a makeshift babushka out of a white pillowcase. It looks ridiculous, but better to be remembered as eccentric than scarred.

The hallway is clear, the stairwell is clear, the lobby is clear, and the parking lot is clear, except for some idiot in a Winnebago blocking the exit. Alex chucks the duffel bag in back, starts the Prius, and drives up over the curb to get past the RV moron, and wonders where to head next.

Wisconsin is out of the question. She's almost as popular with cops there as she is in Chicago. She also left a trail in Iowa, and going back now would be unwise. Michigan is a possibility. Plenty of privacy in the woods. A secluded farm would work too.

A farm.

Actually, for a final showdown, Alex's old homestead would be a perfect place. Private, out of the way, easy to set up. And she'd get a thrill out of seeing their farm one last time.

Alex heads for I-90, and Gary, Indiana.

Soon, this will all be over. Alex isn't sure what she wants to do next. The possibilities are limitless. Hell, she could even get a regular job, become a respectable citizen. Perhaps even join a police force some-where. Wearing that cop uniform was a lot of fun.

It's cold enough outside for Alex to switch on the heat, but that makes the smell from the backseat more pronounced. She opens the windows to compensate, and wonders if she should stop for deodorizer. Or at least something to cover the corpse, other than the blanket cur-rently performing the task. Alex reaches around, tugs down a corner, and catches a quick glimpse out of her back window.

That damn Winnebago is following her.

Adrenaline jolts her. Maybe it isn't the same one. There have to be dozens of them on the road, and they probably all look similar.

She glances at her rearview, trying to see the driver. He's too far back, and his windows have a light tint to them, making it hard to see inside.

That clinches it. The RV back at the hotel had tinted windows too.

Could it be the Feds? They're known for doing stakeouts in vans and trucks. But a Winnebago seems too conspicuous, too elaborate, even for the FBI. This thing is the size of a bus. No one would be stupid enough to use a recreational vehicle for surveillance, except maybe . . .

Harry McGlade.

"Is that you, Harry, you pain in the ass? Let's find out."

Alex turns at the next light, taking Touhy Avenue around the air-port, then turning onto South Mount Prospect Road. This is no-man's-land, acres and acres of undesirable property, too close to O'Hare to be habitable. Many have tried, as evidenced by the crumbling and torn-down buildings in these empty lots, but the sound must have been too much for even the factories to endure.

Alex hangs a sharp, fast right onto Old Higgins Road, the Prius cor-nering bravely, and then a quick left into an abandoned lot, weeds pok-ing up through the cracked asphalt. She jams the car into park, hops out palming her Cheetah stun gun, and sprints back to the ditch near the entrance to crouch in the tall grass.

The Winnebago slows down as it nears, crawling by the lot, the driver obviously spotting the Prius. Alex runs up behind the vehicle, grabbing onto the rear ladder, pulling herself up as it rolls past. The rungs are round, sturdy, easy to hold. The RV comes to a stop, and Alex climbs up the back side and onto the roof. As expected, there's a hatch. She slides over to it on her hands and knees, the slight noise she makes lost in the overhead roar of jet engines. Happily, the hatch is open a few inches, probably for air circulation. Alex lifts it up and slithers forward on her belly.

The smell is awful, a cross between a zoo and a truck stop toilet. Definitely Harry. Alex swings inside and drops onto the sofa. A scream, to her left, and she spins around, Cheetah poised and ready to strike.

It's a monkey, in a cage. And the scream isn't directed at her. It's directed at what appears to be a damp sweater, which he's earnestly humping.

Yes, this has to be Harry's RV.

She creeps forward, to the cab. The door is closed. She can imagine McGlade sitting there, staring at her car, wondering what to do next. But she isn't sure he's alone in there. Jack might be with him. Better to know for sure before attacking.

Alex looks around, finds a Ping-Pong paddle covered in mud. She picks it up.

Yuck. That isn't mud.

She wipes her hand on the carpet, but that's damp with something even worse. Now seriously grossed out, she frantically searches for a towel. The only thing nearby is that sweater in the monkey cage, and Alex decides she'd rather light herself on fire than touch that splotchy thing. She crinkles her nose, decides to just deal with it for the time being, and then throws the Ping-Pong paddle at the cab door.

"Dammit, Slappy, how did you get out of your cage?"

The door opens. McGlade appears. Alex jams the stun gun into his belly, dropping him to his knees, then whacks him alongside the head with her elbow, getting all of her weight and muscle behind it.

He crumples to the floor, landing on something squishy. Serves the asshole right.

Alex checks the cab for other passengers. It's empty. The monkey screeches again. He's still raping the cardigan, but his eyes are now locked on her, the filthy little pervert. Alex considers giving him a little zap with the Cheetah, but she has more pressing things to do, like restrain Harry.

But first things first. Alex hurries to the bathroom to wash her hands. She really hopes McGlade has soap.

CHAPTER 53

STEPPED ONTO VAN BUREN, walking out of the Metropolitan Correctional Center having just been given back my personal belongings. The night in lockup had flown by—I'd actually slept pretty well — and the morning was taken up by the bond hearing at the Northern District courthouse. My professional record, ties to the community, and the fact that obstruction of justice isn't really that big a charge meant I walked with only a ten-thousand-dollar bond.

The day was cool, almost cold. I walked around the block, checking for tails of the Feebie variety—I got the impression Special Agent Dailey thought I knew more about Phin's and Alex's whereabouts than I actually did.

No Feds were following me. But I did notice a Ford Bronco without a front windshield. I walked up to him. Time to bury this particular hatchet.

"Need a ride?" Phin asked.

"You know that large oppressive building behind me is a federal prison, right?"

"Yeah. Harry told me you were doing time. Is it like those old Roger Corman movies?"

"Exactly the same. I took a shower in slow motion, then fought off the advances of a big-breasted lesbian warden."

"Sounds hot."

"Can you take me home?"

He nodded, and I climbed in. Phin and I had some unresolved is-sues, and now that Alex was off my mind I actually had a clear head. We were wrong for each other, for a million different reasons. I was mentally preparing the "let's still be friends" speech when he launched into a speech of his own.

"I never said thanks that you covered for me. You could have turned me in. I'm a thief, and an addict, and I don't deserve your friendship. Es-pecially since I want more than just friendship. So it's probably best we don't see each other anymore."

I wasn't sure how to reply to that. While I didn't want Phin as a boyfriend, I didn't want him out of my life.

He pulled into traffic, and I found it hard to talk with the wind blowing straight into my face. I had to wait until we reached a stoplight, ready to argue with him, to make a case for friendship. But my mouth said something else.

"You've always been there for me, Phin. I call, you come. Thank you. It means a lot. And if you think we should go our separate ways, that hurts, but I'll respect that."

Phin nodded. I felt my chest get tight, my eyes well up. But this was for the best. I didn't love this man. I couldn't ever love this man.

Then why did this feel like the totally wrong thing to do?

My phone rang. I dug it out of my purse, answered.

No response. I looked at the screen, saw I had a text message.

THIS IS HARRY. HE'S YOUR BROTHER.

Oh shit.

"Phin, when was the last time you talked to Harry?"

"This morning. Why?"

"Alex has him."

A picture came next, McGlade duct-taped to a chair, his face bleed-ing, his eyes desperate. Then the phone rang again. I answered.

"Hello, Jack. Harry just told me some nonsense about you quitting. Did I give you permission to quit?"

The wind howled in my face. I put my finger in my ear to drown out the noise.

"Where is he, Alex?"

"He's with me. We're reliving old times. Right, Harry?"

A crackling sound, followed by a howl. Every muscle in my body tensed up.

"What do you want, Alex?"

"A showdown, Jack. Just you and me. No cops. No Feds. No special forces yahoos swooping in on helicopters. I've got enough explosives to level a city block, and if I even suspect that you're not alone, I press a little button and you get to bury what's left of your brother in a matchbox."

"Don't come, Jackie!" Harry yelled in the background. "I got this bitch right where I want her!"

Another crackle, and another howl. I guessed Alex was using a stun gun on him.

"I'm just west of O'Hare," Alex said. "Be here in twenty minutes. For every minute you're late, Harry loses a finger."

"I got a finger for you right here!" Harry yelled. The yell became a scream when she juiced him again.

"Twenty minutes, Jack."

"I don't have a car. You remember what happened to my car."

"Where's your buddy Phin?"

"He's out of the picture."

"That's your problem. Twenty minutes."

I turned to Phin. "Remember what I just said about going our separate ways?"

"Where is he?"

"O'Hare. We have twenty minutes."

Phin jammed on the gas. I buckled up. Calling for reinforcements seemed like the right thing to do. If I did, Harry was dead, but he was probably dead anyway. So were Phin and me. The only way to win this was to call in the troops and nuke her.

I dialed 9 and 1 and then stopped.

"Do you still have the rifles?" I yelled at Phin over the wind.

"In back!"

"The radio?"

"Yeah!"

He hit the horn, blowing through a red light, causing a car to swerve and smash into a bus. Alex didn't know Phin was with me. Maybe Harry had a chance to make it through this after all. A slight chance, but better than none at all. Much as I didn't like the guy, and much as I hated the thought that there was a remotely small possibility we were related, I had to try to save him. He'd do the same for me.

It's what any brother and sister would do.

Phin found the expressway, riding the shoulder and passing cars while squinting against the wind. I figured our best shot was setting up Phin someplace elevated, far enough away that she wouldn't see him. We'd never finished zeroing out his scope, but hopefully he'd learned enough in our brief tutorial that he'd be able to compensate.

If not, Harry and I were dead.

And, surprisingly, I realized I didn't want to die. I wanted to live a long, happy, fruitful life, as something other than a cop. I wasn't sure what yet. While lying in my holding cell, I actually toyed with the idea of opening up a bar, maybe with some pool tables. With a name like Jack Daniels, how could it lose?

But now I could lose. I could lose a future I never even dreamed I could have. And I was scared.

I tucked my head down and turned away from the wind screaming in at us, blowing my hair into Medusa snakes. If there was the possibility I might be killed, I needed to make a call first. I hit speed dial. She picked up on the third ring.

"Mom?"

"Jacqueline! You've got to come on a cruise with us! We're having a fabulous time!"

Mom sounded loaded. Happy, but loaded.

"Mom, I want to tell you something. Something important."

"Is it about your father? We bumped into each other at bingo. He told me he was gay. Can you believe it? I married a homo!" Mom laughed. "He never told me all of these years because he didn't want to hurt me. What a sweet man. We've been having such a wonderful time together. Did you know he was at your wedding?"

"Yes, Mom. Glad you two made up."

"There's a senior social tonight. We're going to cruise men together. I'm letting him do my hair. He used to do that back when we were married. How could I have not guessed he was gay?"

"Is Dad there?"

"He just went to the bathroom. I wonder which one. You think it was the men's or the women's? We're having such fun! They make a drink called a cherry bomb. We've been drinking them all morning. I wish you were here with us. The whole family together again. We simply must go on a cruise when I get back, if my liver is still working."

More giggles. I closed my eyes. Last good-byes were really goddamn hard.

"Mom, I need you to tell Dad that I love him. It's important that he hears that. Okay?"

"I will, Jacqueline, but don't you think you should tell him yourself? He told me you hadn't said that yet."

"I need you to tell him, Mom. And I love you too. And I . . . I want to thank you."

"Thank me? What in heavens for?"

I choked up a little bit, then got it under control. "For raising me. For loving me. For being my hero. You're one of the best people I've ever met, and it's been such an honor being your daughter."

"You're such a sweetheart. Have you been drinking too?"

"Just know that I love you, okay?"

"Okay, honey. My phone is dying, so I'll call you later tonight. If I don't call, it means I'm getting lucky. Bye-bye."

"Mom?"

The phone went dead.

I closed my eyes, letting the wind blow away the tears on my cheeks.

Then I reached into the backseat to check the rifles.

CHAPTER 54

"HEY! NORMA BATES! You're the one who needs to cover up her face, not me."

Alex sets down the blasting cap, walks to Harry—taped to his computer chair with a red velour pillowcase over his head—and punches where she thinks his nose is. His head snaps back and he makes a satisfying grunt.

"I thought we were clear, Harry. Every time you talk, I hit you."

"If I answer, are you going to hit me again?"

Alex sighs. She has a good reason for keeping McGlade in the dark, but realizes she should have gagged him first.

"This pillowcase smells like monkey pee," Harry says.

"Jesus, McGlade, do I have to cut out your tongue?"

"If you did, I could still make sounds with my throat. See? *Wooooaaaaaaaaaaaaooooooo!*"

Harry continues to moan like a ghost, and Alex questions whether it isn't better to simply kill him right now. Instead, she finishes hooking up the detonator and then gives Harry another punch in the face.

"If I take off your hood, will you shut the hell up?"

"I can't make any promises. Your face is pretty frightening. I may scream."

"You're going to scream anyway," Alex says, yanking off his hood.

McGlade opens his mouth, no doubt to make some smart-assed comment, but instead his eyes begin to wander around the RV. Alex has used every last bit of Lance's explosives decorating the interior. It's sort of like Christmas, except with dynamite, det cord, and PENO instead of tinsel, ornaments, and colored lights.

"Jesus H. Tap-Dancing Christ," Harry says.

"Impressed?"

"No. I just forgot how ugly you are."

Alex gives Harry's cheek a not-too-gentle pinch.

"Don't worry, Harry. You're not going to die here. This is all for Jack. I'm taking you with me. We're going to spend some real quality time together before I punch your clock."

"I've got a question for you, Alex. And I'd really appreciate an honest answer."

Alex waits.

"You're a chick," he says. "Do red velour sheets make you hot?"

Alex swings a leg over Harry, straddles his lap.

"Do you know what will make me hot, Harry? Using some pliers to peel all the skin off of your face."

"But what about the sheets? They match those hooker boots you're wearing."

Alex gives Harry a peck on the forehead, then climbs off. His stupid jokes don't bother her. He's scared out of his mind, trying to use humor to cope. Once she starts drawing some serious blood, the joking will be replaced by begging. She was more impressed by how he found her than his current bravado. Tracking the cell phones through the SIM cards and a Bluetooth signal was clever. As soon as he told her, after a liberal application of the stun gun, she switched off her Bluetooth and call forwarding. Alex doesn't want Jack to find her before she's all set up.

She turns, going to check the bedroom one more time. That's where the second Claymore is. But before she gets two steps away McGlade tilts his chair over, falling onto his side. He reaches out an arm—his fake hand had apparently been able to break through the duct tape—and hits the release button on the monkey's cage door.

"Get her, Slappy! Like I trained you!"

McGlade points at Alex. The monkey leaps out of the cage, screeching like a hellspawn. Then he runs right past Alex, jumps through the side window, and tears down the street, disappearing into the distance.

Harry frowns. "There's six hundred bucks shot to hell."

"I think you paid too much."

"It was him, or a gibbon with just one limb."

"The gibbon couldn't have run away."

"Point taken."

Alex checks her watch. Almost time to call. She hopes Jack is late, because Alex feels a little jumpy, and severing a few of Harry's fingers would help take the edge off. She unclips her folder knife, thumbs open the blade.

"I'm sorry, Harry. I don't have my blowtorch handy this time. So it looks like we're going to get blood all over your carpeting."

"It was pretty much ruined anyway." Harry's voice is an octave higher. The fear is taking over.

"Which one should we start with? The thumb?"

"I have a better idea. Why don't you take that knife and jam it right up your— Slappy! I knew you'd come back, buddy!"

Alex checks the window, and sure enough, the monkey is perched there, teeth bared. He slaps himself in the head a few times, giving Alex a pretty good idea of how he got his name.

"Attack, Slappy! Attack!"

Slappy hops into the RV, screeches at Alex, then runs into his cage and grabs the sweater. Two seconds later he's out the window again, dragging it behind him and running off into the distance.

"You really should have went with the gibbon," Alex says, closing and locking the window.

Then she fishes out her cell phone to call Jack.

CHAPTER 55

"*IT'S AN ABANDONED LOT,*" Alex said. "*On Old Higgins Road, just northwest of the airport. Look for the recreational vehicle.*"

Old Higgins, I mouthed at Phin. Into the phone I said, "I want to speak to Harry."

"*He's busy bleeding right now.*"

"Put him on, or this isn't gonna happen."

A pause, then, "*The whole place is wired to blow, Jackie. Get the hell away from—*"

Another zapping sound, and McGlade crying out. The poor bastard.

"*Two minutes,*" Alex said, then hung up.

We made it to Old Higgins in ninety seconds, while I fussed with the walkie-talkies. The area resembled a war zone: crumbling buildings, overgrown lots, cracked concrete. Through some tall weeds, about a thousand yards away, I saw the Crimebago, as out of place as a beached whale.

Phin hit the brakes. I tried to find the words, tried to tell him that maybe I was wrong about us after all, maybe we should be together, but I wimped out and instead said, "Your last shots were too high. Aim lower. And compensate a little for bullet drop. It's a much longer distance than you've tried before. Remember you've only got four shots. Wait for my signal."

"What's the signal?"

I considered it. "When I say *Latham*, let her have it."

Phin nodded. His face looked pained.

"Be careful," he said.

"You too."

We stared at each other for a few more seconds. I shivered. Not from the cold. From fear.

Phin clipped the walkie-talking to his front pocket and reached for the door handle, ready to climb out of the truck.

Dammit, Jack. Say something.

"You know," I managed to sputter, "a little while ago, I was going to try to talk you into still staying friends."

Phin turned, looked at me.

"Is that how you feel now?"

"No. Now the only thing I want in the whole damn world is for you to kiss me like you mean it."

He leaned over, his lips finding mine, his tongue finding mine.

I was sure he meant every second of it.

"Don't die on me, Jack."

I smiled at him, my eyes glassy. "Just try not to shoot me."

He grabbed his rifle and climbed out of the truck, blending into the weeds. I crawled over to the driver's seat, shifted gears, punched the gas, and headed for whatever hell Alex had in store.

I parked a dozen yards away. McGlade was in the parking lot outside the Crimebago, next to the side door, taped to his computer chair. Alex crouched behind him. She had a gun in one hand, holding it to Harry's temple. The other held some sort of detonator, the wire trailing from it and into the open side door of the RV.

I made sure the radio was on, the talk button depressed, and hung it under my armpit, clipping it to my sports bra. The sweatshirt was loose enough that you couldn't tell it was there. I hoped. Then I grabbed my gun and climbed out of the truck.

"Hold it! Drop the gun! Hands over your head!"

I let the gun clatter to the pavement.

"Raise your hands, turn in a full circle!"

I complied, searching for Phin when I faced his way. I didn't see him. And then I had a really bad thought—did he grab the right rifle? If he took mine by mistake, the sights would be way off because they'd been configured for me. And with his bad elbow . . .

"Walk toward me slowly, Jack, keeping your hands raised."

Her gun had switched from pointing at Harry to pointing at me. Right at my heart. Alex liked the chest shot. I felt a cold, dead spot where the bullet would hit if she pulled the trigger. It made me want to run into a corner, curl up fetal, and suck my thumb. I managed to get my legs moving, even though they felt like wet noodles.

"Stop there."

She made me halt ten feet in front of her. Alex was an excellent marksperson, and at this distance she might as well have been holding the gun directly up my nose. She wouldn't miss. Even if Phin fired on her. My only chance was if his first shot was a kill shot.

I didn't hold out much hope for that. This plan was looking worse and worse. It would have been smarter to just drive up really fast and run her over.

"Let Harry go," I said, with a lot more strength than I felt.

"I'm going to."

"You're going to?" Harry said. "My ass."

Alex patted him on the head. "Don't worry. I'll come back for you eventually. But Jack and I are going to go away for a while. I'll send you some pictures. Maybe you'll even be able to recognize her, under all of the blood."

I shook my head slowly, my eyes fixed on her gun. "I'm not going with you, Alex."

"Yes you are. You'll do whatever I tell you to do. You've given up, Jack. You're a shell of your former self. I knew that when I saw you at Latham's funeral."

I tensed, waiting for the shot. It didn't come. Was I in Phin's line of fire? Or did he know that was Alex talking, not me?

Was the walkie-talkie even working?

Jesus, this plan sucked.

"Even if you kill both of us, I'm not going anywhere with you, Alex."

"You can walk over here, Lieutenant. Or I can shoot out both your knees and drag you over here."

"No you won't," I said. And the fear washed away, being replaced by cold, hard anger. "This is for *Latham*."

The shot came from my left, plugging into the Crimebago only inches above Alex's head. She reacted instantly, ducking down and diving inside through the door.

Phin fired again, his shot aimed at where she disappeared.

Save your last two, I thought, willing him to hear. Then, in a crouch, I ran toward Harry.

Phin fired again, apparently not hearing my telepathic message, his shot pinging into the side of the RV.

"Stop firing, you knucklehead!" Harry screamed. "The whole thing is one big bomb!"

I grabbed Harry's chair—which thankfully was on coasters—and began to pull him back toward the Bronco. My thanks were short-lived. The parking lot surface was rough, uneven, covered in gravel. It would have been easier tugging him through mud.

"Dammit, sis, pull!"

"I'm pulling, McGlade! There are rocks stuck in the wheels."

We'd only gotten halfway to the truck when gunfire erupted, coming from the RV. Bits of asphalt flew up from the ground, peppering my legs, making me fall. It felt like being hit with a birdshot. I clawed my way back to my feet, calves bleeding, and dragged McGlade another few steps.

"Try pushing me!" Harry ordered.

I thought about telling him to shut up, but every ounce of energy I had was being expended trying to get him away from the bomb. One of the coasters snapped off, forcing him off balance and making him tip onto his side. I let go, pitching forward, my legs screaming at me. I crawled back to Harry, meeting his eyes.

"Come on, Jackie. You can do it. We have to get farther away." He grinned at me. "I ain't heavy. I'm your brother."

I thought—absurdly, considering the situation—that Harry had kind of a nice smile.

Then the Crimebago exploded, tossing us through the air like rag dolls.

CHAPTER 56

*I*OPENED MY EYES, stared up at empty sky.

A moment later, the sky wasn't empty. There was a plane flying over me. A jumbo jet, so close I could almost touch it.

But I couldn't hear it. All I heard was a dull, droning hum.

Then the pain hit.

My head felt like it had cracked open and was leaking. My arm was behind my back, twisted at a funny angle. My legs were on fire.

I blinked. Checked my head. No major leaks, but a helluva lump, and my stitches had opened up. My arm hurt, but didn't seem to be broken. And my legs weren't actually burning, just cut up.

I looked left. I was lying next to the Bronco, when I'd been several yards away from it before.

I looked right. The Crimebago was mostly gone, leaving a smoking crater where it had been parked.

The lot had become a debris field. Harry's scorched sofa. Part of the Murphy bed, red velour sheets still clinging to it. Half a computer monitor. The top part of a bucket seat. A severed human leg.

I squinted at the leg. It wore jeans, and a red boot with a stiletto heel.

The boots Alex had been wearing.

"Told you I wasn't going with you," I said to the leg.

I sat up, the world spinning, making my stomach unhappy. After swaying a little, I found my balance and began looking across the landscape of detritus for Harry.

He was ten yards to my left, taped to the broken remains of the chair.

I crawled to him, wincing at a dozen kinds of pain, navigating bits of engine and a burning spare tire that stung my eyes and nose.

"McGlade . . ."

His eyes were closed, his face a mess of gore. But he was bleeding. That meant he was alive.

I wiped some of the blood off his face, and was horrified that his nose came off in my hand. I resisted the urge to drop it—maybe surgeons could sew it back on somehow. I turned his head down, so the blood dripped away and not into his lungs, and then checked his pulse.

It was strong. I might have actually smiled a little.

Harry coughed, wet and garbled.

"Jackie?"

"Yes, Harry?"

"I can't . . . I can't feel my nose."

"It, uh, it came off, Harry."

"Fuck me. Where is it?"

I held up his nose, for him to see. He grunted, and I realized he was laughing.

"You got my nose," he said.

I grinned at him.

"My ass hurts Do I still have an ass?"

I looked him over.

"Except for the nose, you're pretty much intact."

"I'm lying on something hard."

I wasn't thrilled to reach under him, but I quickly found the object causing him discomfort. A cell phone. And, incredibly, it still seemed to be working.

I dialed 911, told them to send everything they had.

"Is the bitch dead?" McGlade asked when I got off the phone.

"Yes, bro. She's dead."

"Good. I was getting kind of sick of her."

I glanced over my shoulder and realized I had to make sure. "Be right back."

I made the long return journey to the severed leg, winced at it, and then worked the zipper on the back. These looked like the boots Alex had been wearing, but I wanted to confirm it, grisly as the task was. When the zipper was down I reached inside . . .

Grabbed the ankle . . .

Began to pull it out . . .

Felt a hand, on my shoulder.

I spun around, terrified, thinking it was Alex, still coming after me like the Terminator, refusing to die even missing a limb.

It was Phin.

"Jack?"

"Toenails," I told him. "Alex told me she was painting her toenails."

I tugged the boot free, exposing her foot.

Five toes stared back at me, their nails fire engine red.

This was Alex. She was finally dead.

"Phineas Troutt, this is the FBI! Drop your weapon and raise you hands up over your head!"

Phin and I exchanged a panicked glance. Feebies were all over the place, rushing in from all directions. How the hell could they have followed us? Was there some sort of transmitter on me? Or on Harry? Had he made good on his deal and turned Phin in?

"Go," I told Phin. "Run."

He shook his head.

"Please." I held on to his shoulder. Squeezed.

"You're not going to jail for me, Jack. This is the only way to make it right."

"Phin. . . ."

He dropped the rifle and raised his hands.

Twenty seconds later they had him in cuffs and were dragging him off.

Special Agent Dailey approached me, looking prim and proper in a neatly pressed suit.

"Is that Alex Kork?" he asked, indicating the leg.

"What's left of her. How'd you find me?"

"Your cell phone."

Dammit. The call to my mother, and the calls from Alex.

"Phin's a good man," I said.

"I'm sure he is. But it's not my job to get personal. It's just my job to catch him. Getting personal would take more than I have to give."

He appraised Alex's leg again, then nodded to himself.

"Nice work here, Lieutenant."

Someone found a fire extinguisher and was killing one of the burning tires. I watched for a moment, then looked beyond him, into the distance, into the world. A world that I was finally ready to be part of again. But not as a cop.

"It's not *lieutenant*," I said evenly. "Not anymore."

CHAPTER 57

"I'M READY TO SAY GOOD-BYE."

The day was gorgeous, sun blazing, birds singing, a warm breeze whistling through the tombstones. I wasn't wearing black this time. I had on a floral print dress, one I'd bought decades ago, something casual and flirty and created for a much younger, happier woman. Someone optimistic.

The grass over Latham's grave was green and lush, like it had been growing there for years rather than just four days. I crouched down, placed a single red rose on the ground. Six feet above his heart. I stayed like that for a moment, the two dozen sporadic stitches in my legs protesting.

"I'm sorry for everything. Mostly that I didn't reach this conclusion earlier. You never pushed me into quitting, never made any demands. Thank you for that. But I'm retired now, and if there's anything beyond this world and you're listening, I hope you can forgive me. I also hope I gave you even a tenth of the happiness that you gave me. I love you, Latham."

I stood, wiped the tears off my cheeks. My purse rang, and I fished out my cell.

"Thank you for the gift," Herb said.

"Did the Turduckinlux come?"

"Did you send me that too? How about steaks?"

"Assorted steaks, Herb. I got you the Meat Lover's Package. It also comes with an angioplasty."

"I appreciate it, Jack." He cleared his throat. "Bernice also gave me the other thing. Your badge. Are you sure?"

"I'm sure."

"I think it's a good thing."

"Because now I can't boss you around anymore?"

"Because you deserve to be happy. Now you have a chance to."

I stared at Latham's headstone and pursed my lips.

"When are you getting out?" I asked.

"You know hospitals. They want to milk every last cent out of you. I could actually use some milk right now. Or ice cream. Do you like ice cream? I like bacon. They should make bacon-flavored ice cream."

"Hi, Jack," Bernice was talking now. "The latest morphine dose is kicking in, he's babbling."

"He'll be okay?"

"Everything looks good." A pause. "Will you be okay?"

I glanced at the grave again, then looked up at the sun.

"I think so."

"Good. Stop in later, that will cheer him up. But don't bring any food."

"Bring food!" Herb thundered in the background. "It's horrible here!"

"Don't bring food," Bernice repeated. "Doctors have him on a liquid diet."

"It's horrible!" he wailed.

"I'll be by later."

I hung up, popped the phone back into my purse, and it rang again. I put it to my face.

"Hello?"

Another ring. But it wasn't my phone. It was coming from my purse. I hunted around, found the cell Harry had had in his pocket, the one I'd used to call 911. I checked the caller ID. Four-one-four. A Wisconsin area code. I answered.

"Hello?"

"Is this Gracie?" A woman's voice.

"I'm sorry, no it's not."

"Do you know anyone named Gracie?"

"I don't. This is Harry McGlade's phone."

"Do you know Samantha Porter? I'm her neighbor. I'm watching her daughter, Melinda." The voice was frantic, and picking up speed. "Sam's been gone for two days, and I finally got the landlord to let me into her apartment. I found this number with the name Gracie written on it. She was supposed to go shopping with Gracie, but I haven't heard back from her in two days."

"I'm sorry, I don't know any of those people."

"I don't know what else to do. I've called the police, but they haven't been able to find her. Sam didn't tell me much about Gracie, only that she was a dancer too before the car accident scarred her face."

My core temperature dropped ten degrees.

"Gracie had a scarred face?"

"Just one side, Sam said."

"Can you describe Samantha for me?"

"Tall. Athletic. Blond hair."

"Did she have a pair of red boots?"

"She was a dancer. She had a lot of boots."

"I've got your number. I'll call you back."

I hung up, feeling numb. This wasn't Harry's phone. It was Alex's phone. The last phone in the daisy chain.

It all came to me in a rush. What Alex had done. How she'd pulled it off.

Alex was still alive. And she was getting away.

And I knew what I had to do to stop her.

CHAPTER 58

NOT PERFECT, but not bad.

The plan had been to grab Jack and drive the Winnebago to the Prius parked a few blocks away. Then she'd blow up the RV, with Samantha Porter's body inside, and Harry would ID the body from the ugly Enrique Perez boots. But things had gone a little squirrelly, and she had to abandon both Harry and Jack.

Still, the plan mostly worked. After her date with Sam, they'd gone back to her apartment. Alex had taken Sam's passport, ID, and some of her belongings, then marched the naive stripper back to her Prius and shot her in the backseat.

Now Alex was Samantha. They looked enough alike that she should be able to cross the border into Mexico without any hassle. Once there, the plastic surgeon she'd been exchanging e-mails with would fix her scarred face, turning her into an exact copy of Sam, for the tidy sum of forty grand cash. After recuperating, Alex could go after Jack, Harry, and Phin at her leisure, without worrying about the law breathing down her neck.

Alex smiles, half her face immobile, and runs her hand along the My Ass jeans she's wearing. Samantha's jeans.

I knew I'd get into your pants.

Alex looks at her reflection in the rearview mirror, adjusts her bangs.

"Hello, Sam. I think I'm going to love you."

For the first time in a long time, Alex has hope for the future. And it feels wonderful.

She checks out of the hotel using the TV remote control, grabs the duffel bag full of money, and notices that her cell phone, plugged into the charger, is blinking like it has a message.

Odd. No one should know this number.

She picks it up, sees the call forwarding is still on. Alex thought she'd turned it off. Maybe that's what's blinking. She turns it off for sure this time, and also double-checks that the Bluetooth is disabled.

Not that it matters. No one knows she's alive. No one is coming after her.

Alex leaves the hotel and walks into the parking lot. It's a gorgeous day, sunny and warm. She left the windows open on the Prius last night, and the death smell is just about gone. There are some stains, if you look really close. Alex decides she'll stop at the next car wash she sees and give the carpet a shampoo.

She climbs in, starts the car, and gets ready for the long drive south.

A few moments after pulling onto the expressway, her cell phone rings.

Alex's breath catches. There's a simple explanation. There has to be. It's a wrong number. Or a telemarketer. Something stupid and harmless.

She picks it up but doesn't answer, squinting at the caller ID.

555-5555.

What the fuck?

There has to be something wrong with the phone. That's the only thing that makes sense.

Then it beeps, indicating a text message.

THIS IS ALEX. SHE'S A SERIAL KILLER.

It's followed by a photo.

Alex's mug shot.

THIS IS NOT SAMANTHA PORTER. AND THE BORDER PATROL KNOWS THAT.

This can't be happening. This really can't be happening. Alex has worked out every detail. This plan is perfect. Who the hell could have figured it out?

Another beep.

THIS IS JACK. SHE'S REALLY PISSED OFF.

A photo. Jack Daniels, staring right at her. Looking colder, harder, meaner, than Alex has ever seen before.

And Alex feels something she hasn't felt since she was a little child, hiding in the basement from Father so he couldn't punish her.

Alex feels absolute terror.

Someone honks, and Alex looks up and slams on the brakes, the Prius fishtailing, barely avoiding a collision with the car ahead of her. She pulls onto the shoulder, heart hammering, a giant lump in her throat preventing her from swallowing.

The phone rings again. Alex jumps in her seat.

Another ring.

Another ring—it seems to be getting louder.

Alex reaches for the phone, jittery and fearful, like it's a scorpion, then tentatively holds it up to her ear.

"I know the ID you're using," Jack says. "I know the car you're driving. You can't leave the country. Once I call the state cops, you won't even get out of Illinois."

"What do you want?" Alex asks, surprised at how weak her voice sounds.

"To meet. We're ending this, Alex, once and for all."

Alex forces a laugh. "You're insane. I'm not meeting with you. If I show up, I'll be surrounded by cops."

"No cops. Just us."

"You're out of your mind."

"I'll have my passport on me. Samantha Porter's name is worthless to you. I've made sure of that. But if you kill me, you can be Jack Daniels. You'll have to dye your hair from blond to brunette, but I'm betting you can manage."

Alex considers it, then dismisses it almost immediately.

"No way. I've got no reason to trust you."

"I'm not going to arrest you, Alex. I'm not going to make that mistake again. We're meeting so I can kill you."

Now Alex does actually laugh.

"You don't have it in you, Jack. You've tried before and always lost."

"I won't lose this time."

"Why? Because you'll have one of your dumb-ass friends backing you up?"

"Harry and Herb are in the hospital. Phin is in federal custody, his bail set at a million dollars. This is between you and me, Alex. It's always been between you and me."

"And if I don't show up?"

"Then I'll be following you. Every day. Every hour. Every minute, I'll be on your ass. But I won't be playing it your way anymore, running around trying to save people. Latham left me a fortune, and I'll spend every last dime hunting you down like the animal you are. If you want to live constantly looking over your shoulder, that's up to you. But I want to finish this. Now."

Alex drums her fingers on the steering wheel, her mind churning. She's always been smarter than Jack. Outsmarting her one more time shouldn't be hard. And if it actually came down to a fight, Alex is stronger, and faster, and a better shot. The only thing to worry about is being lied to, but Alex doesn't sense any deceit on Jack's part. One of the good lieutenant's many flaws is her honest streak. Like a forty-seven-year-old Girl Scout.

"Fine," Alex decides. "Same place as yesterday, behind O'Hare. If I sense something is funny, I won't show up."

"Twenty minutes," Jack says.

Alex pulls back onto the expressway. Jittery—from nerves, excitement, and anticipation.

How fun it will be to live life as Jack Daniels.

CHAPTER 59

IT ISN'T MURDER. Like my dad said, killing a rabid dog is actually mercy.

Which is why, when I pulled into the vacant lot and saw Alex parked in the distance, sitting behind the wheel of a Prius, I floored the gas and headed straight for her.

I had no idea what Alex had been expecting. Maybe a gunfight. Maybe a fistfight. And maybe she could have beaten me in both.

But in a demolition derby, a two-and-a-half-ton Ford Bronco truck beat a compact Toyota hybrid any day of the week.

By the time I got close enough to see Alex's expression—pure shock that I wasn't going to stop—she hit the accelerator. But it was too little, too late. The Bronco crashed into her front end with a satisfying, metal-crunching clang, the four-wheel-drive climbing up onto the hood of the tiny car, a heavy steel-belted radial smashing through her front windshield.

I jammed it into reverse, my tires found purchase on the gravel-covered asphalt, and I rocketed backward off the Prius, bouncing high in my seat from the shocks.

Alex was buried under an airbag, the front end of her car smashed to half its height. I backed up until I was a good fifty yards away, then punched it and rammed her again.

The Prius lurched sideways, its tires shrieking, the big truck push-ing until it reached a divot in the cracked pavement and rolled up onto its side, and then over the top, rocking upside-down like a big metal turtle.

I backed up again, but after a few feet something begin to whine under the floorboard. I tried to pop it into gear, and the truck jerked, then was still. I'd killed the transmission.

No biggie. I was just getting started.

I tugged on the door handle. It didn't budge. So I stuck my Beretta in my teeth and climbed out the missing windshield onto the hood of the Bronco. I slid off the bumper and onto my feet, then went after her.

When I got within twenty feet of the Prius I fired three shots, bursting all three airbags. Keeping the Beretta aimed, I pressed on the airbag fabric, deflating it, ready to fire at the first thing underneath.

But there was nothing there. The car was empty.

I spun around just as I saw the blur. The kick connected solidly with my hand, my gun taking flight and arcing through the air, clattering to the concrete a few dozen feet away.

I pivoted, brought my own leg around, aiming at Alex's chest. She turned into it, absorbing the kick on her shoulder. Then she shoved me away, backpedaled, and assumed a tae kwon do stance, legs apart and fists raised.

I got in the same stance.

"I'm going to rip your fucking head off," Alex snarled at me.

"Bring it, bitch."

Alex advanced, feinting with her left, hooking with her right. I ducked my head down, her knuckles grazing off my skull, and then I brought my knee up, driving it into her ribs.

She recovered quickly, spinning to my left, whacking me in the neck with the back of her hand. I staggered from the blow, and she followed up with a scissors kick, her body taking to the air.

Her foot met my jaw, hard enough to bring the stars out. I spun with it, and kept spinning until I hit the ground, slapping both palms against the tarmac to cushion my fall.

Alex was on me quick as a snake, punting one of my kidneys up into my lungs. I screamed, but managed to pin her leg on the second kick, shifting with it, flipping her onto her face.

I kept hold of her ankle, rolling her up, getting on top of her.

Then I grabbed her bleach-blond hair and introduced her face to the pavement. Once. Twice, three times, and then she tangled her hand in my hair and yanked me off.

We both rolled to our feet. Alex spat out blood and teeth. Her face was the picture of rage, the scar tissue stretched so taut it was pure white. She lunged, but anger had replaced form and I easily sidestepped the move, giving her a one-two punch to the nose.

She wiped a sleeve across her face, mopping off blood.

"You're all alone, Jack. No one is here to save you this time."

I thought of every major case I'd ever been on. Each time, someone had come to the rescue. Herb. Harry. Phin. None of them were here now to watch my back.

Alex was right. This time I was totally alone.

But this time I didn't need any help.

I moved in, kicked at her instep, dropping her to one knee, then hammered a right cross home, jerking her head back. Alex brought up her fists, swung and missed. I followed the right with a left, rocking her sideways, then another right, and another left. It was like hitting a heavy bag, except heavy bags don't whimper.

She fell onto both knees, not even fighting back, keeping her head covered up.

I grabbed her arms and my knee met her nose. If it hadn't been broken before, now it was.

Alex slumped onto her ass. She wasn't getting up again.

"Lucky," Alex said, blood dribbling down her face from eight different places. "You got lucky."

"Wrong. I'm better than you. And I just kicked your ass."

I scanned the empty lot, found my Beretta only a few yards away. I strode over to it and scooped it up. Then I returned to Alex, sticking the gun in her face, pointing it at her eye socket so she could look up the barrel.

Alex tried to smile, all red gums and broken teeth.

"You're not going to kill me."

"Yes. I am. And I don't want your last thought to be a hopeful one, so stop trying to convince yourself of that. In five seconds, I'm pulling this trigger."

"You can't do it."

"You'll find out in four more seconds."

Alex's half grin faltered. "You're a cop."

"Not anymore."

And there it was. The sneering, mocking face that had haunted my dreams for so long became something pitiful, pathetic, filled with fear.

"Jack. Don't do this."

"This is for Latham, and Alan, and Coursey, and the dozens of others you've slaughtered. But mostly, it's for me."

"Jack, please—"

"When you get to hell, say hi to Charles."

Alex cried out, "Jack—no!"

The bullet took off the back of her head. She flopped onto her side, blood spraying the broken concrete. I put two more into her skull, kicked her over, and fired three more into her dead heart.

Dad was right. It was like killing a rabid dog.

I checked her pulse, found none.

But just to make absolutely sure, I waited ten minutes before calling the police.

CHAPTER 60

I WAS SWEEPING UP my wreck of a house—something I'd put off during my three-week bout of drinking and depression—when a car pulled into the driveway.

"How's the nose?" I asked when I opened the door.

"I've got an extra nostril." Harry's voice was nasally, for obvious reasons. He had a big white bandage across his face, with some sort of nose brace, and his black eyes made him look like a raccoon.

"Nice," I said.

"Doc said it came off pretty clean, so it should look more or less normal when it heals. Thanks for giving it to the EMT. And thanks, you know, for coming to my rescue and saving my ass."

"My pleasure, Harry."

Harry looked down at his feet, then scratched himself in a bad place.

"So I was thinking. Alex is dead, right?"

"Yeah."

I'd found Alex's gun in the wrecked Prius and given it back to her, so it looked less like an assassination and more like self-defense, but otherwise told the authorities everything that happened. There would be a hearing, but I'd learned from on high that no charges would be filed. Stopping a serial killer's multi-state crime spree and recovering over eighty thousand dollars in stolen money counted for a lot, and supposedly no one was anxious to prosecute me.

The only weak link was Officer Scott Hajek. After leaving the cemetery I'd visited the Crime Lab with the phone Harry had found, asking Hajek to get Alex's number off the SIM card. He agreed, and promised he'd keep quiet about helping me, as long as I promised to go out with him sometime.

Sometime wouldn't happen anytime soon.

"And you're not a cop anymore, right?" Harry asked.

I nodded. "I start getting my retirement pension next week."

"Well, I've been thinking, since this is the big day—"

"Big day?"

"DNA Day. Today we get the test results."

Oh, brother. Or in this case, *Oh, I hope it isn't my brother.* "Yeah, it's supposed to be today."

"Did you call yet?"

"Not yet."

"Good. I wanted to be there when you called. Anyway, I was thinking that since you aren't a cop anymore, maybe you're looking for some gainful employment."

I narrowed my eyes at him.

"What are you saying, Harry?"

"I'm saying that the Crimebago is gone. So is my partner."

"You had a partner?"

"Slappy. He wasn't a very good partner, but he was all I had."

I tried to look concerned, but didn't quite make it. "I'm sorry your monkey blew up, Harry."

"No, he didn't die. He ran away before the explosion. Haven't you been watching the news? All the monkey attacks in Rosemont?"

"Missed it."

"Well, he's at large, and when they catch him there's no way in hell I'm claiming him, because I'm not paying the medical expenses of all those people he bit. He also assaulted a Chihuahua. The papers didn't go into tails, but I think there was sex involved and I don't think it was consen

"I'm not quite sure how to reply to that."

"Anyway, he's out of the picture and I figured, maybe, if the DNA tests show we're actually related, maybe, you know . . ."

I folded my arms. "Maybe I can join your private investigation business?"

Harry nodded, smiling. "Full partners. Fifty-fifty. Think about it, Jackie. We'd be the only brother-and-sister crime-fighting team in the country." His eyes danced like candle flames. "Mom will be so proud of us."

"We don't even have the test results, Harry."

"Okay. Call."

"Now?"

"Now."

I led Harry through the shambles that was my dwelling, made my way into the kitchen, and picked up the phone. The number for the DNA place was written on a pad.

"Biologen, this is Dr. Stefanopolous."

"Hi, I'm calling about a DNA match check. The name is Daniels. The batch number is 8431485."

"Hold on, please."

Harry poked me. "What did they say?"

"She's checking."

We waited, Harry's eyes pressing on me, his ruined face awash with expectation.

"You're looking for the results of the Daniels/McGlade comparison?" the doctor finally asked.

"Yes."

"Negative. No relation."

"You're sure?"

"We'll mail the detailed results to you within the next five business days. Thanks for choosing Biologen."

She hung up.

"Well?" Harry asked.

I'd known him for over twenty years, and had never seen him so ex- so happy, his face so lit up.

Then I thought of Mom, and how pleased she was to have found her long-lost son. She'd be so disappointed.

I weighed that against the ickiness I felt. But, strangely, now that I knew we weren't actually related, some of the ickiness was gone.

"Come on, Jackie! Don't keep me in suspense!"

I frowned.

"Welcome to the family, Harry."

I had to endure a big hug, which hurt like hell because of my various aches and pains.

"I gotta call Mom," he said, breaking the embrace. "She gets back in a few days. We should all go out to eat. Celebrate."

I tried not to roll my eyes. "Sure."

"Then we can get our matching tattoos."

"That's not going to happen."

"Awesome." I don't think he heard me. "I'll call you tonight about signing the lease."

"What lease?"

"Our new office. It's a primo location, Jackie. Needs a bit of a fix-up, but it will be perfect for our business."

"Harry, I haven't—"

"Gotta run." He slipped in fast and gave me a peck on the cheek. "I'll tell Mom you said hi."

And then he was out the door, leaving me to wonder about the monster I'd just created.

Since I was already in the kitchen, and since it was just as messy as the rest of the house, I grabbed a broom and dustpan and began sweeping. It was mindless work, rewarding in a menial, repetitive way. Being domestic wasn't something I did much of, but I felt like I could get used to it. Maybe even start to enjoy it.

At around noon I got hungry and ordered Chinese food—my domesticity ended at cooking. Half an hour later there was a knock at the front door. I grabbed some cash, brushed some dust off my jeans, and went to pay the delivery driver.

But it wasn't the food. It was someone else.

"Hey," he said.

"Hey."

Phin wore jeans and a white T-shirt, tight in all the right places. He had his hands in his pockets and a boyish grin on his face that made him look ten years younger, which would make him twenty years younger than me.

"Thanks for putting up the bond money."

"I've got a little extra in the bank."

"A hundred grand is more than a little."

"Let's call it even. I know you talked to the Feds, got the charges against me dropped."

"We're not even. Not even close."

"I trashed your truck," I said.

"I can steal another one. But the money . . . Jack, I can't pay that much back."

I nodded. "I know."

"And chances are high I'm not going to appear on my court date."

I nodded again. "I know. It's okay."

He moved a little closer to me, his gaze intense.

"Look, Jack, I know how you feel about me. And if you really want to just be friends, I'd rather have your friendship than none of you at all."

I stared at Phin, and felt something I hadn't felt in weeks. Happiness. I was actually happy. It was such an alien feeling I wasn't sure what to do.

My mouth made the decision for me, locking onto his with a heat, a passion, an intensity that made me realize maybe, just maybe, things might work out after all.

"Are you sure this is what you want?" Phin whispered. "I come with some pretty hefty baggage."

I smiled, wicked, free, and wonderfully alive. Maybe for the first time in my entire life.

"Well, Mr. Troutt. I guess we'll just have to take it one day at a time."

Then I grabbed him by the shirt and pulled him into my house.

Acknowledgments

SPECIAL THANKS TO Don Oakes and John Nebl, two very smart cops. Any mistakes in this book are mine, as they don't make mistakes.

A toast to my fellow writers Raymond Benson, Blake Crouch, Barry Eisler, Jack Kilborn, Henry Perez, James Rollins, Marcus Sakey, and Jeff Strand for their unwavering support.

Thanks to my family and friends, everyone at Dystel & Goderich, Hyperion, the booksellers, the libraries, and the fans.

And finally, to a select group who continue to spread the word, including Ben Springer, Brenda Anderson, Brian Prisco, Corky Mayo, Dan Blackley, Dave Eaton, Elizabeth Brux, Greg Swanson, Jan May, Jeanne Donnelly, Jim Munchel, Joe Menta Jr., Karen L. Syed, Kathy Cox, Melanie Williams, Michele Lee, Nick Goodrick, Patricia Reid, Patrick Balester, Paul Pessolano, Robert Mosley, Robyn Glazer, Sean Hicks, Steve Jensen, and all the JAKaholics on my message board.